He was there for a reason...

"Sam—" she used his first name, though he'd never told her to "—what's going on? Can I help?"

When he shook his head, her heart sank. *Please, God, don't let this man have done something bad enough to put him in jail.* A world without him in it. Santa Raquel without him keeping it safe.

The idea left her bereft.

His expression cleared. "Yes, you can help." He seemed to have fought some internal battle and...won?

"Okay." She smiled. Couldn't seem to stop smiling at him. Wanted to put her hand on his knee where it rested close to hers. Or on the hand he had resting on it. "What can I do?"

"I need you to do me a favor."

"Sure. Fine. What?" This was Sam Larson. He'd saved her life. She owed him far more than she'd ever be able to repay.

"I need you to pack up whatever keepsakes and possessions you most value, along with clothes and personal items, and be ready for me to pick you up late tomorrow afternoon."

Dear Reader,

I'm a bit envious of you. You have this story ahead of you. I've already finished it. For me it's one of those books that leaves you feeling bereft at the end because it's over. I can't really even tell you why. I love Sam. He's not perfect. Far from it. But he's completely honest. With himself. And with others. He stands by what he says. Does what he says he's going to do.

And then...he finds out that he's not in control of the whole world...that sometimes he can't do as he says because it's out of his control. He does not take this news well.

And Bloom, she's an incarnation of so many things. She's a genius, like the one I raised. But beyond what I was personally bringing to the story, Bloom... bloomed...into so much more than these little details that I knew about her. She found an inner strength that I didn't know existed, but that I've taken upon myself. Mostly I love her because she found a way to walk through the fire with an open heart.

I hope you enjoy your time in Santa Raquel, and that you come back to visit often. We're giving you many "vacation" opportunities. But rest assured, each "package" takes you, in some way, through The Lemonade Stand, Where Secrets are Safe. Welcome!

I love to hear from readers! You can find me on Facebook at Facebook.com/tarataylorquinn and on Twitter, @tarataylorquinn. Or join my open Friendship board on Pinterest! Pinterest.com/tarataylorquinn/ friendship.

All the best,

Tara
www.TaraTaylorQuinn.com

USA TODAY Bestselling Author

TARA TAYLOR QUINN

——

The Promise He Made Her

HARLEQUIN® SUPERROMANCE®

Recycling programs
for this product may
not exist in your area.

ISBN-13: 978-0-373-60994-9

The Promise He Made Her

Copyright © 2016 by Tara Taylor Quinn

Printed in U.S.A.

www.Harlequin.com

An author of more than seventy novels, **Tara Taylor Quinn** is a *USA TODAY* bestselling author with more than seven million copies sold. She is known for delivering emotional and psychologically astute novels of suspense and romance. Tara is a past president of Romance Writers of America. She has won a Readers' Choice Award and is a five-time finalist for an RWA RITA® Award, a finalist for a Reviewer's Choice Award and a Booksellers' Best Award. She has also appeared on TV across the country, including *CBS Sunday Morning*. She supports the National Domestic Violence Hotline. If you or someone you know might be a victim of domestic violence in the United States, please contact 1-800-799-7233.

Books by Tara Taylor Quinn

HARLEQUIN SUPERROMANCE

Where Secrets are Safe

Wife by Design
Once a Family
Husband by Choice
Child by Chance
Mother by Fate
The Good Father
Love by Association
His First Choice

Shelter Valley Stories

Sophie's Secret
Full Contact
It's Never Too Late
Second Time's the Charm

The Moment of Truth

It Happened in Comfort Cove

A Son's Tale

HARLEQUIN HEARTWARMING

The Historic Arapahoe

Once Upon a Friendship
Once Upon a Marriage

MIRA BOOKS

Street Smart
In Plain Sight
The Second Lie
The Third Secret
The Fourth Victim
The Friendship Pact

Visit the Author Profile page at
Harlequin.com for more titles.

For Rachel: You chose a difficult path to help many and keep us safe. May you also always be able to walk through the fire with your heart open.
All my love, forever. Ma

CHAPTER ONE

PHYSICAL BRUISES HEAL. It's the mental ones that can kill you. Bloom shook her head and hit the delete key. Looked for a more genteel way to get her point across. She didn't want to lose her audience during the first minute of the two-hour-long psychology symposium. They'd given her a room with seating for three hundred, which could feel cavernous if she failed to entertain.

Back in her old life, her teaching life, she'd have filled the screen with visual aids, provided a handout—and probably pens, too. She'd have sent around a bowl filled with individually wrapped peppermints. All actions designed to increase memory retention in lecture situations, and she'd have been content to get 5 percent retention after seven days.

But those were the old days. Her associate college professor days. Funny how so much could change in just three years.

Physical bruises heal. It's the mental ones that can kill you. Her second try ended up exactly the same as the first.

And if she started her keynote address at the psychiatric conference that way, people might not physically exit in droves, but she might lose her credibility.

One in four of the audience members—the current statistic for the number of the victims of domestic violence in the United States—might even take offense. Get angry.

How could she belittle the bruises that took so many lives? How could she say that "bruises heal," dismissing the fact that intimate partners lifted fists to those who loved them?

She had two hours to impress upon her peers the very real disease that ate away at more of the population than any other disease. Domestic violence.

Medical personnel had been made more aware of intimate partner violence in recent years. After all, some professional sports leagues had been forced to shine light on the problem as a way of warding off the negative press that resulted from some of their stars being abusers.

But the fact that every minute twenty-four people were victims of intimate partner abuse in the United States was not just a problem for police and hospitals, doctors and nurses. Her profession—psychiatrists, psychologists, counselors—needed to step up to the plate.

Because bruises, broken bones, even cracked

skulls healed over time. But without awareness, without help, without a "movement" to tend to the mental bruises left by domestic violence, not enough of the victims of that violence were going to heal...

The soapbox is not going to work with these people.

Bloom's self-talk was trying to help. She knew that.

But...unhealed mental wounds often drove victims to the other side—they became abusers.

Preaching, teaching, prophesying or statisticizing wasn't going to reach her peers.

She deleted again.

Sitting behind her mahogany desk, Bloom looked over the top of her laptop screen to survey her office, as though the words she needed were there. The couch and two recliners that faced each other with her favorite old claw-footed chair—an inheritance from the maternal grandmother she'd adored—offered...nothing. There was the coffee table with a floral tissue box holder in the middle of it. Wall hangings, all carefully chosen, in shades of muted reds, oranges, yellows, a splash of purple. Some hearts quilted together. Some quotations in the midst of abstract art.

Clearly a woman's office. She made no apology for that. She was a woman.

Her patients were predominantly women.

A lot of whom were living healthy, productive lives.

But there were so many more out there. And she was booked to the hilt. Beyond the hilt, really, not that she minded the evening hours she put in three nights a week in addition to fully booked days.

Dr. Bloom Freelander, Psy.D, had a thriving private practice.

And it wasn't enough.

She couldn't even come close to serving the needs of all of those calling her office for help.

Nine o'clock on a Wednesday night. Her last patient had been gone almost an hour. Susan, her receptionist, soon after that. She had a 7:00 in the morning—Latoya Markham, who had to be at work by 8:00 a.m. And here she sat, needing to write the speech that she'd be giving at the University of California in just two days.

Physical bruises heal. It's the mental ones that can kill you.

No!

The truth was…true. Physical bruises did heal. In some fashion. They'd fade and disappear. Broken bones reset. Some attacks resulted in death, too. It was the most unfortunate fact of all. One that she was trying desperately to avoid as often as humanly possible. The way to prevent domestic violence deaths was to heal the person. As well as the bruises.

She typed.

The way to prevent domestic violence deaths is to heal the person. Not just the bruises.

She read what she'd typed. Nodded. Yes. There. She still had two hours left to fill.

She read her words again. One sentence. Her fingers lifted to the keys. Began to move. And Bloom quit fighting them.

WTF.

Detective Samuel Larson, thirty-seven-year-old semistar of the Santa Raquel Police Department, leaned back in the old squeaky desk chair he'd inherited, along with the scarred desk, when he'd been awarded his detective's shield.

He didn't give a rat's ass about the desk. Never had. He stared at the emailed report he'd just opened.

Two years? The asshole was out in two years?

How was he going to… "Damn."

"Something wrong?" Brand-new detective Chantel Harris, who'd recently transferred from a beat cop to internet crime investigation, happened to be walking by Sam's desk as that last expletive slipped out.

Sam knew Chantel. Not from any work they'd done together on the job, but because they were both members of the Santa Raquel High Risk Team—an organization of professionals in all fields who came into contact with victims of domestic violence. From nurses to school counselors, cops, doctors, lawyers, the team had formed an intricate communication system geared solely to prevent domestic violence deaths.

"Yeah, something's wrong," he said, running a hand through blond hair that was too long by department standards. No one seemed to care. Least of all him. "One of our High Risk cases just threw up on us."

In silk pants and a jacket that looked like it had cost a year of his car payments, the no-nonsense, no makeup, blond-hair-tied-back cop sat down hard in the varnishless wooden chair beside his desk.

"Which one?" Her lips were white with tension.

"This one was before your time," he quickly assured her.

"But not before yours."

"Right." He looked at his screen again, seething angry energy. Rocking back and forth in the swivel chair that had seen better days, leaning on one elbow as he chewed the side of his finger.

Chantel glanced at the screen. "Arrested three years ago, sentenced to life in prison a year later and now released on a technicality," she read the portion he'd scrolled to.

"The lawyer who prosecuted him was Trevor Banyon." He chewed harder.

Chantel's drawn out curse was only slightly less

harsh than his mental one. "How many are they up to now? Twenty-four? I can't believe that many cases have been overturned. A top prosecutor with an illegal gun trade on the side." She shook her head. "The guy should be shot."

With one of his own weapons, Sam agreed silently.

"I thought all of his cases were drug related." Chantel leaned over and, taking charge of his mouse, scrolled some more. "What was he doing on one of our cases?"

"The perp was a professor of psychology at U of C. The victim, his wife, was an associate professor he'd mentored."

"The authority figure." Chantel's tone dripped disrespect. He knew it because it was a sentiment he shared.

Answering to a boss was one thing—having someone assume that they knew what was best for you better than you did, or thought that they had the right to force their will onto another—the idea pissed him off. Royally.

"So why were we on it?" Chantel, apparently finding nothing pertinent in the brief report, sat back. "U of C is out of our jurisdiction."

"The couple owned a home here on the beach and commuted." An hour and a half four days a week. He remembered the details. Every one of them.

"Still, doesn't explain Banyon's involvement."

"The professor also had a private practice. He was a licensed psychiatrist. He'd been slowly drugging his wife."

"He was killing her?"

"Nothing that kind." Sam shook his head, feeling his lunch threaten to come back up on him. "He'd made up his own little cocktail. Just to dumb her down enough that she wouldn't surpass him."

"He drugged her to keep her in his control?"

"She's genius-level intelligent," Sam said, remembering the woman he'd spent two years trying to forget. Because forgetting was the right thing to do.

She'd been so vulnerable when he'd known her. Nothing like the person she'd been born to be. The person he hoped she'd become after she'd gotten her life back. "He was afraid she was going to take his job." Chantel cut right to the chase. "Or surpass him in his field."

"Yeah."

"Did he hit her, too?"

"Hard enough to break her jaw." And the crooked smile he'd left behind would be her constant reminder of what the man she'd adored, idolized and trusted had done to her.

"He's due out next Monday. That's four days," Chantel said, frowning.

"I know."

"When are you going to tell her?"

It was Thursday morning. He was thinking about…maybe…Sunday night. Give her as much peace of mind as he could.

Give himself some way to figure out how to get the asshole back behind bars before he'd had a chance to take a step out.

"With his conviction overturned there won't even be a probation period."

He knew that.

"What about a restraining order?" Chantel asked the question even as she shook her head.

"Not until he approaches her again," he said what they both already knew. When a case went away, so did all of the painfully collected evidence. At least in theory.

"She needs time to make arrangements."

She had a point. Maybe Sunday night was leaving it a little late. Still, he needed time to make a plan.

"Is she still local?"

"Yeah. She's in private practice now. Has an office in that professional plaza across the street from the hospital." Still living in the beach house she'd bought with the bastard. That was one of the first things they were going to have to fix.

They. As though she was going to want to have anything to do with him when she found out that he hadn't been able to keep his promise to her that once she testified the man who'd hurt her so cruelly would spend the rest of his life behind bars. That *if* she testified he, Detective Sam Larson, would guarantee her safety.

Not that Banyon's sins were on him. But the fact that the asshole professor's wife had testified against him when everything in her had told her not to do so—that was on Sam. He'd ridden her hard.

He'd needed her testimony to make his case.

To keep her safe.

Well, he'd sure as hell screwed that one up.

CHAPTER TWO

"I HAD A degree in psychology from Stanford University when I was seventeen. My master's by the time I was nineteen. And my doctorate at twenty-one."

Bloom spoke with authority. Because when it came to her own life, she was the expert. And that was okay.

"I'm smart. Aware. And a talented right brain, as well." She could talk about her paintings. The artwork on her office walls. She didn't. They weren't pertinent and she had a job to do. A task to get through.

"Unlike many geniuses, I was also gifted with a good bit of common sense. When I was little my mother could get me through most unwanted tasks by telling me that Baby—a rubber doll from which I was inseparable—had to go through them, too. Baby had to get a shot, so I was fine getting one. If it was nap time, Baby had to take a nap, and so I would, too..."

Audience members were looking at her, nodding. A few of them even bore little grins.

"She tells the story that when I was eighteen months old, I announced from the bathtub one morning that I wanted chocolate for breakfast. At which point she informed me that we didn't eat chocolate for breakfast. I frowned for a moment, picked up Baby—who, of course, was in the bath with me—and announced that Baby wanted chocolate for breakfast."

Yep. Three hundred faces were upturned in her direction. Bloom just kept on doing what she was doing. Because she'd told herself to do so.

"My mother told me to tell Baby that we didn't eat chocolate for breakfast. She was one step ahead of me the whole way. Until I held my rubber doll up to her nose and pointed out that 'Baby doesn't have any ears.'"

The entire room erupted in laughter. Bloom started to sweat. It was those bright lights.

She was successful. Capable. And in control.

But she looked to the right, anyway. To the seat at the very end of the front row. She'd arrived early specifically to put a reserved sign on that chair. Lila McDaniel didn't have a lot of time. But when Bloom had called the director of The Lemonade Stand—the unique women's shelter where she'd lived for the weeks it had taken her to come back to herself after it had been discovered that her husband had been drugging her for months—to ask for support for the Friday morning keynote session, for backup statistics and a small informational speech to her colleagues about shelter work, Lila had immediately appointed herself to attend.

As the laughter died down around them, Lila nodded. She wasn't smiling. Yet there was no doubting the warmth in her expression. And it empowered Bloom.

"Mom recovered before I was out of the tub," she continued. The room, when she paused to take a breath, was completely silent. She was speaking to interested bodies. Not walls...

"She explained to me that if I gave Baby chocolate for breakfast I would make her sick. And I told her that she couldn't give me chocolate for breakfast because she'd feel bad if she made me sick."

A collective sigh moved around the room. There were men there. Many of them. All with psychiatric doctoral credentials.

She glanced at Lila again. The woman just looked at her without even so much as another nod of encouragement. To anyone in the room, Lila was just another attendee. To Bloom, she was fresh air in her lungs.

"I can stand up here and fill the next two hours with my mother's tales of my greatness. I can talk about the long-distance call I made when I was five to reassure my grandmother, whose purse had just been stolen, that she would be just fine because I loved her and so did other people, so she hadn't lost what mattered. I can entertain you all day long. To a room full of psychiatrists, my childhood is fascinating stuff. But entertaining you is not my purpose here today." Heads tilted, a few people frowned, all eyes were still on her.

It could be, a small voice inside her said. She could wing this. Be a huge success. But this invitation—to keynote for her peers on whatever topic she chose—gave her a chance to fulfill a higher purpose.

And to grow as a person, too. To take back another piece of herself that the bastard had tried to steal from her.

"I'm a smart woman. A wise woman. And a victim of domestic violence."

Many of them knew. Bloom's husband had been an esteemed colleague to some of them. Even if just through professional organization memberships.

Knowing and wanting to hear were two different things.

She forced herself to look out at them. To continue to connect. All but a few heads were turned away or bowed. People were suddenly interested in loose threads in their clothing. Their shoes. The carpet. A clock on the wall.

"I am also a survivor," she said, her voice imbued with emotion. "I am strong and capable, successful and healthy. Because I was able to get out. To get help. Because I had a counselor who was educated to my specific needs, who not only knew the kinds of things I was experiencing, but who knew what would most likely come as well, who was able to prepare me to handle those things, sometimes even on my own, when they did come.

"It's been two years since my recovery, ladies and gentlemen. And I stand before you today, a fully alive, contributing woman who truly enjoys life. *My* life. I got lucky. I landed in a perfect place—The Lemonade Stand—a place you all will hear about before this session is through.

"But first, my challenge to each and every one of you is to listen. To hear what I have to say. And to look inside yourselves. To ask yourselves the tough questions. And for those of you who receive positive answers, to help. Even if you are in the field you need to be in, you can still help raise awareness of the need for counselors who specialize in intimate partner violence. And for those who don't have special training in that particular field, you can help by being willing to refer their own clients to those who do…"

Bloom was on a roll. Confident. She gave statistics. Mixed in with difficult, but potent personal anecdotes. She grabbed her scholarly audience by the throat. Figuratively.

Much like she'd once been grabbed physically.

She took them down her road with her. As a victim and also as a psychiatrist with a successful practice.

Sparing them nothing, she made them feel her pain.

And brought them to her happy ending.

Thanks to a counselor who was a specialist in treating intimate partner violence, she was no longer a victim.

She was a survivor.

And it was up to all of them—herself included—to save every other victim out there.

SAM'S HOUSE WASN'T MUCH. The fact that it was a cottage not far from the beach was the nicest part. Inside, the floors were linoleum—old linoleum that, before his time, had likely been laid for its ability to withstand sand and water more than for its ambience.

For his current purposes, however, the house was near perfect. Set up on a cliff, on private land, with only a skinny, private, fenced path down to the beach, it was the perfect place to hide.

Or to have someone else hide.

He'd spent Saturday morning cleaning the floors, the bathroom. Changed the sheets on both beds—his own and the one in the spare room. She could use whichever one she wanted.

He'd even thrown the rug in the front room, the one Lucy thought was hers, in the wash.

Probably should have given the Irish setter a trip to the tub, too, but his five-year-old mistress preferred to take her baths in the ocean—an arrangement which benefitted his bathroom walls—and he'd run out of time to make it down there.

He'd stocked the fridge with vegetables and several salad dressings, eggs and milk. Chosen two different kinds of bread. Brought in a box of sensible cereal and a box of sugared, too. Three types of crackers, microwavable popcorn and ice cream bars. Colombian dark coffee and breakfast blend.

He'd bought a new set of towels, two kinds of body wash, extra tissues, paper towels and toilet paper.

He'd packed a bag. Found a room he could rent by the week where Lucy would be tolerated.

And if he didn't get his ass in gear, it would all be for naught.

He had a plan. Possibly not his best, but the only one that was going to work.

And just a little more than twenty-four hours to put it in motion.

A little over twenty-four hours to convince a confident, intelligent, determined woman-in-charge that she was going to have to leave her home, her life and do exactly as he said.

Bloom was in her office late Saturday morning, just a few miles from The Lemonade Stand, having finished with her last client. She had a busy day planned—shopping to do, friends to meet in LA for a coffee house concert one of the women was playing in, a run on the beach—but was taking a moment to reflect.

To breathe. And be present.

Her speech the day before—and the lunch following—had been successful beyond her hopes. Lila had names of volunteers, counselors had Lila's card and many of her peers had exchanged cards with each other—those with specific domestic violence training and those without. She'd given out contact names for members of the High Risk Team.

And she'd talked Lila in to staying for lunch, her treat. She'd seen the woman, who was in her fifties, smile more that day than she could ever remember.

And hoped it wasn't just a reflection of the success of the morning. Bloom had no idea what Lila's personal life looked like. The woman was like a phantom—at the Stand seven days a week and some nights. She had an apartment someplace close by, but didn't appear to have any family. Or friends.

Which wasn't natural. And raised Bloom's professional radar above comfort level.

If anyone deserved to be happy, it was Lila.

And she hoped she was.

Because she had a few minutes before she had to leave for the city, Bloom caught up on enough world and state news that she'd be able to contribute to conversation at dinner that night.

A headline caught her eye. Because of the name. There couldn't be too many prosecuting attorneys named Trevor Banyon in Southern California.

He'd been arrested on gun running charges. She wanted to open the article. Like a bystander wanted to get closer to a car accident. You just had to see. To know.

But she knew better. Reentering any part of Banyon's life would take her places she didn't need or want to go. She'd left her past behind. And wasn't going to let it pull her back.

The past was an unhealthy place for her. The present, which contained her hopes for the future, was the road she was consciously traveling. A road that was already giving her a happy life.

Closing the news app, she gathered her things, planning to leave straight for LA from the office. Her overnight bag was in the trunk of her six-year-old hunter green Jaguar.

A gift from Ken—Dr. Kenneth Freelander—after he'd verbally brutalized her the first time. Before he'd started drugging her to keep her in line. She loved the car, as she'd once loved him.

And kept it as a reminder that lemons could always be made into lemonade. That thorns had roses.

That it was up to her what she saw when she opened her eyes in the morning.

Out of the office, door locked, she nodded at a couple of people she knew, professionals who shared her office building, as she walked down the hall. Shared the elevator with a woman and a young girl, presumably patients, as they'd pushed the button for the fourth floor, which housed all pediatric and dental specialties.

Bloom exited the elevator and then the building, blinking as her eyes adjusted to the bright sunlight. Even in July the California coastal air wasn't smoldering with heat. But it was warm enough to be a comfort to her skin after spending several hours in air conditioning.

A man approached her on the sidewalk. She moved to one side in preparation for their eventual passing, not really noticing him any more than she noticed any of the other patients who came and went.

But she noticed enough to take a second look. Did she know him? Was he, perhaps, the husband of one of her patients? The tempo of her heart upping just a small notch, she looked more closely. If he was an ex…

Hand on the jeweled canister of mace attached

to her key ring, Bloom made one deft move with her thumb, unlocking the release.

And almost as quickly returned the safety catch. She did know the man. But not because of any of her patients.

She knew him because of herself.

Detective Samuel Larson was the man who'd saved her life.

CHAPTER THREE

HE ALMOST DIDN'T recognize her. Hell, what was he thinking? If it hadn't been for the fact that he'd memorized every bone in that face when he'd studied the crime scene photos, he wouldn't have recognized her. Her high cheekbones and that little bit of a squaring off of her chin gave her away. That and the slight bit of crookedness on one side of her jaw.

That auburn hair, more brown than red but with a hint of fire that had drawn his attention every time, was longer now. Softly curled.

Her body stood straighter, was fuller without losing the slenderness that drew eyes to her when she walked.

Bloom Freelander had…bloomed. His body took note.

WTF.

Had he left his mind back at the cottage? In the toilet he'd cleaned?

Still several yards away she didn't appear to have seen him yet. Which gave him time to get his head out of the plumbing and back to the case at hand.

Maybe the fact that he was dreading the next minutes, the fact that her life could very well depend on his ability to force her to do his bidding, was the reason he'd gone so far south.

He'd thought about her often over the past couple of years. Had wanted to check in on her. But he'd had no reason. No right.

Had thought it was not good or fair to remind her of the time in her life she was working so hard to escape.

Maybe he'd hoped he'd run into her. Maybe, when he'd been at the beach, or the grocery store, he'd kept an eye out for her.

Fate hadn't seen fit to bring them together.

But it had damned sure seen fit to put her in danger again.

He was no fonder of the fates at the moment than he was of his overresponsive nether region.

No doubting now that she'd seen him. She was staring right at him.

As if she couldn't believe it was he? Or was trying to place him?

Didn't matter.

Either way, it was showtime.

"DETECTIVE LARSON." Bloom slowed down, stepped off the walk into the grass as he drew closer, so as not to block traffic into and out of the building. If he had a medical appointment, she couldn't keep him. But...she'd thought of him so often during her months of healing. Wanted to let him know that he'd helped. A lot.

"Dr. Freelander..." He stepped off the walk, too.

"I told you," she said with an easy smile— something she'd been unable to give him when he'd known her. "Call me Bloom. Dr. Freelander is someone else in my mind. My former self. And the nemesis of my former self, too."

"Did you get your divorce?"

From anyone else the question would have been rude. But Sam Larson had been in every intimate crevice of her life as he'd built the case that had put her diabolically intelligent and demonic husband behind bars.

"I did," she told him, smiling again. "It was final just last month." Because Ken had fought it tooth and nail. From the throne he seemed to think he sat on in his prison cell.

Detective Larson's frown was something she remembered well. It gave her stomach a sexy little jolt to see it now.

Not an altogether comfortable experience. She was healthy. Happy. Just as she was. Without sex. Been there, done that. Didn't want the complication. The physical experience just wasn't worth what it put you through, exposed you to, made you vulnerable to...

Besides, she was professional enough to recognize that any feeling she might have for this particular man was transference—a former captive gravitating toward the safety net offered by her rescuer.

"I thought you were going to change your name."

The fact that he remembered gave her another jolt. Nice to know that of all of his many cases she'd been...memorable.

Or he just had one hell of a memory. Which was impressive, too.

"I was," she told him. "But it's on my degree. My doctoral certificate. And on the deed to the house I was just awarded as part of my settlement."

And that was enough about her. "You look good," she told him, smiling again.

"Thank you. So do you." He would know, as closely as he was looking her over.

Just as he'd done in the past. As though he didn't miss a single freckle. She'd thought the intensity of his regard had been due to the fact that he'd been the detective in charge of investigating her case.

But there it was, two years later, still searching out her secrets...

"I imagine you have an appointment to keep,"

she told him, pulling the strap of her black leather satchel more closely to her body. "I just wanted to thank you. You have no idea how many times I've thought of you since Kenneth went to prison and I could begin to heal, and I wanted to let you know what a difference you've made in my life. That you helped. So much. That the work you do…it matters so much…"

It wasn't like her to babble. Those brooding brown eyes of his, the flop of blond hair that never seemed to be in place, they were…familiar. As though she took them with her everywhere she went.

The idea was shocking, and yet recognizable, too. His calm, his strength, they'd been like examples of a parent to her. Something she'd been emulating as she rebuilt her life.

Rescuer, rescuee. Safety net. Sense of security.

"I don't have an appointment," the detective said, rocking back on the heels of the black slip-ons he'd always worn. They looked like the exact same ones from back then. Did he buy several pairs at a time? Were they some kind of detective issue? Uniform to go with the dress slacks and button-down shirts he'd always worn? With a sedate tie in varying shades of blah.

"You're here on a call?" she asked now, adrenaline rushing to the fore. Knocking out the other… inappropriate emotions his unexpected presence had raised in her. "I'm so sorry, I shouldn't have kept you."

Even as she said the words she realized that if he'd been on an emergency call he most likely would have had a partner with him and wouldn't have stopped to chat.

Which meant he was following up on a lead of some kind. Investigating every angle. Just like always.

"You might say I'm here on a call."

Sliding his hands in his pockets, he continued to peruse her, an odd glint to his eyes. Sadness?

What? She didn't look recovered enough to him?

The thought left her wanting to march him straight upstairs to her third-floor office, show him her walls and furniture and big mahogany desk. The drawers of patient files, proof of her success, and the awards that were hanging on the walls of the private bathroom attached to her suite. They were there so she would see them several times a day to remind her who she was. And so only she would see them. She wanted to instill a sense of comfort in her clients. Not intimidate them. Not to spill her ego over onto others.

"I'm here to see you, Bloom. Is there some-place we can go?"

Bloom. She liked the inflection he put on her

name. Liked that he'd finally used it. Honoring her request.

Liked the fleeting sense of power that it gave her. But knew it for what it was. A change from her past when he'd insisted that he wasn't comfortable using her first name. That he needed the distance of formality between them.

Because she'd looked horrible with a broken jaw, drug-blurred eyes and black-and-blue skin?

He'd seen her later, too. Physically healed and pretty enough to turn heads...

"Bloom? Is there someplace we can go?"

She didn't move. Inside or out. "Why do you need to see me?"

The part of her life where she had a detective in it was done. Forever. No more trouble with the law. Of any kind. She'd promised herself. Never again.

"I just... Is there someplace we can go to talk?"

They could go back up to her office. But she didn't want him there anymore. Her car? No better.

She took him to a bench out in the yard behind the building. It was in a garden. With several benches. And a winding walkway with trees for shade. She chose to sit in the sun.

"What's going on?"

Even as she asked the question, she had a flash

of the news headline she'd seen less than an hour before.

Trevor Banyon.

Had the jerk said something untoward about her? Released some confidential information pertaining to her case? Were his files being turned over as part of the investigation against him? Was there something incriminating to her reputation there? Something that would embarrass her professionally?

"I assume you've heard about Trevor Banyon…"

She started to breathe again. Relaxed against the seat. That was it then. Something from her case was going to be exposed.

She wouldn't wish for it. But didn't care all that much, either. In her new life she kept no secrets. So there was nothing to hold over her. And thus, nothing to fear.

Not that he'd know that. The Bloom Freelander he'd known had been afraid of her own shadow. When she was even aware of it following her around.

"I just saw something this morning," she said, looking him over again, glad to have a few minutes with him now that she knew she had nothing to worry about. He was there as a courtesy. She got that now. And liked him all the more for it. It was so like him to follow up. "Something about him running illegal guns on the side?"

Sam Larson nodded. That flop of blond hair coming down on his forehead. The man had to be nearing forty, but you wouldn't know it by his hairline.

Maybe the lines at the edges of his mouth gave a hint of experience...

"Do you think he'll go to jail?" she asked now, trying to keep her mind on topic—something that usually came naturally to her these days. "Locked up with all those people he put away..." She didn't wish it on him.

The man had done her a great service—putting Ken behind bars. He'd fought hard for her.

"That's what I'm here to talk to you about."

"What does Trevor Banyon going to jail have to do with me? Do they need me to testify on his behalf? To talk about the good he's done? The lives he's saved? Because while I don't condone anything to do with illegal arms, he really did help save my life...and I'm sure many others. Are they thinking that if they have enough mitigating circumstances he'll just get probation?"

She had no idea how serious the charges were against the man because she'd closed the app without reading the article.

It was about that time, when her voice dropped off and nothing else filled the silence, that Bloom realized part of the reason she'd been rambling so much. He was letting her. His long silences almost begging her to ramble.

"What's going on?" Was he in trouble? Did he have something to do with Banyon's side career?

She'd never have thought so. Couldn't believe it. Maybe Banyon had something on him?

He was clearly having difficulty saying whatever it was he'd come to say…

Just like that she switched from a previously needy woman with her earthly savior to psychiatrist mode. Wanting to help him as he'd helped her. Whatever he needed…

"Sam…" she used his first name, though he'd never invited her to do so. "What's going on? Can I help?"

He was there for a reason.

When he shook his head, her heart sank. Please, God, don't let this man have done something bad enough to put him in jail. A world without him in it, Santa Raquel without him out there keeping it safe…

The idea left her bereft.

His expression cleared. "Yes, you can help." He seemed to have fought some internal battle and… won?

"Okay." She smiled. Couldn't seem to stop smiling at him. Wanted to put her hand on his knee where it rested close to hers. Or on the hand he had resting on it. "What can I do?"

"I need you to do me a favor."

"Sure. Fine. What?" This was Sam Larson. He'd saved her life. She owed him far more than she'd ever be able to repay.

"I need you to pack up whatever keepsakes and possessions you most value, along with clothes and personal items, and be ready for me to pick you up late tomorrow afternoon."

She felt the blood drain from her face. Didn't know her mouth was hanging open until she felt the dryness on her tongue.

"You're abducting me?" They were the first words that came to her mind. He was in that much trouble?

"Of course not!" He shifted next to her and she felt the holstered gun he always wore under his jacket. He'd have one strapped to his ankle, too. "Well, not in the way you make it sound."

"But you are planning to take me away against my will." Her insides were frozen. Not shaking. She wasn't even sure her heart was still beating.

And she didn't give him time to answer. "I trusted you."

He was wearing his badge. She'd seen that hooked to his belt, too, when he'd first taken a seat. He was on the job. Not committing a crime.

Didn't feel any different to her.

When he bowed his head, she started to shake. Just her hands. Nothing else.

"Banyon." She managed the one word past the sting in her throat. A tainted prosecuting attorney.

"He was selling guns to certain disreputable persons while prosecuting their competition. Twenty-four of his cases have been thrown out," Detective Larson was saying. "Drug dealers are going to be back out on the street."

"I don't know any drug dealers."

"You know someone who provided drugs to one in exchange for protection in prison. Drugs he'd been slowly, illegally, siphoning for years."

To use on her. And others?

"Ken gave away the evidence."

After a lot of intricate tracking of hidden trails, Sam Larson had found proof that Ken had been writing prescriptions for the various ingredients in the cocktail he'd been feeding her. But they'd never found drugs that correlated with the prescriptions. If he'd fed them all to her, she'd have been dead.

Her mind was working on facts. The rest of her was silent.

Gone.

"I need you to come with me, Bloom. Just for a few weeks."

"I'm not running from him. I won't let him make me a prisoner in my own life. Not again."

"I'm not suggesting that you quit living your life. I'll have someone posted to watch you at work and anywhere else you want to go. I just need you out of that house. Word came up from his cell block that he has plans for the place…"

"So I'll sell it."

"That's fine. I need you safe in the meantime."

She wasn't afraid. Didn't he get that? At least not of Ken hurting her. What scared her most was giving up control of her life again.

"No. If I run, he wins."

"If he hurts you, he wins."

She saw a friend of hers, Dr. Molly Higley, a woman who had an office on her floor, leave the building and get in her car. Bloom wanted to be as free as Molly was. Free to get in her car and drive off to a normal Saturday afternoon.

"I…know some people…inside…"

He had informants. Who'd say anything for favors.

"Word is that he's going to see you pay…"

But, of course, there was no evidence that Freelander had said such a thing. No way to restrain a man before he committed a crime.

"I need time to build another case against him. Without any of the evidence Banyon presented."

"With what then?"

"We've got this new information about him ditching the drugs to a dealer, for one."

In exchange for protection in prison.

"Let me guess, some thug's going to testify to that." She'd learned how it all worked. Knew far too much.

His shrug wasn't enough. Because he didn't have enough.

"And you want me to believe that a thug's word that a respected professor gave him drugs is going to be enough to convict Ken in court?"

When two and a half years before only her testimony would have been strong enough? And now they wouldn't have that. Double jeopardy wouldn't allow it.

"It won't be enough. No. But it's a start." His gaze was piercing. "You're in danger, Dr. Freelander."

So they were going with formality again. Fine by her.

"You're trying to scare me."

"That depends."

She hadn't been asking a question. She'd been stating a fact. She knew what he was doing. What he'd done from the first time she'd met him in the emergency room. Frightened her so much she'd felt she had no choice but to appear in court, face her ex-husband, the man she'd given not only her heart, but her entire future, and talk about how he'd been responsible for her broken jaw. The detective had been right to ask things of her then. She'd taken the stand and taken back her life.

"Depends on what?"

"On whether or not it's working. I need your cooperation on this, Bloom."

Bloom again. Back and forth. Push and back off. Forcing her and then letting her choose. He knew how to manipulate, that was for sure.

"How long do you propose keeping me hostage?" She wasn't going. At least not with him. Maybe she'd check herself into a hotel. Until she could figure out what else to do.

"Not long."

She studied him. Wanting to trust him. But she'd trusted him when she'd been adamant about not testifying against Ken, and Sam had assured her that they had such an airtight case that nothing could possibly go wrong.

She'd trusted him when he'd told her that the way to ensure freedom from Ken for the rest of her life was to testify...

She'd trusted Ken, too, when he'd promised to love and honor her.

Turned out he'd been more threatened by her intelligence, her ability to surpass him in their chosen field, than in love with her.

And the self-admitted wedded-to-his-job detective needed her to close his case. Again.

Two very different men. Both serving their internal drive to be the brightest stars in their career universes.

"How can you sit there and calmly tell me that

it won't be long? If what you say is true, you can't possibly know how long it will be before Ken does something else to get himself in hot water. Because if what you're telling me is true, he's going to be after me until he finds me, right? If you have your way, he doesn't find me at all. Which means I have to stay hidden forever."

Or be found.

She might be slow to see some things, but she was not stupid. Far from it.

"I have a plan."

It wasn't the look on Sam Larson's face that stopped Bloom's thoughts cold. Or even the words. It was the tone of his voice.

Like he wasn't bullshitting her at all.

Like he was deadly serious.

"Will you at least give me a chance to lay it out for you before you decide?"

The choice was hers. To listen or not. To decide her course of action. Either with him or not.

It would be stupid not to avail herself of all the information.

"I'll listen," she told him. And she would.

But listening did not mean agreeing with what she heard.

It did not mean doing what she was told.

She was no longer a woman who could do that.

She'd rather die first.

CHAPTER FOUR

SAM HAD HER. He always knew when a subject he was interviewing was going to give him what he wanted. It was some kind of sixth sense he'd been given.

Sick sense, his ex-wife used to say. After she'd fallen out of love with him.

Whatever. He hadn't asked for it. And he used it for good.

This wasn't about having her. It had been. But now that he'd crossed that hurdle, he faced another.

How to make her think capitulation was her idea? How to make it her idea? Because the second he'd seen the spark of fear return to her eyes he'd known what he didn't want to have to do. Control her. Manipulate her. Scare her back into the woman he'd met in that hospital emergency room.

"First, I have a place you can stay that will cost you nothing…"

"I'm not a charity case," she interrupted, and he swore silently, giving her time to add, "I can afford to pay my own way. And then some."

"I expect you can afford to pay my way, too," he told her with complete honesty. "And then some. This isn't about what you can afford. It's about not letting that bastard take another thing from you. Or cost you more than the thousands you already spent on legal fees and counseling…"

She knew he knew the intimate details. So why did he feel as though he'd just knocked on the bathroom door while she was inside?

"And you think leaving my home won't do that?"

He didn't like feeling like a failure in an interview. Had no practice at it. "It also has to do with making you less easy to trace," he said. "Hear me out, please?" Demanding was going to defeat his purpose.

The one where she was the one in charge and still chose his course of action.

"The place I have, it's everything you told me you love about your house. It's right on the ocean—closer than your house actually. It's not as big—you'd said that you always thought that house was too much space just for you and the bastard. It's higher up so you have the view you'd said was most important to you. And…it's more private."

She'd pictured a more peaceful setting for their beach home, but Ken had needed people around him. Rich people. All the time. At least that was what she'd told him close to three years before when he'd asked her permission to search her home without a warrant.

"You remember every word I ever said? Or have you been reading my case file?"

"My notes aren't that good. Did you catch the part about this place being private, Bloom? It's set up on a cliff, on private property. Fenced property. There's a small trail down to the ocean. One that can be easily guarded. You'll be safe there."

Her expression softened. Everything in him pushed for the close. He gritted his teeth and sat there.

"I don't like how easily you can play me," she told him. And he started to look for angles again. Was much more comfortable doing so.

So…his angle was to get her to agree without losing any sense of the control she'd gained over her life.

"Are you telling me it doesn't sound good to you?"

"It sounds heavenly."

Good. Hopefully he could get her to agree before she actually saw the place.

"But I need to be right here in the city. I've got early morning appointments and sometimes I don't get home until nine o'clock at night as it is…"

Hours he could relate to. And didn't like to hear her keeping. As if she had no life…

"It is right here in the city."

"A place like that, here in the city, and it's available?" Her tone had lightened. He took that as a win.

"Yes."

"That's hard to believe."

Not as hard as she thought. As she'd soon find out. He'd gotten the place for a steal, on foreclosure, after years of neglect and abuse.

The toilets had been replaced. And the faucets. Structurally it was fine. He'd added braces beneath the porch. Done some painting—so far only on the inside. And covered holes in the walls with cheap prints...

"So, do you think it's a good idea for you to stay there where it'll be easier to keep you safe? At least for the time being?"

The way she stuck her out lower lip, as though she was considering, that was new. Drew attention to how full that lip was...

"So that's your plan?" Her disapproving tone didn't coincide with his thoughts at all. "To have me move to a safer place? Be guarded? Held hostage for the unforeseeable future, in case someday Ken decides to act on a threat that he might not even have made?"

He'd made it. Sam was 100 percent certain of that.

He just had no proof. Yet.

"You honestly expect me to believe if you aren't guarded that you won't be looking over your shoulder every second of every day, living in fear, in case someday the bastard decides to act on a threat that he might not even have made?" The words burst from him. He'd rather scare her than have her beat up again. Or worse.

She had to move. Within the next twenty-four hours. Period.

He'd made a promise to her to keep her safe and he was damn well going to keep it.

HER INSIDES MIGHT be clenching to the point of pain, but Bloom was not going to give in. Fear would not rule her life. Ever again.

Sure, she'd experience the emotion now and then. It was an inevitable part of the human experience. But that didn't mean she had to live it.

Feel it. Breathe. Move on. And it would pass. Fact. Not just theory. Or wishful thinking.

Nor was she going to dumb herself down by refusing to see, or to think about, the fearful challenges that could be in front of her. Having once been robbed of that chance against her will, without even knowing that it was happening to her, she now cherished her ability to face situations and make her own choices in how to deal with them.

"I won't be living in fear," she said after a minute of careful thinking, in answer to the detective's challenge. "And I already look over my shoulder. Unless my back is against the wall," she added. A timeless "gift" from her past. An awareness that there is always that which is unseen acting upon you.

His expression didn't change. Nor did his posture. But she knew he was changing tactics even before he spoke. Because she was trained to hear the things people didn't or couldn't say. To see the things that they didn't know were there.

Except for where Kenneth Freelander was concerned. That's what love had done to her. It had used her to prove the truth in the old adage "love is blind…"

"My plan doesn't end with getting you to a safe house."

She was listening.

"A batterer will batter if he's met with the provocation that brings out that tendency in him," he continued.

Now he was in her territory. "Unless he's had counseling and learned how to redirect those tendencies," she said. "Or to recognize the circumstances that prompt them and distance himself from them before they get out of hand."

Not all abusers were destined to lives of abuse. Science told her that. And she believed it, too. On a professional level. Personally, she couldn't be objective…

"Kenneth has had no counseling."

He'd know what she'd had no way of finding out.

Bloom looked at his shoes. Those uneventful black loafers. And flashed back to a gray-and-white-tiled floor. Industrial tile. Hospital floor tile. She'd been in the emergency room. Unable to make herself look up from the floor. She'd been too drugged to care enough to try.

And too embarrassed by what had happened to her to face another human being eye to eye. She'd listened as medical personnel spoke to her. She'd heard the voices. The kindness in them had only made everything that much more difficult to bear. She hadn't felt like she'd deserved their kindness. She'd been a fool. The worst kind. Because she'd had the intelligence to know better…

His shoes had been her indication that someone else had entered the room. He'd said something about being on call for the High Risk Team. It was the first she'd heard the term. And had thought he was a doctor. Called in either because she was suspected to have brain damage and could hemorrhage. Or because they'd thought she was a suicide risk.

"I'm Detective Larson," he'd said then. "And I need you to look at me." There'd been no kindness in his voice. No demand, either, really. She'd never understood why that voice had moved her. Why she'd raised her head.

Or why she'd instantly trusted him.

"Bloom?"

She looked at him.

"I'm going to see that Kenneth is met with the provocation that will force him to hang himself."

"That's entrapment." She was in his territory, but she'd learned a lot since her debut in the court system. Knowledge was power. And inner power led to healing. With her IQ Bloom had had a head start to healthy living.

"Not if it's done right," he said. "I've already spoken with a detective who is also on the High Risk Team…"

She knew the term now. Intimately. The team, comprised of industry professionals—if you could call intimate partner abuse an industry—was designed to prevent death due to domestic violence.

She'd been in danger of death. At Kenneth's hands. The thought came with the same internal hiccup as always. It was possible her mind would never completely wrap around that truth. She could live with hiccups.

"… Chantel did some undercover work for the team a few months ago…" Sam was saying.

Bloom didn't like that she'd missed part of what he'd been saying. A residual from her drugged days. Already he was sending her back.

Kenneth. And Sam, too.

"I read recently about this village in Northern Kenya," she said, consciously switching focus, taking control of her thoughts. "Umoja, that's the name of the village…"

She looked Sam Larson in the eye, challenging him to leave her alone.

"It's fully inhabited by women and children, only. No men allowed."

His eyes narrowed.

"And before you doubt its veracity, you should know that it's thriving, as much as any village in that region thrives. It was founded in 1990 by fifteen women who'd been victims of rape. In Kenya, when a woman is raped, she is blamed, considered unclean and unfit for marriage. If she was unlucky enough to be married at the time of the rape, she is oftentimes subjected to beatings by her husband…"

Drawing a shaky breath, Bloom turned her head, focusing on the flowering bush several yards away. Filled with reds and oranges, the plants reminded her of the paintings in her office. Bold. Vibrant. Sunrise and sunset. The circle of life.

"Women are survivors, Detective," she said when she could speak calmly. "Many of us have not yet learned our strengths. We aren't raised to know about the core of steel inside of us. But it's there. We nurture. We spread softness, and care for our own, but don't mistake us as being incapable of taking care of ourselves."

"When I first met you, you said there was no one I could call," he responded immediately. "That you had no family close by. But I need to know if you have any family, period. Anyone Freelander might contact."

The tiny voice crying out inside her had to be diminished. She would not crumble. Would not allow Kenneth to have squeezed the heart and soul out of her. She was smart, but she was so much more than a mind that made people curious. Her whole life people had concentrated on that part of her. Her own parents had shipped her off to a university to be raised as a lab rat.

No...she reined in her thoughts again. Those were Kenneth's words, hurled at her in one of his many verbal attacks when she'd been to blame for something he'd done. Carl and Betty, as she'd always called her parents, had loved her to distraction. And had given her some of the best memories of her life during her summer vacations and holidays with them. Betty had sobbed every single time they'd had to say goodbye. And there'd always been moisture in Carl's eyes, too, as he'd stood there with one hand on the big golden retriever they'd purchased the year after she left and who'd been a "child" more suited to the older couple, and the other hand at his wife's waist.

Maybe, if they'd been younger when they'd had her...or prepared to ever have a child...

"My parents are both alive. And I have an aunt and uncle and some cousins. All older than me."

She never talked to anyone anymore about who she'd been before she'd attracted the attention of the handsome and charming star of the university psych department.

"Are they local?"

She stared at him. Thinking of Ken contacting Betty and Carl. And knowing he wouldn't.

"Because if they are, we need to make certain that they're safe, too…"

"They live in Oklahoma," she said now, still watching him. "They have a house, and a couple of acres on the farm my father's family owns."

Her father and father's older brother jointly owned and worked the farm. The final decision to ship her off had been made by the two of them. She'd been six.

Sam nodded. "Good."

She nodded, too. It was good. And maybe in the fall, if her schedule slowed a little bit, she'd make time to spend a week on the farm. To get back to her roots and know that, no matter what, she was okay. Because she mattered to them all.

They didn't understand her. They were always afraid they were going to do or say the wrong thing. They were intimidated by her. At least her father and uncle were. But they did love her.

And she had to get to LA. Missing an evening

out with her friends—most especially because of Ken—would be as unhealthy for her as a heart patient neglecting to take her beta-blocker.

She stood. "Tell me what time you'll get me tomorrow and I will be packed and ready," she said, facing the detective as he stood, as well. His shoulders were broad. She liked them, anyway. "But I will only go on one condition…"

He hadn't been smiling. His expression still fell. "What…"

"…I will be the provocation used to drive Kenneth Freelander to his rewards."

There was no other option.

CHAPTER FIVE

SAM DIDN'T LIKE misleading her. And he damned straight wasn't going to lie to her. He'd tell her the truth—that there was no way he was letting her get anywhere near that bastard ex-husband of hers again—as soon as he had her safely out of that house.

He made the promise to himself, and silently to her, Sunday afternoon during the entire fifteen minutes it took him to get from the foot of his dirt drive to the fancy winding street that housed the two-acre beach lots where Freelander had brought her to live. With a stop at the room he'd rented to drop off Lucy.

The girl had not been pleased with him. At all. Hadn't cared a whit about the meaty bone he'd left her. No, she'd been 100 percent into the guilt. Giving him that big brown-eyed stare, the drooped ears and lips.

Just like a female...

Sam shook his head. Lucy was the best. Loyal. A great companion. And best of all...forgiving.

She might be displeased with him at the moment, but she'd be as thrilled as hell when he got back. And she didn't hold a grudge.

Bloom was not outside waiting for him. Her car wasn't in the driveway.

In his usual cotton dress pants, shirt and loafers, he stepped out of the car, straightening his tie as he prepared for battle.

When he knocked, she had to unlock the front door to let him in. But she did so. And stood there looking more gorgeous than ever with her long legs mostly covered by the calf-length, short-sleeved, multicolored T-shirt-style dress she was wearing. With sandals.

She'd pulled her hair back, loosely. Was wearing no earrings—though he noted a second piercing in both of her ears—and stepped back to let him in.

He'd have told her he liked what she'd done with the place, except that she'd thrown white sheets over everything minus the shiny wood floors.

"You have bags for me to carry?" He wanted to get this done. With as little conversation—and chance for something to go backward on him—as possible.

"They're out in my car. And before you tell me I have to leave that, too, I'm telling you right now, I'm not going to."

The damned Jaguar. "Why you hang on to a car he bought you, I have no idea." Sam shut his mouth so fast he almost bit his tongue. See, these were the things that could go wrong, he reminded himself.

"Make no mistake, Detective…"

He didn't like the formality one bit.

"…I paid for that car. Dearly."

Still, who held on to anything that was a part of, or came from, someone who'd brutalized you so cruelly…

Unless, in spite of everything, she wasn't really over Kenneth Freelander. Was possibly even still in love with him. It happened. He knew only too well from his work with the High Risk Team.

And if she did still hold feelings for her ex… his job just got that much more difficult.

"I didn't ever intend for you to give up your car," he said now, hoping he could backpedal enough to get her safely ensconced in his home.

His temporary ex-home. For as long as this took.

"I just figured you'd need to put some things in my SUV. It's bigger."

"I've got what I need."

Had she understood? "You won't be coming back here. Not even to pick things up."

"Unless the laws have changed overnight, or I'm under arrest, I can go anywhere I please. Whenever I please."

True. But…

"However, I've agreed to be under protection, with the understanding that I am your bait, dangled in front of my ex-husband under your auspices, not his. And I'm good for my word. I expect, if Kenneth really is out to get me, he'll take our bait fairly quickly and this will all be over. If not, it will be over anyway because I won't be in any danger."

"I don't expect him to jump on you the second he's out, Bloom. You know him better than I do, but from what I've gleaned, he's a man who plans carefully before he brushes his teeth in the morning."

A bit of an exaggeration. But not much.

"That's true," she said, eyeing him with something that looked a little bit like respect. It was the first time she'd met his gaze since she'd let him in the door.

"So…if I find I need something I've left behind, I'll let you know and you can come get it for me. How does that work?"

He could live with that. And wanted to leave it alone from there. But…

"Do you at least have everything that means something to you?" he pressed. "As in, if this house were to burn down, you'd have everything that was irreplaceable?"

Freelander had threatened to burn down the

place. But he could just as easily trash it, or anything that mattered to her, depending on his mood.

"Most of what I can't live without, along with my will and all important papers, are locked in a safe in my office." She'd surprised him again. Wasn't nearly as naive as she'd been when he'd known her before. But then, she wasn't drugged anymore, either.

He made a mental note not to underestimate her again.

"I've got the rest in the car."

Picturing the backseat of the Jaguar, he wondered what she'd put there. Wanted to know what she couldn't live without.

Crazy. Other than Lucy, he wasn't even sure what *he* couldn't live without.

"You ready, then?" He didn't want to admit to a case of nerves. You had to have nerves to get nervous. But there was no kidding himself. Getting her out of there was the easy part of this day.

"I'll follow you," she told him. She had to follow him. She couldn't very well lead when she didn't know where he was going.

And she could turn off at any point, which was why Chantel was a half block down, waiting to follow Bloom in the old Mustang Chantel insisted on driving even now that she was engaged to a millionaire. Chantel was as adamant as Sam that Bloom get moved to a safe house.

Sam always had a backup plan. It was the only way to stay alive in his business.

BLOOM WASN'T AS unsettled as she probably should have been. Leaving the home she loved…

She'd return soon enough. And appreciate it all the more. Absence made the heart grow fonder.

"I'm having an adventure," she said aloud to the Jaguar's interior. And wondered if, in the spirit of adventure, when she got back, she should get a bird. Something that would talk back to her on occasion.

Probably not, though. A bird would need care and company and Bloom gave everything she had to her job.

Keeping the detective in sight was proving a bit more difficult than it could have been. There was no way she was going more than five miles above the speed limit—being led by a cop or not. The law was the law.

She'd have expected him to be a bit more thoughtful, though. To be aware that if the light was soon to turn yellow, he should stop, because she'd have to do so. Or wait until there was enough of a clearing in the traffic for both of them before making a turn.

He got better at it, though. After he'd twice had to pull over to wait for her. She almost smiled, but then worried that he'd see her in the rearview mirror and find her odd, smiling alone in her car.

She didn't really care what he thought about her.

Ah...ah...ah. Her internal companion butted in. So yeah, okay, she cared a little bit. She was entrusting herself to his care for the next brief window in time. And would be trusting him with her life when she became Ken bait.

The idea didn't scare her as she'd have assumed it would. Pausing in the thought, Bloom waited for the small voice inside of her to chime in. Surprised when she was met with only silence. She really wasn't afraid of Ken as much as she was driven to take this step. To stand up to him. Free herself of any power he'd ever had over her, free her heart from that last vestige of tenderness for having once loved the man so completely.

With the help of Sam Larson. That internal voice of honesty that was what she placed her trust in now added to her thought.

And she knew it was right. Without Sam Larson's backup, his protection, his willingness to do what it took to get Ken back in jail, his drive to make Ken pay for his crimes, she wouldn't be able to face Ken and succeed.

Not because she thought she'd cave in. But because she wasn't powerful enough. Ken had the superior physical strength. Friends in low places.

And he had friends in high places where the court was concerned, as well.

Not high enough to defeat the law, though. Or a detective set on upholding the law. Especially not in Santa Raquel. While Ken was busy building an army of thugs in prison, the Santa Raquel police force had been cleaning up house. Some people with money had been getting favors, to the point of a privileged son getting away with rape and, with the help of an undercover beat cop, a way of life that had been going on for decades had been stopped. The commissioner had been exposed. A rapist was awaiting trial. And Chantel Harris, the cop, was now a detective.

Like everyone else in Santa Raquel, Bloom had followed the whole thing on the news. Perhaps not everyone had followed as closely as she had. The rape hadn't been the only cover-up. A powerful man had been getting away with raping women within his society. One of them was now one of Bloom's patients.

Bloom wasn't Sam Larson's compliant, needy charge anymore, though. She wasn't going to sit back and let him take care of her as she had in the past. Which was why she wasn't telling him about the number that had shown up on her caller ID that morning. The call she hadn't answered.

Ken had called her a few times from prison. The first time she'd taken the call because she hadn't recognized the number. The second time, she'd taken it because she'd still been under his manipulative influence. And probably still a bit in love with the man she'd thought him to be.

She hadn't actually spoken with him, other than that first time. After that she'd just answered the calls and as soon as she'd heard his voice she'd hung up.

This most recent time she'd just let it ring. He hadn't left a message.

And Bloom wasn't telling Sam. The detective already believed that Ken was a threat to her. That he wanted her. And she was giving him no reason, no excuse, not to use her as the bait that would reel him in.

Sam Larson turned his nondescript SUV. Bloom turned the Jaguar. They weren't far from her house. A few miles, maybe. But the meticulously manicured landscape that stretched along all of the roads around her part of town had disappeared, giving way to tangled growth, underbrush with thorns, weeds and as much roadside trash as there ever was anywhere in Santa Raquel city limits. Because this area, on the outskirts to the north of town, was last on the day's cleanup schedule.

Curiosity rose inside her. Maybe even a hint of excitement. She was a thinker. And like Ken— worse than Ken—a planner. Her mind never rested.

Which left very little room for anything akin to adventure.

Still, north of town? With beaches that were more rocky than sandy and cliffs that prevented easy access to the water, the area was only popular with those who could afford no better.

On the coastal road, she sped up as the speed limit increased, thinking about pushing the button on the steering wheel that would allow her to make a call and find out just where Detective Larson was taking her.

She'd stressed to him her working hours. Her need to be close to the office. And as far as she knew, there were no other habitable places in this direction until they came to the next town, more than ten miles away. She saw nothing but roadway ahead, lined on the right by brush and trees and on the left, hills and cliff face that fronted the ocean down below. He signaled a left turn.

There was no road to the left. He slowed, anyway. Almost to a stop. Heart pounding, Bloom wondered what was wrong. And wondered why she was overreacting so much since she wasn't afraid.

She saw the two dirt tire track paths as he turned onto them. And because he was Detective Sam Larson, the man who'd saved her life, figuratively if not literally, she followed him. The track wound back and forth up the hill beneath a thick canopy of trees that were growing so close to the track that branches scraped against her car.

Clearly the detective hadn't driven a Jaguar lately. He should have warned her that getting where they were going could scratch the paint job on a vehicle she couldn't afford to purchase a second time. If she was going to drive her dream car—a Jaguar—this was it.

She worried about the car so that she didn't have to think about where they might end up. He'd said the house had private beach access. Or rather, what he'd said was that there was a single path down to the water and that the property was fenced off.

They hadn't driven through a fence. Anyone could access the road from down below. They wouldn't be able to hang out down there, though. The busy highway didn't have enough shoulder to allow anyone to hang out without being noticed. And in the way.

Almost as though he'd read her mind, Larson pulled to a stop, and when she crept up as close to his bumper as she could get without hitting him, she saw the newish-looking double-story gate that had prevented him from going any farther. The iron bars were slowly opening.

Looking to the right and left of that gate, she also saw the ten-foot-high fencing that went as far as she could see. Iron poles that were cemented into the ground, placed only an inch apart, criss-crossing at the top. No way for anyone to climb the fence, or shimmy up a pole, either, since there wasn't enough room in between them to wrap an arm around.

Holy crap, she thought. He hadn't been kidding about getting her someplace safe. He'd lied to her when he'd promised her that, if she testified, she'd never have to deal with Ken Freelander again. Not that a crooked prosecuting attorney was anything he could have predicted or prevented.

But the point was, he made promises he couldn't possibly keep.

Like promising her that he'd protect her this time around. He was only one man. So many things were out of his control. So much could go wrong.

Still, at the moment, she was better with him than without him. And it was good to know that he hadn't lied about the place being protected from easy intrusion.

Keeping her mind focused on the goal in mind—getting Ken back behind bars—she followed the detective through the gate.

CHAPTER SIX

THE…HOUSE…WAS a shock. Gray boards, peeling slivers of wood in places, had long since lost their paint. Leaving everything but her purse—which held her cell phone—and pepper spray key chain, she climbed out of the Jaguar and stood for a moment, staring at the smallish building.

It wasn't the Taj Mahal. It wasn't even as nice as the freshman dorm she'd lived in in college. Or the tract home she'd visited the previous week to see a client whose bones were not yet healed enough to allow her comfortable travel to Bloom's office.

Sam Larson wasn't looking to her for approval or even a reaction. He was all business as he headed up decaying steps toward a door. Bloom stepped gingerly forward—not sure she trusted the steps, in spite of the fact that a man twice her size had just bounded up them—until she noticed the new boards giving support underneath the porch.

For some reason that small sign of repair, of attention and care, gave her the impetus to focus on Ken behind bars, and not on the fact that this place was supposed to be her new home. Albeit temporarily. Stepping with as much authority as she could muster, she made it to the front door without shaking.

Or even feeling like shaking.

The door was as ancient-looking as the rest of the house, but it was solid. And bore new dead bolt locks. Two of them. He unlocked them and handed her the keys.

To say the inside wasn't what she'd been expecting would be a huge understatement. Nor did it resemble anything like any of the places she'd lived over the last two decades. But it was…doable. Reminded her of the little place her folks had lived in on the farm when they'd first married. Before they'd built their current, more modern, fancier home. Also on the farm. The old place was a guest house now, of sorts. Nothing fancy. Isolated. But clean if you didn't look too closely.

Sam's choice of safe house was certainly off the beaten path. So far off Ken would never believe she'd inhabit such a place. Or probably ever visit himself. But those trees, the snarls of weedy undergrowth, the dirt road, the…dirt…in general, wouldn't be an impediment to the types of people Ken had supposedly befriended.

"There are two bedrooms," the detective was saying, heading from the entry, past a galley kitchen, through the great room toward a hallway at the back. "One has its own bathroom, the other uses the bath here off the hall." He was opening doors as he went, showing her an iron tub that reminded her, again, of that old house on the farm. It had been a place she'd gravitated to when she'd been home for summer vacations. More home to her than the house she'd lived in with her parents before her uncle and father had decided to ship her away for being too smart.

Before her mother had chosen to side with them.

Plush white towels in varying sizes hung on the rods. She caught sight of a price tag on the back of one of them. The toilet was new. Linoleum, like that in the other parts she'd seen of the cottage, was yellowed and curled around the base of the new white porcelain.

Three types of shampoo, a full bar of soap and a container of body wash lined the back wall of the tub. The shower curtain still had creases in it from being packaged.

Had the house just been made habitable for her purposes? And if so, who'd paid for it?

Could they somehow stick Prosecutor Trevor Banyon with the tab?

The bedroom immediately across the hall was small, but as clean as the rest of the house. An old double bed sat on scarred linoleum. The comforter and pillow cases resembled the shower curtain in their even creases. A window faced the front yard. It was a little low for her liking.

"It's bolted shut," Larson said, observant as always, apparently. She'd been eying the old latch and wondering…

"It's completely reinforced with rebar."

"Rebar?"

"It's steel bar used in construction to reinforce concrete."

She nodded. Feeling a bit cramped standing there alone with him in the small room. She noted a dresser. A door that she assumed opened to a closet. And she moved toward the hall, grateful when he stepped aside to give her clear passage.

Her wedge sandals had a two-inch sole, but her eyes only came to his nose as she passed. She didn't look closely.

Instead, she concentrated on what had to be new paint in the hallway. The same off-color, not bright enough to be white and not golden enough to be beige—that she'd noted on walls in the front room.

He led her to the second bedroom. Stood back while she looked around. A charging station sat on a nightstand on one side of the king-size bed. The comforter, a nondescript beige, had no crease marks. If anything, it was slightly wrinkled, as though it had been crammed into a dryer that was too small for it. A couple of paintings hung on the walls. They were washed-out prints of boats that looked as though they'd come from a dollar store.

They made Bloom want to paint. The entire place cried for her brushes. For color.

I choose joy, her inner voice piped up unexpectedly. Yes. She consciously always chose color—in her clothes, her adornments, her walls, because color brought her joy.

In the bathroom she noticed a used bar of soap in the shower. Along with identical bottles of everything she'd seen in the other, smaller bathroom off the hall. Even the new towels were there. Minus any visible tags.

And the toilet paper roll, as in the other room, was full, as though it hadn't had a single sheet torn off from it.

But that soap...

"Is this someone's room?" she asked.

"Not currently, why?"

"The soap in the shower."

He blinked, looked a tad put out and retrieved the bar. "That shouldn't have been left there," he said, sounding apologetic.

Or annoyed. She couldn't tell which. Unlike Ken, Sam Larson kept his emotions well in check.

He'd said she could have either bedroom.

"You're sure I'm not putting somebody out of a home?"

"Positive."

There'd been new towels in both bathrooms. As though both were expected to be used.

"I'm not staying here alone am I?" For a brief second her heart rate sped up.

She didn't want Detective Larson to stay with her. He hadn't offered, either. But for a second there…

"No, you're not," he said, as though brooking no argument.

The place was remote. And while she prided herself on being self-sufficient, the place was… remote. And yet…she didn't want to stay alone with him.

Transference was a powerful tool the mind used to emulate the sense of safety and security that was on Maslow's hierarchy of needs. Right behind physiological. She was noticing him. Noting odd sensations. She couldn't afford a personal setback. Most particularly not with Ken soon to be back in her picture, however briefly.

"Who's going to be staying here with me?"

"Detective Chantel Harris," he said. "She's giving us some time to get you settled and then she'll be along. I'll introduce you before I go."

She could pretend she wasn't disappointed. Though she'd like to think that for her own good she'd have refused to stay there alone with him. But her inner voice wouldn't let her get away with lying to herself, so she went ahead and dealt with the feeling of dismay right then and there. He was her safety net. What she was feeling was normal. She nodded.

She thought about Ken being free and needed him back behind bars. Those bars that held him had given her her life back. Had taught her about freedom. Given her the first real taste of it she'd ever known.

"So what is this, someone's summer home?" she asked, following Sam back out into the great room. She could see dishes stacked on shelves that a cupboard door had once covered. "If it is, they'll be needing it soon."

It was July. Summer visitors were already there in full force. Ever since Memorial Day the beaches— and bed-and-breakfasts that lined the streets around them—had been filled.

"This house is yours for as long as you need it," he stated, clearly undaunted.

"I'm not going to need it long," she pushed back.

He studied her. Put his hands in his pockets. And said nothing.

Bloom understood the tactic. And didn't like the response.

At all.

As soon as Sam heard Chantel's car coming up the drive, he started to breathe easier. His associate had promised him that she wouldn't say anything to Bloom about the cottage being his house. He knew she'd refuse to stay.

And there was no place else safe enough, that he could afford, that was also close to her work. He'd yet to receive financial approval from the department for his plan, but with Freelander's imminent release, he hadn't been able to wait for it.

Lucky for him he heard the old Mustang just as Bloom was letting him know that she wouldn't be in his house long. All he had to do was hold his tongue for thirty seconds or so and be home free.

He told himself that he'd cut out a minute after introductions because Lucy was alone in a one-room…room, and would need to be let out. And added that Chantel and Bloom were better off getting to know each other on their own.

He was happy with both points. Sam's conscience had learned long ago to leave well enough alone.

He spent the evening with Lucy, walking on the beach. Because Bloom was his responsibility, he chose the stretch directly below his cottage. He'd had to drive through the gate, but had left his vehicle there and then hiked to the side path that led down to the beach. Lucy loved bounding through the trees almost as much as she liked running in the sand, spraying it up behind her. He was glad to see lights flickering through the trees.

Glad, too, to verify that he *couldn't* see enough

of the window to make out anything, or anyone, inside.

He talked to Chantel just before bed. And again the next morning when she showed up for work after tailing Bloom to her office.

Freelander wasn't out of prison yet, but word was that he'd specifically stated that he was going to have the pleasure of watching his wife find out that he was in charge as he taught her about proper respect.

Sam and Chantel were setting their routine for the days to come—when Freelander would be out. Taking it through a dry run. They'd put in a request for a guard to be placed with Bloom throughout the day. For round-the-clock protection.

"So far so good," the unadorned blonde said as, in brown tweed pants, a white shirt and a matching jacket that only partially blocked her holster and gun from view, she slouched down in the chair beside his desk. They weren't partners. Didn't even work in the same area. But High Risk Team aside, he'd heard incredible things about her.

She was tough. She didn't give up.

And she'd risk her life to help someone she believed deserved help. The job aside.

"How'd last night go?" The eagerness with which he awaited her response left him feeling slightly voyeuristic.

"Good. Fine. She worked. I watched TV."

"What do you think?"

"I like her. She's nice."

"I meant about our chances of keeping her safe until we can figure out a way to get the guy to make the mistake that will send him back to jail."

Chantel's pause gave him indigestion.

"You get the idea she's not going to cooperate for long?" He put the concern right out there. He had her in the house. She was cooperating. But keeping her there…

"I get the idea she has a mind of her own and doesn't plan to let that creep husband of hers hold her hostage."

Minor discomfort became not so minor. "Meaning?"

Shaking her head, her ponytail swaying, Chantel twisted her mouth and said, "I don't know, Sam. She's a hard one to read."

Not if you knew her well enough.

The thought came unbidden to his head. He held on to it.

"Anyway, I've got a thing with Colin tonight and I know you wanted to be with Bloom when Freelander's officially released, so can you get her from work? Stay with her until I get there?"

He welcomed the chance. "Any idea how late you're going to be?" he asked, because it seemed like an expected response.

"If that rich and powerful fiancé of mine had his way it would be all night. But I've already told him I'll attend his fund-raiser with him as long as he has me back to my car by eleven."

Which would put her at the house by eleven-fifteen. Give or take five.

"You going to show up in your finery?" He'd heard talk around the station of the astonishing change she could pull off in very few minutes, but he'd never seen it for himself. From what he'd heard, she'd never seen it either until she'd been forced, while working as an undercover dilettante, to buy some designer clothes and learn how to wear makeup.

"I'm stopping by my place to change," she said, shrugging. And then grinned. "It drives Colin nuts, and it's good to keep him on his toes," she said. "Keeps him from taking me for granted."

He harrumphed. Had no interest in being privy to any romantic entanglements between...anyone.

"I thought you were living with him." He only thought about the arrangement because she'd been the talk of the station a few months before. A real Cinderella tale. And he'd had his doubts about how a beat cop tomboy would fit in with the high-falutin lawyer's fanciness. Eating off fine china every day.

"Him and his sister, at the family estate," she said. "But I kept my place, too. Colin's actually started to like slumming with me a night or two a week. Gives us time alone. And gives Julie, his sister, a chance to entertain without us around."

He'd heard about the girl only enough to know she'd been a victim of date rape. He nodded politely, ready to move on, and noticed his captain coming toward them.

The grim look on the black man's face didn't bode well. If it was a case that was going to take him out of commission he'd have to pull some kind of favor and get out of it.

"You'll be getting the email shortly, but I wanted to tell you personally, you didn't get the approval for extra coverage," Captain Salyers said. He didn't sound happy. "With the new regime, with everyone looking, we can't pull favors. Most particularly not for the town's elite."

The words running through Sam's mind weren't for speaking.

Chantel's booted feet landed on the floor. "How is it a *favor* to protect a woman whose ex has threatened her life and who's getting out of jail on a technicality? How is that not a given?"

"That's just it," the captain said, looking between the two of them. "The threat against her life hasn't been substantiated in any official way. And the reversal on the case wasn't our mistake. The commissioner said to take it up with the prosecutor's office. Get them to come up with the money for off-duty cops. If the prosecutor's office does it, it's fair pay for wrongdoing. If the commissioner allots funds, without wrongdoing on the part of the police department, it'll look like he's doing favors."

And the new commissioner had some heavy footsteps to obliterate.

"Because we don't have a crime here," Sam said succinctly. Nodding. He understood. Cops weren't officially in the business of prevention. Only cleanup. It was messed up.

But nothing he was going to change in time for his purposes.

Salyers made a couple of suggestions regarding requests made to the district attorney's office, who to contact, what he might want to say. Sam could feel Chantel's gaze on him as he listened to his superior. He nodded, took down a name and thanked him.

"You think the DA's office will move on this today?" she asked as soon as Salyers was out of earshot.

"I'm not going to risk it," he told her. He'd put in the request. Stupid not to. And if approval came at some point, great. But in the meantime, "I'm on to plan B," he told her.

"You can't afford to pay for round-the-clock protection on your own, Sam."

"I made a promise to that woman. I promised that if she testified she'd be safe."

"You promised her her ex would be in prison for the rest of his life."

Chin jutted, he nodded slowly. "He will be. And I intend to keep her safe until that happens."

"I'll talk to Colin…"

Sam's head shot up. "I did not ask you to help me with this to get money out of that rich fiancé of yours."

"You didn't ask, period, Larson. I'm on the High Risk Team, too, remember? I offered. And Colin donates money all over the state. He's giving regularly to The Lemonade Stand now…"

A unique women's shelter in town that was changing the world one life at a time. Sam had been there several times, interviewing victims. It was a good place. Necessary. Deserving of any monies it could get.

Bloom had spent time there after the trial…

"Colin's sister was a victim of an unethical police commissioner," Chantel reminded him. "He'll gladly support someone who is now caught in the system due to the commissioner's professional demise. And even if he wouldn't, Julie would. She has half of the Fairbanks fortune."

Sam wasn't feeling charitable. Mostly because he couldn't afford to be as charitable as Chantel's intended. Or Bloom's ex.

Or Bloom, either, for that matter.

All night he'd been aware of the fact that he'd taken the lovely princess out of her castle. Wondering how Bloom was acclimating.

She was "slumming it," as Chantel had just said about Colin. And Sam's home was the slum.

The dichotomy was not lost on him.

And shouldn't matter. He was in her life to do a job. Period.

"I'll make some calls," he told Chantel. "Get a crew together. I'll plan to pay them. If you come up with donations, they'll be appreciated."

He'd only been married once. Hadn't made any more money than his wife had so he hadn't had to pay alimony. He'd acquired the cottage at a steal. Lucy didn't care about diamonds or furs; she ate out of a forty-pound bag. And he made a good salary and had enough put away to pay for protection. For a while, at least.

Plus, he had years ahead of him to rebuild his heirless savings.

What good was a safety net if it couldn't be used to keep someone safe?

CHAPTER SEVEN

SHE'D BEEN EXPECTING CHANTEL. Had been looking forward to making spinach salad for the woman who was giving up time with her new family—living in an old cottage with her instead of the mansion that was now her official home—just because Ken was getting out of jail.

Hating that people were having to rearrange their lives because of her, she was more determined than ever to contact Ken as soon as possible. He knew her, but she knew him, too. Better now than she ever had before. She knew his weaknesses. His vulnerabilities. She knew why he had issues. And her biggest advantage was that he knew she knew.

He had to beat her at mind games. Period. Had to prove to himself that he was superior to any woman. Every woman. Because of the humiliating things his mother had done to him when he was a kid. Making him pay for the fact that he'd been born male right after his father had left her for another woman. For getting in her way when she'd brought jerk after jerk home to take his father's place.

The woman had done bad things. Inconceivable, really, for a mother to do to a son. Nothing as overt as hitting him. She'd left no external bruises. Had inflicted very little physical pain. Bloom had fallen in love with the man that little boy had become. It was only years later that she'd been forced to confront his shadow side.

Or rather, now was when she was going to confront it. She'd only been its victim in times past.

A youngish-looking man waiting in the vestibule opened the door for Bloom as she headed out of her building, on her way to meet the man waiting at the end of the walk to escort her to her car. Chantel had called to let her know that Sam Larson would be picking her up after work.

"Have a good evening," her door-holder said, giving her a head-on, but otherwise situation-appropriate look.

That was when she realized she'd seen him in the hallway earlier when she'd left her office to go down the hall for a soda. Pretending that her insides weren't suddenly shaking, determined to act as though her evening was going to be like any other, she nodded and moved past him, bracing herself for any sudden move he might make. She stared at Sam, hoping he was getting her telepathic message. The able-bodied twentysomething's interest in her was personal.

She was certain of it.

"How was your day?" Sam asked as she reached him, turning toward the parking lot with his hands in his pockets.

"There's a guy up there..."

Though there was no visible change in him, she could feel him stiffen. And heard the change in his breathing. He glanced around them without removing his hands from his pockets, but she saw his elbow reposition slightly, as though he were prepared to go for the gun she knew was beneath his suit jacket.

It was her job to be aware of minute changes in body language. To interpret what they might be telling her about the emotional and mental inner workings of her patients.

Still, she felt him so acutely.

"Up on the steps," she said, continuing to walk. "He held the door for me."

Sam's shoulders dropped. His breathing evened out. Even his pace softened.

"That was Gomez," he said.

"Gomez?"

"You're being provided with twenty-four-hour protection," he told her. "Someone will be in the house with you anytime you're there, and you'll have a bodyguard the rest of the time."

"A bodyguard?"

Gomez's interest *had* been personal. She wasn't losing it. But he'd been there to protect her. Not hurt her.

"An off-duty officer who is being paid to guard you. And before you get all peeved on me, you've been failed by the judiciary system. That entitles you to protection. At least until Ken is settled."

Sam made perfect sense. And she felt better.

Sam was a professional through and through. He could sit with a beautiful, fascinating, independent and curiously needy woman without messing up. Or getting involved. In any way.

Marriage had proven to him, if nothing else had, that his work was his life. Which didn't explain the restlessness trickling through him as he thought of the evening ahead—spending hours in his own home while acting like it wasn't home.

He could come clean. Chantel had already told him, more than once, that he *should* do so. She had been somewhat mollified by his assertion that if Dr. Freelander knew that she was putting him out of a home she'd refuse to stay.

Chantel had been appeased *after* spending the evening with Bloom the night before. But she still thought he could let her know the house was his. Chantel seemed pretty certain that Bloom was in full agreement with their arrangement to keep her in a safe house. At least for the time being.

He led the way out of the ritzy part of town that housed her office, keeping Bloom's Jaguar in sight in his rearview mirror. She was making it easy. Staying close. It helped that she knew where they were going.

And he thought again about the long evening hours to fill. With a list as long as his arm and leg added together of things he had yet to do to the place, there was plenty to keep him busy. He and Lucy spent pretty much every night on one project or another. But it would be kind of hard to explain to the occupant of the home why all of his tools and supplies were locked in the shed a few yards from the cottage.

Lucy was not only going to be disgruntled, but she was going to be wound up when he arrived home at eleven o'clock that night expecting to go to bed. Used to having the acres around the cottage as her playground, and at least running on the beach below his place the night before, his late-night walk around the block with her would not suffice. They'd practiced that morning. Exercising and doing her business that way. That was only after working her for half an hour to get her to agree to walk on a leash. In city boundaries it was the law, her being on a leash, but he couldn't seem to impress the importance of police detectives following the law on her. She'd wanted to run. Once, when he'd made the mistake of getting within a block of the beach, she'd practically pulled his arm out of the socket.

They were only a couple of miles from the cottage. And he'd gotten no closer to a decision on what he was going to do with himself that evening. He could watch TV. He wasn't certain that would be enough of a distraction.

From what...he didn't want to think about.

He punched the newest speed dial on his phone. Waited for the Bluetooth to connect and then ring through.

"Hello?" He could see her talking when he glanced in the rearview mirror. But she hadn't removed her hands from the steering wheel. Of course the Jaguar would have come equipped with in-car calling.

"I'd like to take a bit of a detour, if you don't mind," he said, making one decision only to realize he'd just given himself another problem.

"Of course. I'll follow."

No questions. Just...acquiescence. The woman was a kind person. In his world he didn't see enough of them.

"I... Do you like dogs?" he asked, thinking too late that she might not. There'd been no evidence of pets in her life.

"I haven't been around them since I was a kid. But I used to…"

Her voice faded off. As though she'd gone to a different place. A different time. He wondered what it was like for her there.

And when he realized that his wanting to know had nothing to do with the case, he swore to himself.

"I have a red setter," he stated a bit more baldly than he might have if his brain had been working. "She's…staying…where she stays right now when I'm at work, and I'd like to swing by and get her. It's going to be late by the time I head home and it would save me a stop."

Going back to the room to get her. Taking her down to the beach. And then back home to the room. *That* stop.

But he wasn't about to tell Bloom that he was living in a dingy, converted motel room apartment. Renting by the week.

And while getting Lucy was for the girl's benefit, it was for his, as well. Not because of the walk on the beach, but because he needed the distraction. A third party with him and Bloom at all times. His girl keeping him firmly aware of who and what he was.

And what he wasn't. He was not a man who got *personal* with other human beings. No matter how desirable she might be. Or how alone they were in his very secluded home.

"Oh. Okay…"

He wasn't sure what her hesitation meant, but didn't ask. Sometimes what he didn't touch wouldn't burn him.

Occasionally. If he got lucky.

He was lucky that Lucy hadn't shredded the already threadbare carpet in their room. Or peed or pooped on it, either. The girl nearly knocked him over in her exuberance to see him, and while he might have boxed with her a minute or two—a game she'd grown to expect—he held the door open and said, "Car."

He'd left the passenger door ajar for her before he'd unlocked their room, and Lucy made it from the carpet to her seat in two bounds. He was right behind her.

Bloom, her car still running, was stopped by the entrance to the motel.

His phone rang before they'd pulled out of the lot. "That's an odd place to drop your dog for day care."

Something about tangled webs came to mind. He pushed it away. His life was filled with tangled webs. Just usually ones that had been tangled by others. Not ones he'd tangled himself.

"People who live in these places are usually the ones who need money the most," he said. Shaking his head at the whole situation as he stopped at a red light and rang off.

Lucy was staring at him. Probably because he was talking, and not to her.

He stared back.

Until Bloom honked behind him. The light had turned green.

Half a mile from home, he glanced at his passenger again. "Do you have any idea how it makes me feel, telling her I live in a run-down shack compared to that place she owns?" Or that, outside it, all he could afford was a dingy motel room?

The girl didn't seem to understand the magnitude of his humiliation.

Or maybe she just didn't get why it mattered.

For that matter, neither did he.

AT SAM'S INSTRUCTION, Bloom stayed in her Jaguar while he left the dog whining in his car and checked out the place.

He was back out in no time. Which made the dog turn in circles on the front seat and paw at the door. It wanted out. Or him. Sam told her to go inside. As soon as she'd closed the screen door behind her, she heard his car door open and close. The huge dog was loose, and Bloom suddenly felt twice protected.

The kitchen had come fully stocked. She'd investigated the night before and had planned a week's worth of meals from everything she'd found. So maybe the spinach salad could be a complement to something filling enough for a man.

The dog barked. She nearly dropped the pound of ground beef she'd been reaching for, and, glancing out the window, saw Sam throwing a stick he must have found in the woods. Watched as the big red dog bounded after it, landing both front paws on it before picking it up with its mouth and running it back to him.

Sam wasn't an ounce overweight, but he was a big guy… Lean and muscled in all the right places.

Right. She looked away. Found the package in her hand. Sam was a meat kind of guy. She had one meat dish in her repertoire. Meat loaf. Her mother used to make it at least once a week. It had been her father's favorite. And Bloom's, too. Something they had had in common. Back then she hadn't been able to discern why that meant so much to her—to be like either of her parents.

Back then she hadn't known that there'd been an invisible wall between them. One erected when she was two and made her first long-distance phone call without help. Her parents had been astonished. And then frightened at what that meant. They were common folks of average intelligence, living simple lives. Seeking no more than a good farmer could expect when he shared a moderate-size farm with his brother.

They went to church socials. Liked to watch game shows on television. They went to bed early and were up before the roosters crowed.

All things, they'd determined, that would be a waste for a genius child. She was meant to be more.

More what, she still wasn't sure.

But one thing she knew: more, in their eyes, meant more than they could handle. With them her potential would be wasted, and to good farming people, waste of any kind was criminal.

When she was four they'd had her tested.

And when she was six, they'd pulled her out of local school.

Bloom had hated that. She hadn't said anything, though. Mostly because her mother had been so adamant, certain it was the right thing to do. Bloom, like most girls, adored her mother and trusted her to know what was right.

She still loved her mother's meat loaf.

And Ken had insisted that any time they had meat he'd cook it on the grill. He never even so much as scrambled an egg in the kitchen, but he fancied himself grill master of the universe.

Smiling at the ridiculous verbiage she'd just come up with, she pulled out onions, Worcestershire sauce, bread crumbs, oatmeal, ketchup, barbecue sauce, brown sugar and one egg. Her mother had also added a can of green beans, but

Ken had put his foot down at that, challenging her to find a single recipe for meat loaf that called for green beans.

When she'd been unable to do so, she'd reluctantly changed her recipe. On a whim, she checked the cupboard where she'd seen some canned vegetables the night before. Found two cans of French style green beans and opened one.

She had a feeling Sam Larson wouldn't complain. If he was even planning to eat with her.

Either way, meat loaf sounded good to her all of a sudden.

In less than an hour, her ex-husband would be processed and in the car that would transfer him back into society.

A free man.

CHAPTER EIGHT

HE'D PLANNED ON keeping Lucy outside. After being cooped up in one room all day, being out in the fresh air would be good for her. She wasn't too bad as a watch dog, either. Not that Randolph, the officer watching the property, wasn't perfectly competent.

He'd been inside less than five minutes and was already antsy. He'd had to stop himself from automatically reaching above the stove for the bottle of scotch he knew would be there, thinking one shot with water might be just the ticket to get him through the hours ahead.

Sam was a loner by choice. And his home had been a sanctuary to him.

Pausing now and then to talk to him, Bloom was busy putting various ingredients in the big plastic bowl he used for popcorn. It held three microwave bags' worth, which was just about what it took to get him and Lucy through a movie.

"They got anything stronger to drink in this place?" he asked when she lifted a bottle of water to her lips.

She looked good in the kitchen. Damned good. Not as good as she'd looked coming out of her office toward him that afternoon, focusing on him so intently he'd embarrassed himself and had had to close his jacket.

Not one to be so instantly affected by a woman, the circumstance didn't sit well with him. Nor was it going to get in his way.

The job came first. Always.

"There's a selection of things above the stove," she told him, pointing. "It looks like they've been opened, but I guess, since they're here, they're free for the using, right? Which reminds me, I want to buy my own groceries. There's no way the county needs to pay to feed me while I'm here. I'd be buying my own stuff if I were home."

"Fine." There were some points that just made sense. He poured some scotch and asked her if she wanted any. It didn't surprise him when she shook her head. He didn't suppose she'd purposely cloud her mind with artificial substances after being unknowingly drugged for years.

She was chopping onions. With a knife. He wanted to tell her where the handheld chopper was. But stopped himself.

He'd taken a couple of sips when he heard Lucy's first whine. A warning. She stood at the door, her back paws on the concrete and her front paws up as high as she could reach. She was peering in the window at him.

He turned away and took another sip, knowing he wasn't going to be able to leave her out there.

"You can bring her in," Bloom said. "When I was little we had a golden Lab." She was grinning. "I remember running out to the apple tree with her. First one there got the ones on the ground."

"Why would you want apples that had fallen on the ground?"

"My dad and I used to have gushing contests."

"Gushing contests?" Lucy's whine startled him. He'd actually forgotten that he'd been about to let her in.

"You put the apples on the concrete and then jump on them to see who could make the gushes go the farthest."

Turning his head slightly, he studied her from a different angle. He was pretty sure she was pulling his leg, but...

"Your father taught you that game?" It didn't hurt to play along. Worst that could happen was that she'd laugh out loud.

"Uh-huh." She was taking off her rings and placing them on the windowsill. "He and his brother made it up as kids." She frowned. "That was before they found out how smart I was and decided that the game was a waste of my talents."

"A waste of your talents?" And had to add, "Sounds like you were having fun."

"I was."

Lucy's whines were no longer as easy to ignore. Especially accompanied by the scratching. Sam leaned one hand on the counter, watching her. "So what did you do with them for fun after that? That didn't waste your talents?"

"Nothing with him. He fixed up this old house on the property for me, cleaned it and put in some furniture…made it like my own playhouse, and I'd go there and read. He bought me any book I wanted. That was fun."

Remembering all of the years of hanging out with his old man, Sam couldn't see how being alone instead would have seemed like fun. But the arrangement seemed to make some kind of sense to her. She'd shoved her hand down into the bowl and was mixing all of the ingredients together. Not at all sure what took onion, green beans and oatmeal—three of the things he'd noted going into the bowl—he would have continued to watch her, but Lucy barked.

A very definite warning.

Not of danger, but the girl was growing impatient with him. He was in her home and she had a right to be there with him.

Praying that the two women got along, Sam opened the front door.

BLOOM STOOD AT the counter, continuing what she was doing, when the dog ran straight to her.

She braced herself for a jump, but instead, Lucy sniffed her ankles, shoved her nose slightly under the hem of Bloom's navy blue skirt before walking around to the other side of her and repeating the process.

Seemingly satisfied, she made it to Sam in one bound and put her paws up to his chest level, pawing the air and barking. As Bloom formed a mound with her meat mixture, she tried not to stare as Sam held his fists up and then moved them back and forth as the dog's paws hit them.

She was grinning again, though, as she put the meat in the glass pan she'd already prepared, and washed her hands. Then she turned.

"You taught your dog to box?" she asked, feeling...good.

It didn't seem possible, the hour that Ken was due to be free, but...she didn't lie to herself. She'd made that pact two years before, when she'd gotten her mind back and been able to see that she'd been partially to blame for having lost full lucidity to begin with.

The drugs were none of her doing. And hideously wrong. But she'd known that Ken's jealousy, of her with other men and of her intelligence, was beyond the scope of rational. Or normal.

She'd made allowances. Excuses. And when

she could no longer do either of those, she'd told herself that this action or that, by itself, wasn't enough to lose a good marriage over.

She'd lied to herself. Which had allowed him to live out the lie he'd perpetuated.

The dog dropped her front paws to the floor and went off toward the hall. Like she had a purpose. Most likely exploring, Bloom thought, remembering a few more bits and pieces of her life with Madge. She had no idea how old the Lab had been. She'd been around before Bloom was born.

And had died sometime within the first year after she'd been shipped away. She'd been six. And had thought that Madge had died of sadness. Like she'd thought she might do.

Her father had purchased another Lab before Bloom had come home for break, but it hadn't been the same...

"She taught me to box," Sam said, finally answering her question as he picked up his mostly full glass of scotch and watched his dog smell the corners of the room. "She'd bat at me and more times than not catch my face. I put up my hands in self-defense."

The oven sounded its preheated beep and Bloom put the meat in.

"What's her name?"

"Lucy."

"Lucy?"

"Yeah, I know. Strange name for a dog. But it's the first thing I thought of when I saw her. You know, Lucille Ball. She was before our time, but who hasn't heard of..."

"I used to watch *I Love Lucy* every night."

He sipped. She stood.

"Besides, I don't think it's strange. My dog's name was Madge."

"When you were growing up?"

"When I was little, yes."

"Why Madge?"

"My mother named her. After the lady on the Palmolive commercial, she always said. I never saw the commercial, but..."

"Ha!" Sam let out. And, glass in hand, walked over to the wall of DVDs behind the flat-screen TV. Lucy joined him, wagging her tail as he picked out a DVD without really even looking at the more than two hundred choices, flipped a couple of buttons, slid a disc into the Blu-ray player, picked up a remote, pushed a couple more buttons and said, "Watch."

She *was* watching.

And wondering how he knew...well, not how to work everything with such efficiency...guys seemed to have a knack for that, but...

Her thoughts were interrupted by the video's caption. One hundred and one of TV's best commercials, she read. Stood silently while he scrolled.

And then watched as a beautician, Madge, she was called, while in the process of giving a woman a manicure, told her she was "soaking in it"—referring to the deep green dishwashing liquid that was visible.

Bloom's throat closed up as a wave of homesickness washed over her so acutely she almost had to sit down. She hadn't missed her mother like that in…two decades. Not since she'd figured out that she wasn't going to get to go back home no matter what and just had to find a way to make the best of things.

She was emotionally self-sufficient. Didn't need Mom fixes like most girls.

But Ken was out of jail. And gunning for her. Her. Bloom. Betty's daughter.

"Dinner's going to be ready in about an hour," she said, reaching for her phone. She walked down the hall, dialing before she could analyze her reasons for doing so.

And waited for her mother to pick up. It wasn't like Betty was going to have any wise advice for her. Or, more accurately, wouldn't think it worth sharing. Because according to her, Bloom was so much smarter than she was.

"Betty?" she said when she heard the click on the other end of the line.

"Bloom?" Betty's tone sounded as happy as it did every single time Bloom called. At least once a week. Not nearly often enough. "It's not Sunday, dear. Are you okay?"

"Yeah, Betty, I'm fine. I just wanted to tell you, I saw the Madge commercial." She needed to connect to the child she'd been before she'd been tested. Back when Betty had thought she knew more than Bloom did and protected her little girl from the bogeyman.

Before she'd been intimidated by her daughter's higher intelligence and had been afraid that her unschooled way of seeing the world wasn't accurate. Had been afraid of dumbing Bloom down and making her less than she'd been born to be.

And, Bloom figured out many years later, had been afraid of having her daughter think she was dumb.

"You're soaking in it," Betty said, and chuckled. "Where on earth did you see it?"

She'd called to tell her mother about Ken. To know that she wasn't alone in her battle to be strong enough to beat him at his own game.

"A…friend…has a DVD of old commercials," she said, ad-libbing. In her mind, Betty might have been the mother she needed. In reality, the other woman wouldn't understand that while Bloom's intelligence made her mind work quickly, it didn't mean she knew all the things that Betty had learned from living life.

Things Bloom needed to hear.

"That's really cool," Betty said, and Bloom could tell she was smiling. Which felt good. Betty letting her share something on an equal level, rather than constantly holding Bloom up on a higher shelf. "I'd like to have one of those."

She made a mental note to order one off the internet and have it shipped to the farm.

And so it went. Betty told her about the no-peek chicken casserole they'd had for dinner. About the mushroom soup she'd made herself from mushrooms she'd canned. Talked about her father's arthritis and how it was making it harder for him to tighten the cinch strap on his saddle. About how she worried he was going to slide right off that huge mare he still insisted on riding around the farm even though he had a perfectly good side by side.

And she told Bloom that they were getting ready to watch *Wheel of Fortune*. Wishing that Bloom was there watching it with them, but knowing that she was where she needed to be, helping people who needed her.

"I wish I was there, too, Betty," she said, the child in her hoping that her mom would hear the need in her voice and offer to…do something. Come be with her. Give her some words of strength. Tell her how she'd handled the fear when Bloom's father had been trampled by a bull several years before and they thought he might die.

"Your father and I understand, though, Bloom. We know you do very important work and we're so proud of you, sweetie. You know that."

"Yes."

"Why, just this morning I was down at the vegetable market in town and I was telling Cora Sue how you helped women whose husbands abuse them. Cora Sue's afraid that her daughter's new boyfriend is the type to be a wife beater. I told her that I'd have you send me a brochure of warning signs and the name of someone she could call if it ever came to that. Funny how you called tonight, out of the blue, right when I had a favor to ask…"

Betty had a way of going on. Which had a tendency to irritate Bloom's uncle. But not Carl. Bloom's father seemed to tune out his wife's chatter while still managing to hear pretty much everything she said.

"I'll get one out to you in the morning," she said when she could break in. And then, when her mother asked again if she was okay, assured her that she was perfectly fine. That her life was business as usual. And waited while her mother put her father on.

Turning at the end of the hallway, Bloom saw Sam in the living room.

He was staring at her.

She should never have called. Had no idea what

she'd been thinking. Or why she hadn't realized, with today's technology, that she could have Googled that damned commercial and seen it years ago.

If she'd thought of Madge even once in the past ten years she might have. So much of that part of her life had been cut off, shut away, because to remember, to long for what she'd needed from her parents, for the years lost, was pointless.

Turning her back on the man who had a penchant for asking her questions no one else asked, she concentrated on listening to her father. His always slow speech was slower now, but he was still very much in charge of his portion of the world. A world he'd decided didn't fit her. Or that she didn't fit it.

He asked how she was. She wanted to tell him the truth. That she was afraid.

But she wasn't going to let fear defeat her.

She wanted to tell him about Ken. To think that if her father knew a man was after her, he'd load his gun and come save her.

But she knew better than that, too.

She almost told him that Ken was getting out of prison just so they'd know. But thought about how worried they would be, while feeling powerless and unable to help.

She wanted his sage advice, but wasn't even

sure anymore if he had any. He'd certainly never shared any of it with her, that she could remember.

She definitely did not want them coming to town.

So she told him she was fine. He hemmed and hawed for a moment. Probably looking for something smart to say.

It was always that way with them. Awkward at best. But then, other than vacations, they hadn't lived in the same home together since she was six years old. In many ways, her parents were strangers to her.

When he finally gave up and simply told her he loved her, she teared up. Her relationship with her parents was what it was.

Her abusive husband being on the loose wasn't going to change that.

CHAPTER NINE

THE ENTIRE TIME Bloom was on the phone, Sam told himself he wasn't going to pry. He sipped scotch. Slowly. He was driving later that evening, which meant he'd only drink one.

He texted a contact at the prison to see if Kenneth Freelander was out as planned and got confirmation that he was. Because his case had been thrown out, he wasn't on probation. Wasn't being watched. He was just…free.

Exactly as Sam had known would happen. He texted the investigator he'd hired to keep tabs on Freelander. And heard back that the ex-con had checked himself into a five-star hotel on the beach fifty miles south of Santa Barbara, almost two hours away. Freelander was at the open air bar buying drinks for a couple of women. And getting drunk.

Kind of what Sam had expected there, too. The bastard was going to take care of his physical needs first. And take his time with his big picture goal. Bloom.

"Tell Betty I'll mail the brochure tomorrow."

Sam moved to the kitchen, looking for something with which to occupy himself as Bloom continued to talk. Not as softly as she'd started out. "And you guys can email me, you know. Just to let me know how you're doing. You got the computer set up that I sent you, right? And the satellite is working okay?"

What in the hell was going on? Who were Betty and Carl? Why had she purchased them a computer? And why had she called them about seeing the commercial that had inspired her mother's name for her childhood pet?

"I know," Bloom said after a moment. "I don't care about your spelling."

There was another pause. Sam finished his drink. Looked down as Lucy came into the kitchen and sniffed at the cupboard from which he'd recently moved out her bag of food. He'd fed her that morning, but she was out of her routine. He wondered what to give her to tide her over until they got back to their room.

"Then have Betty write it."

Another pause. And then, "I know, but it's not hard to learn. Please, Carl? I sent you guys that computer so we could stay in touch. I know if you'd just give it a try, you guys would love it. Betty could do most of her shopping online. And save a bunch, too, considering how high prices are in town. It would save her trips to the city. Which would save gas…"

Begging. Her tone had a definite "beg" to it. Something he'd never heard from Dr. Freelander. Even when her face had been smashed in.

Lucy's tail thumped against the cupboard as she continued to look up at him. The kitchen had been stocked for Bloom, but by his "department," so surely he could take a piece of cheese.

Sam reached into the bottom drawer of the refrigerator. Opened the new package of American cheese, peeled off a slice and handed it to the dog.

Bloom was in the living area, standing by the window. Freelander was drunk off his ass but Sam still didn't like Bloom by the window.

"What was that all about?" he asked, wishing he had some scotch left in the glass he'd just refilled with straight water.

She turned. Shrugged. He thought she blinked away tears, but then wasn't sure. She left the window and he was glad he didn't have to ask her to do so. He'd need to instruct her about windows and protection safety—you didn't stand in front of them when you were being protected—but the lesson could wait. Maybe even for Chantel.

Bloom returned to the kitchen, patting Lucy's head as she walked past the dog who was still hanging around in the galley—as though her presence there would award her another snack. Too bad for her, Bloom didn't speak Lucy's language.

The psychiatrist withdrew two plates from the shelf above the dishwasher. The middle shelf of three without a door in front of them. Because he wasn't sure if he was going to keep the same cupboards or build new.

"Who are Carl and Betty?" he asked her. He could get the silverware. Help set the table. But he wasn't sure if he should know where the silverware was kept. Just how thorough had he been of his inspection of the place when he'd arranged for her use of it?

Who, for that matter, had stocked it? She hadn't asked. He hadn't come up with an answer in case she did. Maybe Chantel had said something.

She carried plates to the table. "I'd like something from my house," she said, moving to the silverware drawer without having to look for it. Or pulling out the wrong drawer first. She'd certainly learned her way around quickly enough.

But then, he was dealing with a genius. A woman who'd graduated from college at an age when he'd been figuring out ways to climb out his bedroom window without his dad knowing so he could hang out at the beach with his friends.

"I can run by your place on my way home tonight," he told her. Get in and get out while Freelander was safely two hours away. "Why don't you make a list for me?"

She nodded. "I want placemats," she said. "But I'll make a list. There might be another thing or two."

She'd set the table. Was standing by one of the places, her hands on the back of the chair.

"Who are Betty and Carl?" If they were close... someone Freelander might try to get to in order to get to Bloom...he had to know about them.

And it was bugging him that she was upset and he didn't know why.

"My parents." She moved as gracefully as always back to the galley. Pulled open the oven, bent down to peek inside.

Hiding from him?

"Your parents."

"Mmm-hmm."

Made sense regarding Madge and the commercial. But...

"You didn't sound like you were talking to your parents." To put it mildly. At least not like he'd ever talked to his dad. What adult needed to beg their parents to stay in touch? Usually it was the other way around at that age...

The refrigerator door received her attention next. "There's a bottle of Chardonnay in here," she said, pulling it out. "I'm not sure how good it is, but...you want to join me in a glass?"

He'd made the scotch weak. And only had to wait an hour per drink before being able to drive without the effects of alcohol. Two hours tops. He was still good.

"Yeah," he said, wishing he could be sure it was any good. They had a couple of well-known wineries right there in Santa Raquel. One that had only recently begun producing and was already starting to make a name for itself. A lot of Californians were wine drinkers. He wasn't one of them.

He'd purchased based on price—low—not on name. Or any pretense of knowing what made quality wine. She unscrewed the top. Poured two juice glasses full of wine and set one down for him on the counter. Leaning back against the sink, she took a sip from her glass and didn't cringe.

He sipped, too. Also didn't cringe. But he didn't like the acidic drink any more than he usually did. He was grateful for it just the same. Could use a bit of the edge taken off. Even if only for the hour it would take for its effects to be gone from his system.

"My parents are older. I was…unexpected… and when they found out I was of above average intelligence, they thought I needed more than they could give me, so they shipped me off to an institution, which is where I grew up." Her words were so nonchalant, for a second there he thought she was kidding—like, *I drive my par-*

ents crazy so they were happy to be rid of me.
But she wasn't smiling.

"Come again?"

"They figured it out when I was two. Had me tested when I was four. And sent me away when I was six. They were afraid they were going to 'ruin' me. That my extraordinary 'talents and abilities' would be wasted."

Not much surprised him.

Sam yanked out the chair behind him and sat, taking another sip of the wine. She was telling him that she'd been rejected by those whose love and acceptance she'd needed most.

"Are they your biological parents?"

He had to hand it to her. She didn't flinch at his lack of tact. But…

"Yes."

Of course. She'd said she was unexpected…

"Don't get me wrong," she quickly added. "They loved me. Betty cried buckets every time a vacation came to an end and I had to leave again. They just didn't think they could give me what I needed."

He couldn't wrap his mind around any of it. How did… Well, it just went to show that… Wow.

"What about unconditional love and constant support? Security?" were the words that finally came out of his mouth.

Bloom sat across the table from him, her elbows

where he suspected her placemats would soon be, both hands resting on the sides of the juice glass. "My folks showed their love by sacrificing their own happiness to give me the best opportunities."

None of this was his business. At all.

But whose curiosity wouldn't be on overdrive?

Yet, his need to know didn't feel like mere curiosity. He needed to know Bloom.

For the case. Right?

The doubt scared the shit out of him and he almost left the table.

And might have if not for the things she wasn't saying.

She sipped wine. He held his glass. Lucy lay down by the front door. He was good at asking tough questions, but also knew when to sit silent and listen.

Even if he just heard silence.

"My folks live simple lives. Not because they couldn't excel in college or a busy career—they just never wanted anything more than their life on the farm. My father was born on that farm. As was his brother, who now shares the business with him. My mother and aunt were born and raised in the small town that is closest to the farm. They've got two thousand acres, which in the world of big business farming isn't a lot, but it supports both families and that's enough for them. But it was pretty clear to all four of them that I didn't fit in."

She told him about making a long-distance phone call at age two—to a friend of her mother's who'd moved away. She'd memorized the number from watching her mother make the call.

"Did you know someone would be on the other end?" he asked. Fascinated.

For the case. Cataloguing things in the event he might need them. Profiling. To protect her.

She nodded. "I said, 'Hi, Jac.' That was my mom's friend's name. And then I hung up. She called back, upset with my mom for just hanging up. That's how they found out I'd called."

She wasn't smiling. And yet the memory should have been a good one.

For her, it marked the beginning of a diagnosis that was going to strip her of her home, her family, and send her off to face the world alone.

"When I started school I kept asking the teacher for more work. More to do. She was frustrated and felt like she wasn't doing me justice. There were meetings. And in the end, my father and my uncle took her suggestion and went farther afield to see what the world had to offer me. They found a university that had a program for genius children—run by the psychology department. And before I even knew what was going on, I was enrolled."

A psychology department had become her parent figures? Ken Freelander had headed up the psychology department where he'd met Bloom.

The thought of the man made him more sick than ever. As intelligent as Bloom was, she'd clearly had some challenges and would have been prone to a father figure type of worship. The noted psychology professor should have known that.

Sam gritted his teeth as things became so much more clear to him. Freelander *had* known. And had taken advantage of a much younger Bloom…

"I LIVED IN a home with other kids during the week and then went home with various staff members on weekends when the other kids went home to their families."

"For how long?"

"Until I'd completed a course of study that equaled high school graduation."

"How old were you then?"

"Nine. I probably would have finished sooner, but I was a little…behind…when I got there.

"I knew how to read. But I'd spent so much time playing alone my peer interaction skills were non-existent. I was so much younger than my uncle's kids so I'd had no other kids around…"

He wanted her to say more. To tell him how she felt. How she'd coped.

Her wine was almost gone. He took another sip of his. And topped it with one more while she retrieved the bottle from the kitchen, stopping to peek in the oven at the same time.

"Why do you call them Betty and Carl?" Not a case question. It would be his only one.

"No one taught me any differently," she said. "That's what they called each other around me. They referred to each other that way. My aunt and uncle called them that. No one ever said, 'This is your mom.' Maybe when I was a baby, but not once they knew I was different. They thought I knew best."

He shook his head. "But..."

Bloom's smile stopped him. It was warm. And sweet. And just that tiny bit crooked. "They all did the best they could, Sam." The kindness in her voice was like a knee in the groin.

But this was only a case, and that was all it could be. No matter how much thoughts of Bloom Freelander had lingered over the past two years. And the past few days.

He'd never met anyone like her. The dichotomy of supreme understanding, of core strength, determination and incredible vulnerability. It drew him.

And she was just a case.

"They were in foreign waters with no rule book to guide them. And they did what they thought best. Thinking of me, not themselves. And I have to say, when I look at my life now, at the work I do, work that I love, and the people I help—their choices produced a decent result."

She was a successful psychiatrist who probably made more in a month than he made in a year. But she'd never had a mama or a daddy.

The significance of that—the loneliness it would have caused her—hit him hard.

CHAPTER TEN

THE MEAT LOAF tasted exactly as she remembered it. While, considering that she'd just shared her deepest secrets with a man who wasn't even a friend, she'd expect to have little appetite, she helped herself to two slices. And ate the rice and spinach salad with equal gusto.

She had another glass of wine, too. A regular glutton. When normally she monitored and contained every single choice, every movement, she made. Every nuance of her behavior.

Lucy sat beside Sam. She didn't beg. She just stared. Bloom would have liked to have called her over to sit in the chair next to her—as she'd done with Madge—to give the dog her own plate at the table. But she knew better. Far better.

Table food wasn't good for dogs. She knew the science of it now. But still had a hard time really believing that it was wrong to feed a dog table scraps.

Eventually the dog wandered away—heading slowly down the hall as though exploring the rest of the house. Sam had had her out to do her business just before they'd filled their plates. Sam told Bloom that Kenneth's release had been confirmed and that he'd checked into a hotel down the coast. He assured her that her ex-husband was being watched and they'd be notified the second he was on the move.

She believed him. But was prepared either way. The whole point of the exercise was for her to interact with Ken and get him to threaten her life in some way. Or to give new proof of his abuse of her, something that would allow prosecutors to place new charges on him.

Double jeopardy wouldn't allow him to be charged for the same crime twice, but there were things he'd done for which he hadn't been formally charged. Instead, there had been charges that had been made and then dropped so that they'd be guaranteed a clean and solid conviction.

She knew how it all worked. Was prepared.

The sooner they got going on it the better…

Lucy returned, a half-chewed rawhide bone, with a dust bunny the size of a grapefruit on one end, between her jaws.

And the earlier part of the hour came flooding back to her. The part where Sam had walked up to a wall of videos and had known just which one to pull out.

He was observant—and had clearly checked over the place before he'd brought her there—but even he wasn't good enough to have memorized more than two hundred discs from a cursory look.

Nor would he have had cause to learn the video's content to ensure that the place was sufficient for her needs…

He was staring at the bone—his mouth open like he'd just heard bad news.

Or was about to get caught in a lie?

Lucy hadn't just found that bone for the first time. Bloom supposed she could have. If dog senses had led her to it. But she knew she hadn't.

Because Lucy hadn't been gone long enough to have discovered it. It had been someplace the dog knew about since she'd known right where to go get it when begging for food at the table had yielded her nothing.

Getting up, Bloom picked up the big plastic bowl Sam had filled with water and put down for the dog while she'd been getting dinner out of the oven. Lucy hadn't touched it.

"Where is her water usually kept?" she asked. She could have asked specifically where *he* usually kept Lucy's water, but that could have been taken as accusation.

She wasn't ready to accuse him of anything.

Or rather, wasn't going to let her emotions get the better of her. There was no logical reason for her to feel betrayed. Or to care if he hadn't been completely honest with her.

She already knew that Detective Larson said things he couldn't possibly mean. Made promises he couldn't possibly keep.

Her current situation was proof of that.

"In the laundry room."

He got a point for choosing not to further insult her with an attempt at keeping up the pretense.

Bloom called to Lucy, carried the bowl into the laundry room, put it down in the only free wall space that looked like a dog's bowl could live there without being in the way and watched as Lucy took a drink. She left her to it.

"Where is she staying now?" she asked, getting her plate from the table and taking it to the sink.

"You've seen it."

The seedy motel. She spun around.

"You're living in *that* place?"

"Compared to your house, you could take the same tone about this one." He folded his arms against his chest.

A defensive move that softened her heart more than it should have.

"I'm assuming you gave up your place because it's so obviously perfect as a safe house—or as perfect as we're probably going to find close enough to my office—but why not use money allotted for my safe house to get yourself someplace nicer to stay?"

He opened his mouth, as though starting to

speak. Closed it again. He met her gaze. And then looked down at his plate. Picking it up, he started toward her. Then stood there holding it.

"Sam?"

His chin jutted as he looked at her.

"The department is paying for this, aren't they?"

"Define 'this.'"

She wished she hadn't eaten as much. Or at all.

"My being here, this isn't official business? No one thinks I'm in danger?"

His head shot up. He brought his plate to the sink, placed it on top of hers and stood so close she could see the creases in his lips as he said, "Everyone, from the commissioner on down knows that you are in danger. If you need me to, I will get a signed affidavit from the commissioner himself to that effect."

She was somewhat appeased. "But they don't think I need to be out of my home?"

"Everyone knows you are not safe in that home. Everyone knows that you are here. Because Freelander's early release is in no way the fault of the police department, we have no reason to allot funds needed due to that release. Unfortunately, due to the unethical behavior of our former commissioner, we find ourselves in a gray area here. And gray is not allowed in the Santa Raquel Police Department right now. Not for any reason. No matter how legitimate it is."

He made sense. Real sense.

"So you offered your house."

"I offered my house because, as you said, it was right for the job."

"What about the round-the-clock detail?" she asked, using a word she'd heard on a television police show at some time or other and hadn't known she'd retained. "Are you paying for that?"

"I had confirmation this morning that money is forthcoming..."

"From you?"

"No. I put in a formal request."

"You're sure?" She stood toe-to-toe with him. Staring him down. "Because I am not staying here if this isn't officially sanctioned. I'm not going to let my stupidity in husband choosing cost you or anyone else. I can't take my own comfort over yours. I wouldn't feel good about that. Nor am I going to put everyone through this drama if it isn't absolutely necessary."

"I can tell you for absolute certain that it is necessary."

His tone alone would have convinced her, but the look in his eye gave her such certainty it sent a shot of fear through her body.

"I don't know yet exactly how the money is going to work to pay for the detail, but I can tell you with the same assurance that I have been given it will be there. That's how important everyone knows this is."

"Who paid for the groceries? The new sheets and towels? And toiletries?"

"I did."

"I'll write you a check."

"Fine."

Good. He was learning. Accepting the fact that she was in charge. Understanding that she was in control of her life now. And would take orders from no one unless she specifically and rationally chose to do so.

"Call Chantel. Tell her there's no need for her to come back tonight. She's newly engaged and should be at home with her fiancé. And Julie, too. They're family now. They need each other."

As she talked, her tone softened. She and Chantel hadn't talked late the night before. Maybe only for an hour or so. But it had been enlightening.

She'd told her to bring Julie in to see her. Would have liked to tell her that she was already counseling Julie's friend, Leslie Harrison. A woman who, like Julie, had been raped by a son of the previous commissioner's best friend—and had received no justice. Until recently.

Sam stepped back. She assumed to call his partner in crime and tell her they'd been found out. Turning on the water, she started to rinse their plates, readying them for the dishwasher. It wasn't as fancy as hers, had fewer functions, but it was newer.

"I can't leave you here alone." His hand appeared in her line of vision as he took a plate from her, opened the dishwasher and placed it inside at an awkward angle.

He was supposed to be making a phone call.

"I'm not going to be alone," she said, sounding as though the situation were completely obvious.

When, in truth, her insides were shaking just thinking about the right choice here. She knew what it was. With such certainty that she would act with authority. But that didn't mean she wouldn't experience normal human emotions.

Because she was human. And normal.

And finding herself, with two glasses of wine in her, incredibly attracted to…the man who treated his dog like a person.

It wasn't real. She knew that. It was more of the transference issue—her underlying vulnerability to one who represents safety and security. A little girl craving the protection of those who are meant to love her unconditionally.

She was not at all attracted to the detective who made promises he couldn't keep and who was, in his own words in the past, married to his job.

She still remembered his words on the subject. They'd come in response to her query as to whether or not he'd ever been married. She'd been trying to explain how she could still have feelings left for the man who'd abused her so cruelly. She'd been trying to explain about love and commitment through sickness and health.

Ken had been sick.

It had taken her a while to realize that he also had never loved her. He'd only loved how having her beneath him, physically and every other way, made him feel.

Detective Larson had apologized for his lack of compassion in the matter, explaining that he'd only been married once, for a very short time, and that his wife had helped him realize that he was a man only ever meant to be married to his job. The way he'd taken his ex-wife's words to heart, and felt bad for what he'd put her through, the way he'd hurt her with his inability to make her a priority, was what had first brought Bloom out of the cloud Ken's drugs had put her in. She'd heard a man taking accountability, rather than blaming his wife and it had hit her hard. Her first moment of complete clarity had come to her in an inter-rogation room alone with Sam Larson.

That was the moment she'd agreed to testify against the man she'd promised to love and cher-ish until death did them part.

"I DON'T UNDERSTAND." The rock was back in Sam's gut. She wanted him to cancel Chantel. But she wasn't going to be there alone? He rubbed the back of his neck. Longing for a battle with the waves down below. Didn't even care that the Pacific ocean, even in July, was still cold at night in Santa Raquel.

Dealing with Bloom Freelander was worse than he'd feared. She'd become an impressive opponent. Did his heart good to see it.

But if she thought she was going to call some friend to come stay with her and rely only on the off-duty cop watching the property to keep her safe at night, she was wrong.

Still, if he could get her where she had to be and let her think she was calling the shots...

If only he had the ability to finesse like his old man had...

She handed him the other plate and dropped the silverware in the dispenser, letting her statement that she wouldn't be there alone—and his response that he didn't understand—just...hang in the air.

Did she think it was going to float away and be forgotten?

Was she playing him?

He had to get one step ahead of her—and stay there—if he was going to pull this off.

Only problem was…how did a regular guy, who wasn't great with women in the first place, ever get ahead of a woman like her? Sam closed the dishwasher with his foot, purposely blocking her exit from the kitchen.

She stepped around him, heading to the living area where she sat in the middle of the couch. Where he always sat. Which she could probably tell from the indentation in the cushion.

Lucy, the traitor, settled her butt on the cushion beside her and put her paws in Bloom's lap. Manners told him to call the dog away.

Perverseness kept him silent.

Those slim, feminine, psychiatrist fingers stroked his dog's coat. Lucy laid her head on Bloom's thigh.

Jealousy shot through him.

WTF.

CHAPTER ELEVEN

HE WAS GOING to argue with her. Bloom knew Sam Larson well enough to know that much. Just as she knew that her way was the right one. She just needed a little time to figure out his objections and find responses to them before she embarked on the battle that was to come.

Funny, she wasn't the least bit nervous about going head-to-head with him.

The result—the obvious solution—that made her nervous. And she was just going to have to get over that part. She was the one who'd chosen to marry the wrong man. So she would do all she could to help those who were sacrificing so much to help her.

But to buy herself a little time, she petted the dog. She loved having Lucy so close.

Madge had been both a sibling and best friend to her youngest self. She saw that now.

"She'll be glad to be back home," she said aloud what she was thinking. Making it about the dog. Not about him.

Or her.

"And she's fine at the motel until that happens," Sam said, standing there by his wall of movies, his hands in his pockets and his expression as stern as she'd seen it this time around.

In the past, he'd looked like that a lot. Like everybody just better get out of his way. Like he thought the concept of saving the world rested on his shoulders.

She thought about resting her head on one of those shoulders. Like she used to lie with Ken. Back when she'd thought they'd been lovers. In love. She'd been lying in a dream world by herself. But Sam…if he took a woman to his bed, offered his chest as her pillow…she was sure he'd be 100 percent present with her.

But how could she possibly know that? She'd thought the same thing about Ken. So long ago she could hardly remember.

She had no business picturing her head and the detective's naked shoulder in the same frame. Or picturing his shoulders naked at all.

Unless she wanted to fail the task at hand. Which could mean failing, period, if Ken really did plan to come after her. And after seeing the number on her caller ID the morning before, she was pretty certain that was the case.

"How badly do you want me to stay here?" Just like that, the way to get to him presented itself to her.

"I won't consider any other option," he said. "I will not have your death on my conscience."

He was playing hardball. Trying to scare her.

He'd succeeded. The word death was too real. They weren't playing a game here. Ken had threatened her life. And he was mentally unstable beneath a guise of academic and monetary stability.

Laying heads on shoulders wasn't even in the ballpark.

Sam had also just given her the impetus she needed to get her way..

"I'll agree to stay, for as long as you deem necessary, doing as you direct on any matter concerning my safety where Ken is concerned, on one condition."

She drew confidence from the way the muscles in his cheeks relaxed as his head tilted slightly.

"I'm listening."

"You and Lucy leave that hellhole and come home." She looked straight at him. Didn't even blink.

The butterflies in her stomach where his maleness was concerned, her sexual reaction to him, didn't matter here. It was a minor irritation that she'd deal with. Easily. She was a psychiatrist. Knew those wayward feelings were not based in reality. And that was the first step in obliterating them.

It might take a little time. But they'd fade away.

"I become a helpless female if you pay, personally, for the plight I'm in through no fault of your own," she told him. Laying bare the honest truth. "I can't be that person again, Sam. Not ever. I'd rather be dead."

She'd go home and let Ken do his worst before she'd ever give up control of her choices again. She believed, with all of her being, that Sam paying for her protection was wrong.

"Professionally, I need your help," she told him. "I'm good with that. My patients need my help and it doesn't make them any less capable or powerful or strong when they seek me out. To the contrary, it makes them more so, as they are taking action to tend to their needs."

His lips were pursed. His chin stiff.

"But this…you giving up your home…making Lucy stay in that room, listening to the traffic and everyone come and go all day… It's not right. Look at her." She motioned to the dog who was now sound asleep with her head on Bloom's lap. "She's exhausted. And glad to be home."

He did as she suggested. Looked at his dog.

"You told me before…in the past…during one of those conversations where you were trying to impress upon me the importance of my testifying against Ken in order for me to take back control of my life…that you used to do off-duty work in

LA guarding witnesses who were going to testify in important cases."

"Before I made detective." He'd spoken. She took that as a good sign.

"You told me about one woman who was testifying against her father…the head of a drug cartel…"

"That's correct."

"She was in a hotel in San Diego."

"Right."

"You spent a weekend in the suite with her."

His mouth tightened. He didn't respond.

"You can be alone with a woman, professionally. Stay with her overnight. And not compromise your job."

He blinked. Except that his eyes stayed closed about three blinks worth.

"You also told me that you're married to your job."

He leaned a shoulder against the wall. Staring at her now.

"Your job is all that matters to you. My being here…it's because of your job. That's the only reason we know each other or have ever had contact. And your job is to offer needed protection, so…"

"Fine." His interruption was no less powerful for the one word he bit out. "But you're staying in the bedroom you're in. I will not have you walking from bedroom to bathroom and risk me finding you in the hall in any inappropriate state of dress. Anytime you are outside that bedroom door—" he shot a finger toward the hall "—you are fully dressed."

"Including shoes," she agreed.

"Get your purse," he demanded.

She did.

"Lucy, stay," he said as he grabbed his keys and the dog moved toward the door. His jaw was so tight it was a wonder he didn't break a tooth.

Bloom didn't ask where they were going until she was belted into the front seat of his SUV.

"Freelander's occupied tonight. Tomorrow, who knows? I cannot afford to be distracted with relocating once he's on the move."

Made sense.

She didn't bother him with any further conversation. He was tense. She was nervous. And a bit scared, too, knowing that Ken really was out of jail. And could be around any corner. Gunning for her.

Scared enough that when they reached his rent-by-the-week motel, she asked, "May I come in with you while you pack?"

"Come in with me? Lady, you're going to help," he told her. But once they were inside, all he let her do was get Lucy's bed and perpetual waterer. He took care of the rest in about five minutes.

But in those few minutes she'd learned something else about Detective Larson.

He didn't fold his underwear.

AFTER ALL THE HOOPLA, the next couple of days were so uneventful Sam was ready to leap tall buildings in a single bound.

He'd given Bloom her way. He'd moved back into the cottage. But he wasn't spending any real time with her. Chantel still took the after-work shift while Sam caught up on paperwork. And made use of his membership at the local gym. Bloom turned in early, at which point Chantel would text and Sam would go home.

He was missing Lucy like hell. But otherwise the plan was working out just fine.

Bloom hadn't said a word to him about the way he'd turned the tables on her.

But then, she was a smart woman. He'd always known that.

Freelander, on the other hand, was smarter than he'd given him credit for. The man had rented a condo in an upscale high-rise close to the university. He was trying to use the fact that he once again had no record—since the case had been thrown out as though it didn't exist—to get his job back.

And had probable grounds to sue if the university didn't give fair consideration to his request.

To the school's detriment was the fact that they had a professorship available in the psychology department. They'd posted the position, open for application for another week, four weeks before it was known that Ken Freelander would be out of jail, record expunged.

Freelander had made no attempt to contact his ex-wife. Nor had he headed any farther north than the hotel where he'd spent his first night of freedom.

He'd visited the office of a divorce attorney, though. And a request had been made to access the decree that had been filed to officially end the marriage of Bloom Morgan Freelander and Kenneth Charles Freelander.

Sam had to assume that Freelander intended to contest the divorce Bloom had been granted while he'd been incarcerated.

Freelander couldn't force Bloom to stay married to him, but he could possibly be granted new divorce proceedings since he had been imprisoned erroneously.

So much for Sam's promise that she'd never have to deal with the fiend again.

He didn't know which was worse—Freelander showing up in town and Bloom having to hide until he did something they could arrest him for—putting Bloom in physical danger—or his going after her in the courts and messing with her emotions.

If he had his way, he'd choose the former. Clearly, when it came to Bloom, his getting his way wasn't high on fate's list of priorities.

He'd won the major battle, though. She was in a safe house. And during the hours he was spending at his desk, when he wasn't helping his colleagues with research on cases, he was poring through unending files of code and messages, phone records and dates, trying to find solid proof that linked Freelander to the gang he'd supplied drugs to in exchange for protection just before going to jail.

Because, whether she thought so or not, he was most definitely not using Bloom as bait.

The word from his contacts regarding Kenneth Freelander's drug and gang ties was good enough for Sam. But it wouldn't even get him to court—let alone get them a win once they got there.

It really pissed him off, though, that Freelander could very well be the one calling Bloom to court for a win of his own.

Sam could wait for Bloom to be served with formal notice, if Freelander's motion actually hit the courts. Or he could give her a heads-up.

He deliberated on the matter all day Thursday. Stood outside his bedroom door Thursday night, thinking about her in his bed, sleeping soundly, and wondered which would be kinder. To let the false sense of security that seemed to be falling over her continue as long as it could, or to prepare her for the battle that was coming.

There was no question. He knew that. The former could lead her to carelessness, a letting down of her guard.

To allow a court representative to arrive at her office to serve her with notice of a hearing—without warning—would be cruel.

To wake her up in the middle of the night to give her the news was inhuman.

And to put himself in a position to see her in... however she slept...was just plain dumb.

Instead, he took Lucy to the twin bed they were sharing—when she wasn't on the floor outside Bloom's room—and sent a text to Chantel.

She could spend Friday evening with her fiancé. He'd pick Bloom up from work and handle the evening shift as well as the night. The captain, fully aware of Sam's off-duty work, was keeping him on light duty in the office during the day for now.

Before he could put his phone on the nightstand, Colin Fairbanks had texted him saying he owed him one.

A pretty generous thing for a guy to say after having just written a check to cover the cost of off-duty detail to protect a woman he'd never met. A check for an amount that was more than Sam had amassed over a lifetime of saving. Colin had designated any funds that might be remaining after the case ended to be put in a fund for future High Risk Team police use.

The world still had some good people in it. People worth protecting.

Lying on top of the still-made bed in the sweatpants and T-shirt he was sleeping in while on duty, his boat shoes ready for him at the side of the bed, the bedroom door wide open and the earpiece that connected him to the officer outside in his ear and on, Sam pulled an old quilt on top of him and closed his eyes.

CHAPTER TWELVE

BLOOM HAD NO idea why she'd worried about living with Sam Larson. Or been concerned that she might develop the hots for him. Intense hots, that was. Any woman with blood in her veins would find him attractive.

In a detective movie kind of way. Only he wasn't an actor. He was the real thing.

But she needn't have worried.

She'd had zero opportunity to have any untoward feelings where the man was concerned. She hardly saw him. He closed his door in the morning when he heard her open hers. Which she did only after she smelled the coffee he put on when he made his early morning check of the premises.

Tuesday morning, the first morning she woke up with him in residence, she'd assumed he'd made the coffee for the two of them to share as they'd shared the meat loaf dinner she'd made the night before. She'd been wrong. The detective had come out of his room when he'd heard her pick up her keys. He'd been fully dressed, in the previous day's clothes, had said he'd follow her to work and locked the door behind them as they left.

She hadn't seen him again until the next morning. He'd had on a different pair of pants, different dress shirt, different coat, but all looked equally worn. She could only assume that after following her to the office and nodding at Gomez, he'd driven himself back home to shower before going to the station.

She'd considered asking him about that. But then thought better of it. She had a much bigger issue to discuss with him.

Ken had been free four days. Other than that prison number showing up on her phone, he hadn't tried to contact her. And she wasn't going to play his waiting game. It was time for her to go fishing for a change. To be the one who set the trap.

She was ready to take him on.

Cleaning up her desk after her final evening appointment on Friday, she didn't feel as tired as she might have done. Odd as it was, she'd been sleeping like a baby all week. A clear sign that she was on the right track. Making decisions that were conducive to her well-being. In sync with her higher self.

Her inner voice was at peace.

And maybe she had a little extra spring in her step because Chantel had called to let her know that Sam would be meeting her after work. Bloom assumed that, as before, the female detective had a function to attend with her fiancé. She'd made a point of letting the other woman know she'd be ordering dinner in between appointments, just to make certain there was no awkwardness over whether she and Sam were going to share the kitchen table again.

But they were going to talk. She had to let him know her plan to contact Ken. To force his hand— if indeed he had one to play. Sam and his people would want to be prepared when Ken did what they all expected him to do—commit another felony against her. One that would, hopefully, land him in jail for good.

Or…maybe he'd surprise all of them and just let her go. Maybe he'd learned his lesson. Maybe the trauma of getting caught, of losing two years of his life to a jail cell, had brought him to his senses.

Maybe that was why he'd attempted to call her the day before his release. To let her know that she had nothing to fear from him.

Maybe this could all just end peacefully and she could continue living the good life she'd made for herself.

Maybe Sam would find solid evidence to prove that Ken had disposed of the drugs he'd been slowly collecting to use on her. Maybe even a tie in to the gang he'd supposedly given them to in exchange for protection in prison.

But probably not.

Ken was diabolically smart. He wouldn't get himself dirty in a way that anyone could trace to him.

Which was why they'd had to have her testimony to put him away. Why Sam hadn't been able to close his case without her. Why he'd ridden her so hard in the past.

Slinging the strap of her purse over her shoulder, she turned out the lights and locked her office door behind her.

Times had changed.

The men in her life were soon going to find out that she was the rider now.

GOMEZ WASN'T AT his post. She'd gotten used to having the young man around after a week of greeting him every time she came and went from her office—even when she was just helping herself to a soda from the vending machine.

Another guard, a woman, stood at attention just inside the entrance to the building. She smiled as Bloom approached and called, "Good night, ma'am," as she held the door open for Bloom to exit. Gomez clearly had the night off. As one could expect he might after a week of work. And she had no business becoming attached to her security detail like they were all part of a working family.

It was definitely time to put any plan Ken might have into motion. Whether he was ready or not.

BLOOM LIKED TO play cards, Chantel had told him. She played a lethal hand of poker. She also liked to watch police procedurals. His peer had been giving him suggestions for ways he and their female charge could pass the evening spent exclusively in each other's company.

He hadn't yet told Chantel about Freelander's divorce activity, about the possibility that their suspect was planning to contest the divorce granted to him while in prison. He'd felt it decent to tell Bloom first.

He also had no plans to sit around with Bloom all evening. Hard enough having the woman in his home. But to actually spend time with her there…

The one night they'd done that—Monday night— he'd practically tripped over his dick a time or two. The cold shower he'd needed before bed had been denied him by his necessity to be available to protect her at all times. And he wasn't even going to think about the dreams he'd been having.

Suffice it to say he'd had to get it out of his system in the shower the other morning.

He'd put in for weekend day relief. He'd have to find somewhere for him and Lucy to hang out, but his house would be covered. A second off-duty cop would be accompanying Bloom anywhere she needed or wanted to be. From what he'd heard, she would be working at least part of the day.

Maybe he could sand the porch, ready it for sealing. Or power wash the outside of the cottage. He'd been thinking about painting it himself. Didn't much matter if it took him all summer.

None of which helped him that evening. Lucy took care of the first five minutes, greeting them both as though she'd been cooped up for months instead of hours. She did her business in the yard, skidded across the linoleum as she raced for her bowl, wolfed down the food Bloom had put out for her and then headed straight back to the door. He'd barely hung his keys on the hook by the door.

Bloom was back in his bedroom. He didn't know what for, but he hoped she'd be out soon. He had to talk to her. Get it over with.

And maybe spend the rest of the evening with his laptop looking for that one connection he'd missed between Freelander and the known LA gang who'd had his back in prison. She hadn't come out yet. Lucy hadn't come back to the door, either.

"Bloom?" Sam wanted to tackle the first problem.

"Yeah?" She came out of his room in purple leggings and a top with a purple, pink and lime swirl pattern, carrying a pair of running shoes with laces that looked like they'd glow in the dark. "Sorry, I was just getting ready to put on my shoes," she said.

He didn't know why she was apologizing to him. And then remembered that she'd promised not to leave the bedroom without being fully dressed. Including shoes.

"I was hoping maybe you'd go with me down to the beach," she told him. "I walked the beach at home whenever I could. The fresh air clears my head. And the waves…"

She was babbling. His instincts told him this was not good. Bloom wasn't a babbler.

"Sure, we can walk down." What else could he say? They might be in his home, but technically he was working for her.

And needed her cooperation so he could do his job and keep her safe.

He changed into jeans, a long-sleeved T-shirt and boat shoes, tucking his gun into the waist of his pants. His normal at-home attire. Even with the gun he felt grossly underdressed.

Lucy wasn't in the yard when he led the way out.

"Wait." The word was abrupt and harsh. He reached for his gun with one hand, and with the other, held Bloom back, shutting the door between them as he whistled for the dog. His gaze shot around the yard. He listened for the merest hint of unfamiliar sound.

Two seconds later, Lucy came bounding out of the trees, tail wagging.

Panting, she stopped just short of his toes.

"Water." He gave Lucy the one-word command and relaxed when she ran for the path that led down to the beach. If there'd been something in the woods, something that was bothering her, had alarmed her or was just plain interesting to her, she'd have run back to it regardless of his command. If she'd even come to his whistle at all.

Sam let go of the door.

He was off his mark. Too jumpy. Maybe a walk on the beach would do him some good, too.

IT WASN'T THAT it was a hard walk down. Mostly a steep path that would be easy enough even for an elderly person to traverse if there was a handrail along the edge. One of the many plans he had for the future—that handrail.

Sam followed Lucy down, leading Bloom's way. And all the way down fought a strong urge to turn around and offer her a hand. Not that he doubted her ability to make it down by herself. Which made his penchant for being her helping hand that much more suspect.

"Wow," she said, getting her first glimpse of his beach in the setting sun. "This is magnificent."

He nodded. His embarrassment about the house fading a bit as he saw her take in the stretch of private, completely natural, sandy beach. This was the reason he'd bought the cottage.

The ocean was behaving herself, bringing in waves more as a gentle hello then in the form of attack. Lucy barked, and Bloom chuckled as the dog slapped first one and then another paw at something in the sand. Probably a sand crab.

He recognized his perfect opportunity to talk to Bloom about her ex-husband's recent movements. But as she began to walk, he followed along, saying little. To do more seemed disrespectful to the moment.

To the sand and the sea.

Keeping her beneath the several-yard overhang from the brush and tree-covered cliff more than an acre above them, Sam started to relax. Enough to forget, for a moment, that he had no right to enjoy a Friday night stroll on the beach with a beautiful woman.

With this beautiful woman. Her hand brushed his. Sliding his fingers through hers seemed like such a natural thing to do, he almost let it happen. She didn't step aside. Neither did he. But he had to live with himself when they got back up to the cottage.

He had to keep her safe. And if he gave her reason not to trust him, or to feel overtly uncomfortable around him, he'd fail at his task.

The thought cleared most of the untoward feel-

ings from his body. The job came first. Always.
It was a given *he* could trust.

SHE'D ASKED HIM to take a walk because she'd determined that she'd rather talk to him about her
plan, and deal with the immediate negative response she knew she was going to inspire, while
not cooped up in his quaint but rather small living room. She was quite comfortable there alone.
Or with Chantel.

But Sam…he was a big guy…and not just in
physical size. Anytime he was around he seemed
to fill the space between them. Her senses ab-
sorbed him until he almost became a part of her.
He made her uncomfortable. In a purely wom-
anly way. She wasn't ready to deal with that part
of her life.

Might not ever be ready.

But she most certainly wasn't going to fall prey
to the feelings when she knew full well that they
were a product of transference.

Besides, being with a man meant giving up herself. She'd already decided she wasn't going to
take that risk again.

*You didn't count on meeting a man who makes
you sexually hot by just walking in a room.*

She stumbled in the sand and moved away from
Sam before he could reach out to steady her.

"I'm ready to move forward with this whole

Ken thing," she blurted out in reaction to his nearness, sounding more like a high school teenager than a thirty-four-year-old psychiatrist.

She hated it when she did that.

And had to acknowledge that her inner voice was right. As always. Sam turned her on. Made her crazy with wanting to get naked with him. She'd lain awake for a full half hour in his bed that morning, imagining what it would be like if he came through the door, climbed under the covers with her and ran his big strong hands down her body.

Then spent the next hour reminding herself that the feelings, while real in the moment, would fade into nothingness when their proximity and her need of his protection were gone.

"I'm here tonight, instead of Chantel, because I need to talk to you about Ken." The seriousness of his tone jarred her from the imaginary road she'd gone down once again.

That path had become far too familiar over the past week.

Over the past two years.

Yeah, yeah, she'd thought of the detective a few times before he'd been back in touch with her. Had had to fight the feelings of wanting him by confronting herself with what they really were. She had this down.

"You have news?" she asked, her heart still beating heavily, but now for an entirely different reason. She moved a little closer to the cliff face to her left, letting the overhang hide her from view of anything but the ocean. Lucy had made her way back toward them and was walking slowly at Sam's side.

"I don't think he plans to harm you physically," he said. "At least not at first."

Bloom shook her head. She didn't understand. How was the plan going to work if they couldn't get Ken riled up to the point of abusing her? She'd figured one or two meetings with him ought to do it…

"He's seen a divorce attorney, Bloom. Who then put in a request for a copy of your decree. I think he intends to contest the decree."

"On what grounds?"

"It was granted on the basis of proof of what he'd done to you. You got the house, the savings account, your car—and the divorce—because he was a convicted criminal and you were his victim. With the conviction gone as though it never existed…"

She stumbled again.

And this time let Sam catch her before she fell.

CHAPTER THIRTEEN

"CAN WE SIT, PLEASE?"

Sam, still reeling from the feeling of Bloom's body touching his, watched as she lowered herself to the sand against the cliff wall and leaned back.

She'd held on to him for less than a second, and something had changed. He didn't know what. Didn't want to know. He'd had women in his life since his divorce. Not many, but enough.

He was not willing to be a changed man.

So he'd just make certain that whatever it was that had just happened got changed back.

He sat beside her and watched Lucy settle on her other side. As though the dog sensed that Bloom was in some kind of trouble.

"I wanted it to be physical violence," she said, her voice sounding calm. Normal. Not anything like he felt.

But maybe it was just him…this weirdness going on where she was concerned.

No harm, no foul if this was all just in his head. He could control that.

"I planned to tell you tonight that I'm going

to contact him," she said. "To get this going and done with…"

His skin turned cold. It was almost dark. But they'd be safe down here. Safer than in the house—not that he feared that, either. He had her well protected.

As long as she didn't run off and do something rash like…

"Come again?" he said when he could do so without sounding ominous.

"You said the plan was to draw him out, to find a way to get him to implicate himself."

He had. Yes. That was still the plan. If he couldn't find the gang connection evidence.

Word was Freelander had bragged that they didn't ever find evidence of the drugs for trial because he'd already passed them on, right after his arrest.

"Chantel's planning to go under cover," he said now. If they needed her to. If Kenneth didn't give them something on his own that they could use against him.

Bloom shook her head. "Not a good plan," she said. "For so many reasons. Early on in his relationships Kenneth always feels like he's in control. If he meets a woman who comes on too strong, he walks away. He doesn't have to control all women, just those in his sphere. She'd have had to have been his boss, or in some form of authority over

him to even have a chance of setting him off, and
even then it's not guaranteed that he'd do anything
to her. Kenneth isn't violent."

"He broke your jaw."

Her silence bothered him. And he thought back
to the night he'd met her in the emergency room.
Police had been called due to suspected abuse.
She'd never admitted that Kenneth hit her. But
when he'd asked if Freelander was responsible for
the bruises on her face and shoulder, she'd nodded.

It had been in his report.

Mentioned only briefly in court.

At the time, it hadn't mattered.

He and Banyon had been after the guy for more
than a first offense domestic violence charge.
They'd gone after him for drugging Bloom, dumbing her down to what one doctor had testified had
been half her potential.

Even more criminal, now that he knew Bloom
had lost any vestige of a normal home life so that
she *wouldn't* live at half her potential. Her parents
had sacrificed their life with her so that wouldn't
happen.

"He hit you," he said now.

"I never said that."

"Banyon asked you in court if Ken Freelander
was responsible for the bruises on your face and
you nodded. His attorney didn't even mention it in
cross. And when he had Freelander on the stand,

when he asked if he denied breaking your jaw, he said no."

Sam had been in court. And now, after all he was going through to help her, she'd been lying to him?

She wasn't like that...

"He was responsible for them," she said, an uncharacteristic break in her voice.

Sam got the nuance this time around. "But he didn't hit you."

"No."

He'd never asked, just assumed. Hadn't really mattered how the jaw got broken. Only that it was. And that Freelander had done it.

"How did he break it?"

"I'd rather not say."

Oh, no, lady, you aren't doing that. Uh-uh. They'd come too far.

"Bloom." One word. But it better get her talking.

Clasping her hands between her knees, she stared out toward the ocean.

The waves were becoming harder to distinguish beneath the darkening sky. Their sound as they reached the shore and receded, was not.

"I can't help you if you aren't going to be straight with me."

"I am straight with you."

"You're withholding information that could be pertinent to the case."

"It wasn't pertinent back then, why would it be now?"

She was staring out toward the horizon. So was he. There was only a diminishing line between ocean and sky. No boats. No lights.

"I knew what I needed to about your ex-husband to charge him with more than a hundred counts of premeditated dangerous assault that could result in murder. A domestic violence charge didn't matter at that point."

She knew that. They'd talked about it. He'd been completely honest with her when he'd asked her for the ultimate sacrifice—taking the stand and testifying against the man she'd married. Facing him and opening herself up to the cross-examination of his very expensive and skilled attorney.

"What happened to my jaw isn't going to help put him back in prison."

The more she resisted telling him, the more he was certain he needed to know. He just couldn't be sure whether the need was personal or professional.

"No, but my understanding of him will help me know how to proceed in my promise to see that he gets there. He's not in custody now like he was two years ago," he added, to show her he wasn't kidding. "I need to know what I'm protecting you against."

Up until that point he'd have sworn Freelander hit her. Multiple times. But only in one incident. There'd been no other accounts of physical violence involving the two of them, which had painted a picture of a mostly nonviolent man whose abusive tendencies had been escalating.

"As he got older it was getting harder for Kenneth to...get an erection." She spoke like a doctor speaking of a patient. But for that one little hesitation. He tried to listen like a professional law enforcement official in conversation with a doctor, as he'd done countless times before. He'd heard it all.

"He had...fantasies."

The waves became a buffer. Something between them. Between her words and his hearing. A filter of emotion.

"He'd give me orders, and I'd...follow them."

Red hot anger possessed him. The man hadn't just drugged his wife to dumb down her genius mind so that he could be intellectually superior to her. He'd drugged her for...sexual capitulation? And, he'd bet, for any other order he wished to mete out. He'd made her his slave.

Overwhelmed with the sense that no one he'd ever helped had been more deserving of his protection, Sam wanted to stop her words. To spare her. Wanted the secrets to remain just that…her secrets. She'd paid the price once.

He couldn't tell her to stop. She was a victim. And part of his job was to get all the facts. Whether it be a child who'd been molested. Or a beautiful, special woman who'd never known what it had been like to be a child.

"He liked to have me…tend to him while he was driving."

Illegal. He jumped on the thought.

Without an accident it would only be a driving violation. Not even enough for a night in jail.

"That night…"

Her voice had changed. Slowed. Become more thick tongued. And Sam knew that she was slipping back to the medicated woman she'd been for so long. He hurt for her. Not the compassion that came from witnessing a stranger's pain. But real pain. The kind he'd take with him.

"He'd been driving fast. Speed was a part of what turned him on…"

Lucy sat up. Put a paw on Bloom's leg. She took Lucy's paw, as though holding her hand and said, "He slammed on the brakes and my head slid between his knees and the steering wheel. I can remember that feeling…being trapped there. I can remember seeing his shiny wing-tipped shoes and the pedals. There was some kind of under-dash light on or something…"

If she was squeezing Lucy's paw now, the girl didn't seem to mind. Sam's mouth twitched. Biting back expletives.

"That's what broke your jaw," he said between gritting his teeth. "Him stopping so suddenly."

"No, it was how he moved…"

He had the full picture now.

Kenneth Freelander better hope there was never a time when he was alone with Detective Sam Larson.

Not ever.

"YOUR PRISON CONTACT was right." Bloom had lost track of time. She'd asked Sam if they could walk again, and they had been for a long time. Back and forth along the beach that was accessible only from his property. "I am his target. And his ultimate goal," she said. And she told him, "He called me the day before his release. I recognized the number from the prison and his is the only list I'm on, so it had to be him."

Prisons had systems for inmate calls. Predetermined lists. Phone numbers.

When they'd first come down to the beach she'd asked Sam about Ken being able to get to her here by boat. He'd told her about the rocks and boulders that had, over centuries, fallen from the cliff behind them into the ocean, making boat access impossible and swimming dangerous sometimes, too. If the waves were fierce they could throw her against a rock.

And she felt like life had been throwing her against rocks since the day she'd been born.

"This is Ken's way," she continued, touching Lucy's head as the dog walked beside her, sometimes pressing against her leg. Lucy wasn't Madge. And the life Bloom had lived on the farm, the six years she'd been truly happy, had been more of a mirage than reality.

Why Carl and Betty had been given a daughter like her, she didn't know. *You're getting maudlin.*

Right. Feeling sorry for herself would get her nothing.

"Just like drugging me."

Sam hadn't said much since she'd told him about that night in the car. She had no idea what he was thinking. Of what had happened. Of her.

Maybe she'd dropped a notch or two in his estimation. Lost a modicum of respect.

Nothing she could do about that. Any more than she could have made Carl and Betty feel sufficient and capable of raising her. She couldn't change who she was, what she'd done or what had been done to her.

She could only shape her future. Not her past. She walked. He walked. Lucy walked. The night air was chilled. She wasn't cold, though. Or maybe she just couldn't feel much of anything.

"Ken isn't a brute. He's not one to raise a fist. Or a gun. His way is quiet and slow. Insidious. Far more cruel, in a way, than broken bones that can heal. Because most times there's no proof. Or enough proof."

"It's emotional cruelty," Sam said. "And it's a crime."

The sound of the waves took his words and brought them back to her. He meant well. He thought he'd win this battle.

A man like Sam, he didn't give up easily. Or believe that there was a guy he couldn't get with hard work, diligence and determination.

He wasn't just married to his job. He *was* the job.

"It's not a crime you can prove."

"We got him drugging you, Bloom. We'll get him again."

She didn't think so. But knew better than to try to get him to see that. Ultimately people saw what they wanted to see.

And sometimes, depending on their reality, even if they tried to see something differently, they couldn't.

"Power, greed—they're the ultimate diseases, and for most people, there's no cure. It got Ken. I don't know for sure when. Maybe back when he was kid. Maybe it was the way he survived his mother's cruelty to him. But what I do know is that he has to have power and control in order to survive. And for him, the way to feel powerful and in control is to prove that he can outsmart you. Right now he thinks I outsmarted him. He has to prove that I did not. He has to show me that his intellect is superior to mine. And when I play him at his own game—that's when he'll strike."

Her calves were getting tired with the sand sifting beneath her feet. She pressed on, anyway. The ocean was vast. The house, any house, symbolized the trapped state her life had become.

"He had such a great reputation," she said now. "Everyone respected him. Liked him. He was made department head when there were others who were equally qualified and had been there longer. Students clamored to take his classes. He was truly a nice guy."

"Until someone challenged his sense of power."

Sam was right with her. She wasn't alone. She looked back at him.

"I don't think anyone ever did. He was of genius-level intelligence, as well. No one in the field came close…"

"Until you came along."

Until she'd come along. But Ken hadn't known, at first, that she could outsmart him. She hadn't known at all. Until the night she'd ended up in the hospital with a broken jaw and had tested positive for medications that had not been prescribed to her.

Kenneth had insisted, when they'd gone to the emergency room, that she tell them that she flew over the front of their Jet Ski and hit something. There hadn't been bruises on her body, other than the shoulder that had hit the steering wheel, to withstand a falling-down-the-stairs excuse. He'd refused to let the car come into play at all. It was too close to the truth.

The Jet Ski excuse hadn't worked, either. But with the drugs coming up in her system, the broken jaw had taken a back seat almost immediately. When Sam had gotten around to asking her about it, she'd admitted that Ken was responsible. He'd known better than to deny it. He hadn't wanted the truth of that night to get out...

Truth was...he probably didn't have problems with erectile dysfunction. There were things he could take for that. He'd just been using her to act out his fantasies because he wanted to. Because he could...

It was getting late. They should get back. Get some rest. She had a seven o'clock appointment in the morning. And an eight and a nine, too. Chantel's soon-to-be sister-in-law, Julie Fairmont, was coming in.

And something was nagging at her. She fought it off as they climbed the path back toward the house. She didn't want to deal with anything else that night. Didn't want to…

"I might as well return home," she said as soon as the cottage came into view. She couldn't keep using him. Inconveniencing him. "With the divorce thing we can assume that I'm not in physical danger with Kenneth. He's going to drag me through the court system. My physical safety isn't at risk, my security is. The house. My car. My money…"

Sam didn't respond. She hadn't really expected him to, not until he thought about what she was saying. He wasn't going to like letting her live alone so soon after Ken's release, but there was no longer any justification for the money being spent on guards. For Chantel to be away from her family every evening. Or for Sam to be eating dinner out instead of at home. And sleeping in his guest bedroom.

There was also no reason for him to be pushing her down into the brush at the side of the path. "Stay here." His voice was a harsh whisper. "Stay down and don't move. I'm taking Lucy with me. I don't want her giving away your position."

Heart pounding, she stared at him. Doing as he said without question.

"Someone's in the house."

He pulled a knife out of his pocket. "Use this

if you have to," he said. "And don't move unless you have to use it. I'll be back."

Shaking, more frightened then she'd ever been, Bloom watched as, gun in hand, he headed toward the cottage.

CHAPTER FOURTEEN

SAM KEPT TO the tree line, shimmying along with his gun trained on the front door of his cottage, Lucy at his side. Several yards away from Bloom, he told the dog to stay. If anyone came around the house, they'd think Lucy was Bloom. And he'd be alerted when he heard the dog bark. Or squeal.

He prayed he'd hear neither and moved forward.

With no idea how many people he was dealing with, and a helpless woman in the weeds, he couldn't just send Lucy in to fight off the danger. In the first place, she wasn't a trained police dog. And in the other, she could be shot in a heartbeat, leaving him who knew how many alerted bad guys on his hands.

Where was the property guard?

He'd noticed the opened front door the second he'd seen the cottage come into view. And had seen a head pass by the front window in the next second. There were no cars in the yard, but he quickly circled around to the back, which would be reached first coming from the road.

The cottage faced the ocean. Not the road.

It was clear, as well. Closer to the building itself now, he thought he heard his name being called in a male voice he recognized. Tom Sherman, one of his previous partners, was taking some of the night duty shifts as a favor to Sam while his wife and kids were visiting her mother in Wisconsin.

Night shift didn't start until eleven.

Was it that late? He and Bloom had been down at the beach so long there'd been a change of guards?

Where was Tom? Was he in trouble?

Thinking of the property between him and the road, he knew he had to leave Tom down there to fend for himself while he found out what was going on in the house. Bloom was out there by herself. His first duty was to her.

He saw a shadow of light in the spare bedroom window. From the beach path he'd seen a head in the front room. So were there two of them? More?

"Sam?"

He heard his name again. Clearer. Was Tom coming closer? Or not in the woods at all?

Hurrying around to the front of the cottage, keeping his back to the wall of the house, he sought out the head of the path. All seemed calm. Lucy sat, ears perked, right where he'd left her.

He had to go in.

"Sam?" The call came again just as the front door of the cottage opened. "Sam!" His ex-partner said, rushing down the steps toward him. "My God, man, what the hell are you doing? You're supposed to be in the house. With the woman. Where's the woman?"

Tom's urgent tone didn't calm him much.

"She's safe for now. What's going on? Where's Williams?"

"Down by the road. Keeping watch. I got a call from one of the uniforms on night duty," he said. "As you know, I'm down as night watch contact tonight so they called me instead of you."

So Sam could rest. As well as a guy rested when he had a person in possible danger sleeping in the next room.

"As soon as I heard what was going on, I came straight here, told Williams to stay put and came up. Where the hell were you?"

"At the beach."

"At this time of night? You never go down after dark."

"I was already down there," he said, impatient now. "What's going on?"

"Ricardo Gomez called me," Tom said. "He's been roughed up. Came to in a Dumpster less than an hour ago."

BLOOM LIKED TOM SHERMAN. He was younger than Sam, but not by much. A little less lean. Reminded her of a big teddy bear. With a gun.

She liked being back in Sam's cottage, sitting on the couch with Lucy next to her. Her palm against the dog's fur was the only sensation she could focus on. Lucy laid her head on Bloom's thigh. She liked that, too.

She didn't like anything else about the turn the evening had taken.

No one had talked to her yet, other than Tom's brief introduction to her as he and Sam came to get her from her hiding place and walk her up, one on either side of her, to the cottage. Sam had been on the phone. Tom had been focused on him and watching the yard.

She'd gleaned that Tom had come to find Sam, to discuss how they wanted to handle a situation. And to be on hand if Sam wanted to leave or needed more coverage. And that a uniformed police officer was at the hospital waiting to talk to Ricardo Gomez, the young man who'd been watching out for her all week.

The young man who'd been absent when she'd left work that evening.

Poor guy. His one night off and he ends up in the hospital.

Sam had just hung up from him.

"The uniform is just getting in to speak with Gomez," he said. "He'll call back with a report as soon as he has one."

He stood by the wall of movies, looking underdressed in his jeans and boat shoes. Tom sat at the kitchen table, between Bloom and the door, hands on his uniformed thighs, just inches from the belt that held his holster.

He had a radio on that belt, too, and it had just crackled as Brad Williams checked in with an "all clear."

Something more than she knew was going on. She had to deal with it. But didn't want to.

"Did you notice anything odd about Gomez when you left this evening?" Sam spoke to her directly for the first time since he'd come back to get her. He got preoccupied when he was working. She'd seen him in action in the past.

"Gomez didn't work tonight," she said. "He had the night off." Surely he'd have known that. It was her understanding that he had a list of who was working and when on her case. Chantel had said, and he'd probably told her, too, that he was in charge of arranging the guard detail.

"What do you mean he had the night off?" Sam bit out. "Of course he didn't have the night off."

"He wasn't there when I left."

"And you didn't think it important to tell me that?" He didn't move closer. Didn't even sound menacing.

But she knew he was more than a little upset. Things were not going according to his plan. It was a control thing.

"He'd sent a replacement, Sam. Or rather, I assumed you had."

He straightened. Came over to sit on the edge of the couch, forearms on his knees. As though he was trying to look relaxed. She felt more like he was ready to pounce.

"What did the guy look like?" She recognized the tone from the past. She'd been sitting up in bed in a little cubicle in the emergency room, having just been told that she had prescription medication in her system without a prescription, and he'd been sitting in a chair, leaning forward in almost the same way, asking her where she'd gotten the drugs.

"It wasn't a guy, Sam. It was a woman. She told me good-night just like Gomez always does. Held the door open for me and stood there while I headed to my car. You were in the parking lot. You watched it all happen."

"I saw the beige shirt on the arm that opened the door. I didn't actually see the guard. I was watching…"

He shook his head. Definitely angry. But not at her.

"Can you describe her?" Tom asked, an odd look on his face as he glanced between Sam and Bloom.

"She was my height. Not overweight, but not model skinny. Dark hair. Long, but she had it pulled back tight. Hispanic, I think. She didn't really say much. Just good-night, as I recall," Bloom told them. Lucy lifted her head. Sensing Bloom's agitation? She stroked the dog slowly. Letting her know everything was fine and she could go back to sleep.

But was everything fine?

Ken was likely going to petition to reopen their divorce case. She could be back to square one, facing the possibility of losing a lot of her security. And with Ken out of work...could she be made to pay alimony?

He was doing just what she'd known he'd try to do—show his power over her. Make her afraid. She'd been prepared for that, and he was still finding a way to beat her.

And now something had happened to Gomez and... Could that really have something to do with her?

"Chantel's highly intelligent," she said, trying to clear her mind. "She speaks with intelligence. But she still has a tone about her...a command that comes through when she speaks..."

"The streets have a tendency to roughen up anyone regardless of intelligence or social stature," Tom said.

"Right." Bloom looked at Sam. "This woman didn't have that...tone. Is it possible she wasn't a cop at all?"

"Other than Chantel, there is no female on my list," he told her. And looked at Tom, whose expression clearly answered some unspoken question between them.

"What?" Bloom asked, looking at Tom briefly, but then pinned Sam with an unyielding stare. "I'm an adult, Sam. If this has something to do with me, you need to let me know."

"We have no idea what's going until we hear back from the hospital," Tom started.

"Sam?"

"Someone who isn't supposed to be there has taken Gomez's place, then he turns up hurt. It's pretty obvious that this has to do with you," Sam said. "Freelander might be planning to go after you in divorce court, but he probably intends to see you suffer in other ways. He's joined a new league since you were married to him, Bloom. He's got thugs who are willing to do him favors. If terrorizing you gives him pleasure, we can assume he has the means to do it. The tip I got implied that he was going to make you hurt physically."

Things he'd been about to tell her when she'd made her bold statement that she was going home? Before they'd been interrupted by their "intruder"?

His phone rang then, interrupting them. Like Tom, Bloom watched Sam as he took the call. Listening to his terse questions. Trying to glean the parts of the conversation that were unheard to them.

"It appears Gomez was hit on the back of the head, had a rag soaked with chloroform put over his nose and mouth and then at some point was thrown in the Dumpster. He doesn't know how or by who. He'd been walking down the hall, checking alcoves after everyone had left for the day when it happened. He's bruised, has a concussion, but doesn't appear to be seriously hurt."

"It's a warning." Tom was standing now, too.

"Gomez is a big guy," Bloom pointed out. "The woman who was there, posing as the guard, even if she could have somehow knocked him out and gotten him to the Dumpster, there's no way she could have lifted him by herself."

Sam was nodding. "Which is how we know we're dealing with a group here. Whoever they are, they're working at the behest of your ex-husband. It's too much of a coincidence to think that someone is suddenly out to get you the week that Freelander gets out of jail. And you are the only reason Gomez was in the building."

She was a grown woman who'd learned how to wear big girl panties all by herself. She would stand up to this. "You really believe he's going to make good on his supposed threat to come after me?"

"I think that seems pretty obviously the case."

"I agree," Tom told her, still maintaining a position close to the front door.

"What do we do?" She already had three of Santa Raquel's finest right there guarding her. There was a whole city to protect.

"Exactly what we are doing," Sam told her. "While I didn't see the thing with Gomez coming, we're all in place because we expected Freelander to come after you..."

True. But she'd thought it would be her he'd try to get. Not...

"Why didn't the girl hurt me then? Why take out Gomez and then just hold the door open for me and let me walk out?"

But even as she asked the question, she knew the answer.

"He's letting me know he's in control." She didn't look at either man now. Ken played head games. It was like Sam said—Ken wanted to terrorize her.

"And that you're vulnerable," Sam added. "He wants you to know you're safe only because he chose to let you be. He's also trying to scare you into thinking that the guards you think you have protecting you are easily dealt with."

Her head shot up. She stared at the detective she'd somehow begun to see as larger than life. Maybe this was more than just transference. Maybe she'd also seen him, at least a little, through the eyes of hero worship. Considering her odd upbringing, latent hero worship was a plausible diagnosis.

"He's going to get me, isn't he?"

"Hell, no!" Sam didn't hesitate. "What happened to Gomez tonight…that works in our favor, Bloom."

Now she was confused. Frowning, Bloom asked, "How?"

"You might be able to take a good cop by surprise once. You won't be able to do it again. Freelander just wasted his one shot."

She wanted to believe him. Prayed that she could believe him.

But Sam already caught her out with one promise he couldn't possibly keep. She wasn't going to let him do it to her again.

CHAPTER FIFTEEN

THEY'D HAD THEIR WARNING. He'd speak with Gomez himself in the morning. Pull surveillance camera tapes from Bloom's office. Get BOLOs out.

Everyone was safe.

Business as usual. Except, "I'm calling in a second guard to be out there with you tonight," he told Tom.

His old partner, and friend, nodded. "Williams said he'd stay as long as you need him. He's on a four on, three off rotation just starting three off."

"We'll keep him them, but I'm still calling in a second pair of fresh eyes." Just for the night. Until he had time to figure out how big a threat they were dealing with.

"There's another possibility," Bloom said.

Sam was trying hard not to notice her. He had a victim to protect. She could not also be a person of personal interest. And yet…she sat there calmly petting Lucy, her face showing no signs of the unrest she must be feeling.

He'd noticed that about her before, too. Bloom didn't get caught up in her own drama. She was always aware of those around her. Even when she was hurting, as she'd been that first night he'd met her in the hospital. A nurse's aide had had trouble finding a vein when Bloom had first come in and when the aide returned while Sam was there, she'd smiled at the young woman and told her that her veins had always been hard to poke.

But this wasn't about Bloom the person.

It was about keeping a citizen safe.

"What other possibility could there be?" he asked her. If she thought for one second he was going to do as she'd suggested earlier and release her to her own home, she was mistaken. Period. He'd find an excuse to lock her up first.

And lose his job later if it came to that.

"My practice… I see mostly woman who've been victims of domestic violence. I help them to free themselves emotionally from the bonds that keep them in abusive situations. To recover and move on. Build new lives. Which leaves behind a lot of violent, abusive men, any of whom could logically blame me for their loss."

She had a point.

"I'll need a list of your current clients in the morning," he told her.

"I can't give you that, Sam. I'm bound under patient-doctor confidentiality."

"You can release them if lives are in danger…"

She was already shaking her head.

"You can release them if they agree to have their names released to the police due to an investigation that could compromise their safety," Tom suggested from beside the door.

Sam sent his partner a silent commendation. They'd made a good team. Too bad Tom had had no interest in a detective's badge.

"I'm going to need you to make calls to your entire client base in the morning," Sam told her. "Or have someone else do so. I need you to get those permissions and get me that list…"

Too late he remembered who he was talking to. And how important it was that she maintain a feeling of being in control of her own life. Her own choices.

"You think they could be in danger, too? If not from an abusive ex, then from Ken? Do you think he could go after them to show me that I'm harmful to my patients? That seeing me puts them in danger?"

He could almost see her mind at work.

"Anything's possible," he told her. Because it might get him those lists quicker. But also because…it was true.

"I'll get you the list," she told him. "But I'm going to have one of the girls at the reception desk make the calls, too."

He was asking her to sacrifice the one thing

that gave her the most strength. Her business. He hoped it didn't suffer from this.

But he'd rather it suffer, than she, or one of her patients, did.

"So if we're done here, I'd like to get to work," Tom said, reaching for the door.

"If Brad's up for keeping watch at the road tonight, I'll get someone to cover midrange and you stay up here on top," Sam said.

Tom nodded. Then said, "I'll get someone to cover midrange. You get some rest. I'm contact man tonight. I've got this."

His look told Sam that he was noticing more than Sam wanted him to see. Which meant he was slipping.

And needed some rest.

Nodding, he silently agreed to let his friend have their backs until morning.

BLOOM INTENDED TO excuse herself to bed the minute that Tom locked the door behind himself.

It had been a long day. She had to be up early in the morning. Earlier now that she had to get a client list to Sam. Tom was organizing someone to take Gomez's shift in the morning, though word was that the young man intended to be there.

Lucy's head was still in her lap.

She glanced at the blank TV screen. There was a TV in the bedroom, too. Her tablet was connected to his Wi-Fi. There was no reason for her to remain in the living room.

Lucy and he went together. A pair. She couldn't take the dog to bed with her.

"You want to watch a few more commercials?" she asked, remembering her first night in his home with him.

Chantel had put the DVD away. They'd watched a couple of movies since then. She didn't want to watch a movie. Couldn't stay up that long. Didn't want to be that engaged. She didn't want to feel. Just to…escape.

Sam watched her for what seemed like minutes but was probably only a few long seconds.

"Sure." He cued up the DVD player, and grabbed them two bottles of water, without asking if she wanted one.

She did. The ocean air, coming off the salty water, had left her thirsty. She moved over to one end of the couch. He sat on the other. Lucy settled herself between them.

And the commercials started. *Plop plop fizz fizz.* She didn't remember that one. *I can't believe I ate the whole thing.* Not that one, either, but she did identify with the message. Her stomach was feeling rather sick.

And a bit like it was full of butterflies, too. Sam was there. Not too far away while being too far away.

She wasn't so scared when he was close. And she was petrified. What in the hell was she going to do? Was she to pay for her poor choice in husband for the rest of her life? His abuse had been so subtle that she didn't believe Sam would ever be able to pin anything on him.

He was going to play with her. Taunt her. Show her who was boss for the rest of her life.

No. He'd had enough of her years. She refused to let him have more.

Her phone bleeped, indicating a text. Her girlfriends in the city sometimes texted when they wanted to get tickets or arrange a night out. She grabbed her cell, opening the text before she realized...

Before fear struck her stomach with a sharp jab. And then her temples.

I hope you feel safe tonight, my dear. You know you have nothing to fear from me. I love you.

She was shaking so hard she couldn't hold the phone.

When it dropped into her lap, Sam grabbed it and tapped the screen.

"Freelander." The word was almost a spit.

She couldn't speak calmly so she said nothing.

A commercial played. She had no idea what anyone was saying.

"With the case gone there's no restraining order out against him. And nothing in this message to hang him with. Not in court." Sam spoke out loud.

Bloom felt the words like a lid on her coffin, but she wasn't going to lie down and die.

She wasn't lying down for that man again. Ever. The thought brought a curious calm.

"It can't be just a coincidence that he sends that text on the same night that my guard is hurt."

"It could be. Stupid of him to implicate himself that way. But we're not going to take any chances."

Ken was playing with her head. She'd known he would. She had to stay strong. Smart. Focused.

"I know how to drive him to enough anger to commit a crime," she said while an old woman asked, "Where's the Beef?" on the flat screen in front of them.

"How?"

"I invite him to the house. That alone will get him started since, until he gets things overturned in court, he's not allowed in the place without my invitation. Even though his money paid for it."

She loved living on the beach in Santa Raquel. Close to work. She didn't care if she never saw Ken's house again.

"No."

"Once he's there, I get him sexually aroused.

It shouldn't be hard after he's spent two years in prison. And then I mock him."

It was a no-brainer. She'd only done it once before, laughing at him that night in the car. She'd ended up in the hospital, but she'd also been freed of him.

"No way in hell." The words were succinct. Each one with such distinct enunciation she stared at him.

Another commercial played. She missed it.

Okay, so it wasn't something a psychiatrist would normally do. Wasn't something she'd ever want to do. But they had to look at this logically. Kenneth wasn't going to go away until he was taken away.

And he wasn't going to make another mistake like putting illegally obtained prescription medication in her food and drinks.

"We're going to find out who attacked Gomez," Sam said. His gaze was soft as it met hers, and she started to feel warmth inside. Not a lot; she couldn't get carried away. And yet…it felt good… looking at him.

Safe.

She'd been alone a long time.

"When we do, we'll tie him to Freelander. I'm also going to find his drug connection. That I can promise you."

Another one of his meaningless promises. Another one he had no control over his ability to keep.

"And while he can't be charged again with drugging you, we can charge him with purchase, possession and sale of illegal substances with the intent to harm."

"You just said he couldn't be charged with drugging me."

"No, but he can be charged with purchasing the means to do so with the intent to do so and then we can use your case as proof of intent. We could never find proof that he had the drugs, only that he'd written the prescriptions. With his hard drive crashing..." He made quote signs with his fingers in the air. They all knew that the crash had been deliberate. "And his disposing of the system in such a way that no one would ever be able to steal confidential information—"

He'd had it smashed in a compactor and then put in an incinerator.

"—there was no hard proof of him receiving, or dispersing the drugs. The prescriptions we know he wrote could have gone to clients for all a jury would know. Unless we find proof of him dispersing those drugs. Which I will do. I just need more time. I only heard about the prison gang affiliation the week that I told you about it."

She shook her head. "That's another thing that doesn't ring true to me. Where would Kenneth ever have found someone associated with a gang? Let alone had a conversation about an illegal drug trade? You don't understand my ex-husband," she said. But he was going to have to if he was going to be able to help her.

"Kenneth is a blue blood through and through. At least, for his persona to be able to exist, he has to believe he is one. His mother's fifth husband was a scumbag into some really bad stuff, I think, but who had a lot of money. At fourteen, Kenneth was a problem for him so he sent him away to a prep boarding school in Boston. From his performance there he gained a full ride scholarship to Harvard and never looked back."

She drank from the bottle of water, which had had its seal intact when he'd handed it to her.

She wondered if he knew that ever since Kenneth she didn't drink anything anyone gave her unless she was the one who unsealed it.

"There's no way he had a gang association before he went to prison. And I'm fairly certain he didn't have one inside, either."

"You ever been inside a prison?"

Bloom shook her head. He nodded. And they both watched a chubby little boy sing about the name of his bologna without so much as cracking a smile.

CHAPTER SIXTEEN

BLOOM HAD ERRANDS to run after work on Saturday, and Chantel went with her. Which left Sam the entire day to begin running down the client list Bloom had faxed over. And to track down the surveillance video of Bloom's office building.

He received it in time to spend his evening going over it. And then to watch faces speed across his screen as he tried to find a match for the woman seen escorting Bloom out of the building the night before.

He didn't get a hit in any database, including missing persons, military or criminal records.

She'd never been on a police force that he could find and her photo was not registered on any security personnel database.

He called Bloom just after eight. She was at his place. He wasn't planning to head that way until he knew she was in his room.

No repeats of the night before. At one point, when he could have sworn she'd had tears in her eyes over an old card commercial, he'd almost asked if he could hold her.

WTF.

"Hello?" Her voice came on and he blinked. Then remembered that he'd just dialed her.

"Did she have a gun?"

"The guard?"

"Yes."

"Yes. Just like Gomez does."

"You're sure?"

"Yes. I saw it on her waist under her jacket when she lifted her arm to open the door. I'm telling you, Sam, she seemed just like Gomez. Down to the way she spoke to me, wishing me a good-night in the same respectful tone, when I left. I wasn't the least bit concerned."

He wanted her to have been. Wanted her to have noticed something.

"You don't happen to know what kind of gun it was, do you?"

He'd already checked the tape to see if he could see even the handle or holster.

"It looked like the one Gomez carries."

His off-duty weapon was not police issued. That was something, at least.

"Like yours," Bloom added.

His duty weapon and Gomez's gun were not even close.

"Okay, thanks." He pulled the phone from his ear to end the call.

"Sam?" Her voice came from afar.

"Yeah?"

"Come home. You need the rest."

"Soon."

"I'm heading to bed now. You can have the place to yourself. You need a break."

The compassion in her tone made him hard. "Okay," he heard himself agree without even giving himself time to think about whether or not he wanted to do as she asked. Just because she'd asked in the way she had?

He'd go. But he was taking a cold shower the second that he got there.

SAM SPENT SUNDAY at work doing what a detective did…investigating. With Bloom's list of clients' names in front of him, he spent the majority of the day online, looking up addresses and former addresses, police records, domestic violence reports, employment records and license plate numbers. The surveillance camera in the parking lot of Bloom's building had given him some. He cross-referenced those with known clients and their abusers. When that turned up nothing he looked up known abusers' plates and compared car makes and models to those he could see in the surveillance tape.

Unfortunately, there'd been no footage of the

Dumpster out back. And none in the hallway where Gomez had been taken down. He didn't think that was a coincidence. Whoever wanted Bloom's guard gone had done enough homework to know where in the building to strike. And where to take him afterward.

Sam also continued to run searches on Freelander's records from two years ago. He had all of the man's credit card records and was running searches for every establishment he'd spent money in, trying to find out who he'd been with. Who'd worked there at the time.

There were phone records to go through, as well.

Lists. Long unending lists.

From the dealership Freelander went to for service on his Lincoln SUV to the Italian restaurant he'd eaten at the night before trial, Sam was going to search every employee on file at every establishment.

There was a connection someplace to those drugs. And the gang that had protected him in prison. That was a given. And it was Sam's job to find it.

And the woman who'd let Bloom out of the building on Friday night had come from somewhere— at the behest of someone.

He had his desktop doing one search. A laptop

doing another. And was running a search on the computer on the unused desk next to his, as well.

When his butt was sore from sitting, when his nerves were screaming for action and his head ached from staring at the screen, he printed a still photo of the female guard impersonator and visited places in the immediate vicinity of Bloom's building. The photo was grainy at best, and the angle wasn't good enough to get a full look at the woman's face, but if someone had seen her, there might be something about her they recognized.

And if he didn't get a hit nearby, he'd likely be spending the week doing the same at places where clients' abusers worked and places Freelander had been known to frequent in LA.

Unless he got lucky first.

What he got was a text from Bloom.

I'm making cabbage rolls for dinner if you want some.

Reminiscent of texts he'd received from Stella when they'd been married.

Can't. Too much work to do.

Same kind of response he'd sent to his ex-wife. Every single time.

He wanted to go, though. He couldn't believe how badly. And that didn't remind him of Stella at all.

GOMEZ WAS BACK at work on Monday. He apologized to Bloom for his lapse and swore to her it wouldn't happen again.

Bloom figured she owed him for taking one on the head because of her. She told him she was just glad that he was okay and assured him that she had no lack of confidence in his abilities.

She spoke the truth.

And she also knew that no matter how many guards they had on her, or how safe her housing situation was, there was always the chance that the "other" side would win.

No fingerprints or other identifying markers had been found on Gomez's clothes. The kidnappers hadn't taken his gun, which suggested that they were pros. They had guns of their own and didn't need a search for the gun to lead anywhere near them.

Chantel gave Bloom the report that night after work. The new detective never seemed to run out of energy.

"Isn't your family getting tired of having you constantly gone?" she asked as she placed two plates of shrimp linguine on the table. Chantel had already poured, from a bottle Bloom had just opened, the two half glasses of wine they'd agreed was a safe nightly allotment considering the circumstances. It was enough to relax but not impair them in the event of danger.

"Colin's busy with a big case right now," Chantel said, sitting down at the plate that was heaped twice as full. "And Julie's hardly ever home now that she's slowly getting her life back. Frankly, I'm glad for a chance to not be in that big house all alone. If I wasn't here, I'd probably be at my place."

Chantel didn't mention Julie's visit with Bloom on Saturday. And neither did Bloom. But she thought about the young woman. About her determination to beat the demons that still attacked her from the inside out. Not just because of the rape, but because for so long no one had believed her about it having taken place.

That's where Bloom had been lucky. She'd had the authorities on her side when her abuse had become known.

Julie had some work to do, but Bloom had no doubt the woman would come out on top. Julie was a fighter. And, she had a strong feeling, a bone-deep good person.

"Still, you've got to be getting tired of living with me every evening rather than having your own life."

Chantel's chuckle brought a smile to Bloom's lips, too, even before the woman responded. "Right now, you are my life," she said. "Just like the next case I'm on will be."

"But I'm not technically your case. I thought you and Sam were doing this on the side because, without a crime, helping me wasn't officially sanctioned."

"That was last week. The attack on Gomez made it a current crime."

At least something good had come of the incident.

"So, for the time being, you're stuck with us." Chantel ate with the gusto of a guy, though her body never showed a sign of it as far as Bloom could tell.

Bloom didn't have that much of an appetite. "I could think of worse things," she said, emptying her wineglass.

"Have more." Chantel pushed the bottle over toward her. "You're allowed."

Bloom hesitated. And without a word Chantel put down her fork. "The bottle's been sitting there between us," she said softly.

Of course it had been.

"And you watched me carry it from your hand to the table to fill our glasses."

So she still had some work of her own to do. Things took time. And…she picked up the bottle and served herself.

"It's okay, you know." Chantel's voice had softened, losing all trace of the streetwise cop. "Your instinct to not drink when someone who isn't having any more encourages you to do so…that's a good one."

"I was going to have some more." Maybe. From what she'd been told, there'd been times Kenneth had slipped her daily dose into her glass while they were sitting at the table together. He'd bragged about it.

To her. When he'd been trying to intimidate her against testifying against him. When she'd agreed to see him against all advice to the contrary. He'd been trying to prove to her that her testimony would do no good because she'd never be able to take him on in court…

"And if you weren't going to have more, that's okay, too." Chantel rescued her from a road she'd thought she'd left behind. "I'm just saying…you don't have to be all perfect around me. I know you're strong and capable. Hell, I just referred my future sister-in-law to you. And I risked my life for her, so that tells you how together I think you are."

Bloom blinked. Tearing up would be embarrassing. She nodded instead and made herself meet the other woman's gaze, taking a sip of wine.

"If you ever do want to talk about it, you know, to just a person…" Chantel let the sentence drop.

Bloom nodded again.

"Soooo…" Chantel glanced at Bloom half an hour later as she handed her a rinsed plate to put in the dishwasher. "What's going on between you and Sam?"

The plate slipped from Bloom's fingers, but she'd been on the way to placing it in the rack, and it fell smoothly into its slot. "Nothing," she said.

Because there was nothing. She hardly saw him.

Chantel studied her for a moment. Looked at the plate that had landed safely, and went back to rinsing dishes.

TUESDAY NIGHT BLOOM handed Chantel a pair of panties and a bra as she emptied them from the dryer. Her own underthings were going in a separate pile for her to fold. When they'd been caught in a sudden downpour during a walk on the beach, it had just made sense, them throwing their things in together. And because she was doing a load, Bloom had put her other whites in. No sense in running up Sam's water and electric bill for separate small loads of laundry.

"How long have you been keeping a change of clothes in your trunk?" she asked the detective. She'd offered to loan Chantel a sweat suit or anything else she wanted to borrow, but the woman had herself covered.

"Since academy days," Chantel told her. "One thing you learn as a female cop is that you have to be more prepared, more alert, more everything than your male counterparts. Because in terms of physical musculature, they already have one up on you. And a lot of them are hesitant at first, trusting their lives to a woman…"

It was something she'd never thought about, but it made perfect sense. Chantel always seemed so together. And now she knew why.

Was glad to know.

She liked Chantel. And wondered if, when this was all over, they could remain friends.

If friendship was even an option. To Chantel, Bloom was a job.

Just as her patients were her job. No matter how much she might care about them there was always that professional distance that could not be breached.

Bloom bent down to the laundry basket and came up with two of her nightgowns and a pair of…

"Tighty-whities." Chantel looked at them, grinning. "They're all yours, Doctor. I'm not touching them. I gotta work with the guy."

She looked from the nighty to the underwear and then paid close attention to her own folding.

"They must have been left in the washer," Bloom said. "Did you check it before you threw in your things?"

Chantel had changed in the laundry room and put her clothes in first, then Bloom had added hers.

"No." Chantel folded. "I never thought to," she added. There was a definite edge of humor in her voice.

Bloom's chest tightened.

"I am not sleeping with him." It was important to Bloom that she be clearly understood. "His underwear and my nightgown…this is the only time they've ever been in contact. Period."

Her tone must have gotten through to the detective, who turned and met Bloom's gaze head-on. All grin gone from her face, Chantel nodded.

CHAPTER SEVENTEEN

"IT WOULDN'T BE a crime if you were, you know." Chantel was putting the clothes she'd washed and folded in the small duffel she'd carried in from her car.

Sam would be home soon.

Well, home to him. Not to Bloom. To Bloom he'd be back soon. She made certain the distinction was clear in her mind.

On the couch with Lucy beside her, Bloom sipped from the glass of wine she'd poured at dinner. Why she craved the extra relaxation that night in particular she had no idea. But she would rather use a glass of wine as a sleep aid than take anything. After spending six months recovering from what Ken had done to her, she was not going down that road again.

"What wouldn't be a crime?" she asked, starting to feel lethargic enough to face being shut in the bedroom for the rest of the night. And maybe even fall asleep within an hour, instead of sitting up in Sam's bed, against his pillows, listening to him move around in his home.

"If you and Sam—how'd you put it?—if your nightgown and his underwear had contact."

The image obliterated any relaxation she'd gained. Sexual desire, hot and undeniable, flared in her lower region. Bloom didn't move.

"Of course it would be wrong," she said aloud, when the alarming sensation didn't immediately subside.

She'd put voice to intention and then it would happen.

"Not really," Chantel told her. "Being a cop isn't like being a doctor or lawyer. We don't have clients. Or, if you want to look at it that way, everyone, including our spouses, our children, even our parents, are our clients. We are sworn to protect all citizens."

Yes. Fine. But…

"I can't believe they tell you in the academy that it's okay to get involved with a victim."

No! Why was she even entertaining the conversation? It was a moot point.

"I met Colin while working undercover. Did you know that?"

"No."

She'd known that Chantel had been pretty much solely responsible for exposing a corrupt police commissioner. And that she'd been promoted soon afterward.

"I was posing as his girlfriend." The woman perched on the arm of the couch.

Bloom was enormously interested. Because she was coming to care for Chantel like a friend. No other reason. "And you fell in love with him?" She had to admit, the idea was romantic.

If a bit over the top.

"Not willingly," Chantel told her. And then shrugged. "As an officer of the law we're sworn to protect the community. We're given a lot of discretion, to determine what needs further investigation, what doesn't. Who to pursue, who not to pursue. A lot of what we do…we have to make split-second decisions that can cost us our lives. You learn to listen to your gut…"

She had Bloom's full attention.

"It's all about integrity," Chantel said. "If you take advantage of someone for personal gain… you shouldn't be wearing the badge."

She'd never counseled a cop, but could see where doing so would be interesting. And rewarding…

"We're human beings," Chantel said. "And we're encouraged to interact socially with those we protect. It builds a sense of trust that allows us to do our jobs to the best of our ability."

The woman's passion for her job was commendable. Bloom felt lucky to have her on her case.

Lucy inched, one paw at a time, closer to Sam's workmate. Chantel ran a hand along the dog's head and down her back as she said, "It works the other way, too."

Bloom missed Lucy's warmth.

"We're expected to act with utmost decorum even when we're off duty. But, bottom line, we're human and allowed to have sex just like anyone else."

Sipping her wine, Bloom kept her thoughts on Chantel. Of what she knew about her. And wanted to know about her and Colin falling in love...

"So, it's like I said, if there *was* something going on between you and Sam...it'd be okay."

Her hands felt a little unsteady so she set down her wineglass. "There isn't."

Shrugging again, Chantel continued to pet Lucy. "If you say so."

Bloom liked the woman, but she was really starting to make her tense.

"Why are you so convinced that something's going on between us?" she asked, taking care to monitor her behavior, as always.

She just had to find out what Chantel was thinking so she could help her see where she'd gone astray.

"I'm paid to be observant." The dry remark wasn't an answer.

Not one Bloom could work with, anyway. "I don't understand."

"I haven't worked with Sam, but I know him

from afar. I know his reputation. I know how he works his cases. And…every single guy at the station is asking me what's going on."

Blood sped through her veins. Probably because the wine had thinned it. That's why she felt like every nerve ending was on edge.

"What?" Her throat got tight so she took another sip of wine.

"I know, right?" the woman said. "But I'm not kidding. Sam's not himself on this one."

"They think he's screwing up?" The horror of such a possibility made her cold. And hot.

"No. You're perfectly safe. Believe me. His dedication to you, to this case…it's personal, is all," Chantel said, her voice softening. "He's always been great. He's one of the most decorated, respected detectives on the force. But with this case…it's like he's Superman or something. He doesn't quit. Not for a second. Not even long enough to get a beer after work."

"He normally does that?"

"At least once a week."

Her first thought was to talk to him about that. To tell him he didn't have to give up his beer nights to babysit her. And then she realized that she wasn't keeping him from his beer. He had all evening to go drink beer if he wanted to. Chantel had the evening shift.

"There's nothing between us," she said now.

And was afraid the words didn't carry the conviction she wanted them to.

"So you don't... I mean... You seem to... You don't like him? Even a little bit?"

"Of course I like him. He's a nice guy. A great guy."

"But it's no more than that?"

She was a woman who'd promised herself to look deep. To always be honest. In control of her own life. "He saved me." She didn't know what kind of answer that was, but it was what she came up with.

Chantel was watching her. And looking far too observant.

"In the past," Bloom explained. "If it wasn't for Sam...I would never have testified. I'd never have been free of the man who has a diabolical need to control me. I might never even have seen that it was going on."

"So that's it. You don't feel anything personal for him."

She didn't want to. She knew that for sure. "I'm living in his home. It's natural that I'd be curious."

Was that why she couldn't sleep at night until she heard him shut his bedroom door and give Lucy a "bed" command?

"Well, just know that he's a good guy," Chantel said.

"I do know that." And that had nothing to do

with nightgowns. Or… No. She was not going to
think of the underwear.

She'd put it back in the washer. And run it
through a cycle. So he'd find it as he left it. And
if he knew she'd done laundry?

Well…

"Some of the unmarried guys…they talk, of
course. Our group is largely male and we're tight.
They…you know…it's not unheard of for them to
pick up girls. Have a good time. Talk about hot
chicks, that kind of thing."

She watched TV now and then. Got the picture.
And didn't think any less of Sam…

"He's not one of them."

Bloom wasn't sorry to hear that, either. But
didn't take it personally.

"Word is he took his divorce pretty hard."

She knew Sam was divorced. From that conversation in the past when she'd asked him if he'd
ever been married.

And if he was still hankering after his ex-wife,
that was all the more reason she was glad she
wasn't hankering after him.

Now more than ever she had to remain completely aware that her feelings were…a case of
transference. Mixed with a bit of hero worship.
A victim experiencing a measure of infatuation
for her protector. Period.

"He'd kill me for saying this. But Sam…he's

decent. Probably the greatest cop I've ever known. And he's…different with you."

"Whatever you tell me is in total confidence." She heard her words even as her inner voice screamed, *No!* "I'm a psychiatrist, remember. I'm used to keeping my own counsel."

The way Chantel was studying her told her she should have said she didn't want to know what she'd been about to say. That Chantel should keep her own counsel on this one.

She wanted to tell Chantel to drop the subject right then and there. She took a sip of wine. And listened as Chantel said, "From what I hear, he took his divorce so hard that he doesn't take dating lightly because of the guilt."

That got her. "The guilt?" Had his wife died? No, wait. They'd divorced. But…

"He loved the job more than he loved her," Chantel said. "He's determined not to hurt another woman that way."

She'd known his job came first. The reminder was critical.

Everything inside Bloom shut down.

Kenneth's driving force had been his professional reputation. The admiration and respect he had in his field. It was his identity, and she'd gotten in the way of that.

"I understand," she said, when she could. She

took her wineglass to the kitchen, dumped it out and put it in the dishwasher.

"I don't think you do." Chantel was close behind her.

Bloom hadn't heard her approach.

"With you, it's like…his guard's down. I don't know. I just… You're a special woman, Bloom. What you've been through…the way you've helped yourself, and how you help others. Sam…he's like that, too. Anyway…I just wanted you to know. If something was going on between you two, I'm happy for you. And here…if you need to talk."

Bloom looked at her. Wanting to say something. Coming up with nothing.

Grabbing her keys from the table, Chantel said, "He'll be here any minute. I'll wait outside."

Bloom wanted to call the woman back. Chantel had never left the house before Sam got home. And Bloom figured she thought she'd said too much. She didn't want Chantel to feel uncomfortable.

She didn't want there to be anything between her and Sam.

She didn't want Kenneth—or anyone—after her.

Saying good-night to Lucy, Bloom headed to the room she was borrowing, telling herself that one out of three was better than none.

At least there was nothing between her and Sam.

And to prove it, she'd be asleep before she heard him say, "Bed."

She almost succeeded.

CHAPTER EIGHTEEN

ON TUESDAY ONE of the beat cops who was carrying around their female guard impersonator photo checked in to say he'd had a positive hit. A woman at a local convenience store recognized the suspect.

"Was she there last Friday?" Sam asked, instantly alert as he took down the address.

"No."

"No?"

"It was Wednesday of last week," the man said. "She was sure."

"Positive, sir. She was off Thursday and Friday. And remembers it was Wednesday because that's Powerball day and she bought a ticket, saying she hoped it brought her luck. The woman remembered her because of the uniform. She wore it with the bottom button undone, just like in the picture.

"The clerk remembered hoping her luck would help keep her safe on the job, rather than wasting it on the lottery. She was afraid I was asking about her because something bad had happened."

"You assured her otherwise?"

"Yes, sir."

"Good work, MacMillon," he said, and hung up.

He paid the woman a visit himself when he went out to grab a sandwich and learned exactly what his officer had.

Obviously the woman who'd posed as a guard was local.

Question was, was she really a guard? Or was the uniform just part of her attempt to get at Bloom? Bigger question—who'd hired her?

Back at the station, he started searching private security companies in the area. Phoning them this time instead of relying on the Santa Raquel Police Department's extensive databases.

He faxed the picture. He emailed it. He worked all evening, quitting only with enough time to get home before Chantel was off.

He left no stone unturned.

And ended up with nothing.

TUESDAY MELDED INTO WEDNESDAY. Sam worked a missing person's case Wednesday morning at the request of the captain. A three-year-old child not from the area had been at the beach with his family and disappeared.

As it turned out the boy had just wandered off and was found asleep under a bench leaning up against a closed hot dog shack a quarter of a mile up from where his parents had last seen him.

By noon, Sam was back looking at computer screens. There were some similarities in names. A couple of times when Freelander had been at a restaurant and receipts showed that another man had also been there.

Looking at other places Freelander had also been, he found no evidence of the other man. But he drove to LA Wednesday afternoon to show him Freelander's picture, ask if he knew him. And to show around the photo of the female guard impersonator. All to no avail.

He was fifteen minutes from his exit when Chantel called.

"You're going to want to pick her up from work," his coworker said without preamble. No names mentioned. He had twenty or so minutes to get there.

Turning on the bubble inside his unmarked car, he sped up.

"Okay. Why?"

"She just called. She was served today."

Shit.

"She tell you how the order read?"

"Only that it was a show cause hearing set for a week from today."

"Here or in LA?"

"Here. The decree was issued here as this is where Bloom was living at the time of the divorce. And it's still her current address."

Her address was with him. Bloom wasn't fighting by herself anymore.

Her address was still her home. As evidenced by the number of times he, or one of the guys, had collected her mail for her. She was with him temporarily.

And Sam had best not forget that fact. Not for a second. He exited the freeway at fifteen miles over the speed limit.

"Still no other contact from Freelander? He hasn't texted again?"

"Nope."

"I'm almost there," he said, vowing silently that he would be focused only on the case, not the victim, from there on out.

BLOOM WAS SURPRISED to see Sam waiting for her after work. She'd been picturing her and Chantel at home with a glass of wine. Time to deal with the day's event.

Instead, the man who was still keeping her up until he settled in for the night was there, at the bottom of the steps, as she walked out the door.

"Where's Chantel?"

"Colin's home tonight."

Then Bloom was glad the detective had called for backup.

"I thought we'd drop off one car and then head out for something to eat." He surprised her further.

"Just you and me? Going out?" When she said it like that it sounded like...more than she'd intended.

But the idea sounded good. Really good.

"I figured I'd drive and you could drown your sorrows," he said, as plain-voiced as if they were discussing which guard was on duty down below.

"She told you."

Bloom wasn't surprised. The detectives kept in constant report with each other when it came to Bloom. She'd expect as much.

"Yes."

She was glad. She'd wanted him to know. And hadn't wanted to talk about it. Chantel had saved her the trouble.

"Dinner out sounds great," she said as they split to get in their respective cars. She was always in the lead these days, with a detective behind her.

Protecting her back.

Something she was trying desperately not to get used to.

THE PUB HE took her to was no place like anyplace she'd ever been before. There were a few scarred dark wooden tables, a long bar and pool tables.

The place was filled with people who obviously knew Sam. Many of them nodded when he came in. As they made their way past the bar and a couple of "Nice to see you here, sirs," a group of two guys and a woman stood and let Sam and Bloom have their table.

"I didn't even know a place like this existed in Santa Raquel," she said. She hadn't seen a name out front.

"It's private. Law enforcement and their families and guests only. Run by a couple of retired cops."

So this was where he came for that beer he'd been skipping lately? "Won't they think it odd, you coming here with me?"

Wouldn't it start gossip he'd neither want nor need?

Sam passed her the menu—a single laminated sheet.

"Most everyone here knows who you are," he said. "A good many of them have been passing around the photo of the fake guard. They're curious. This way they know who they're watching out for without making a big deal about it."

She supposed he made sense. Kind of. While she was a bit uncomfortable, as though she was on stage under lights, she also felt...welcome. And safe.

And that was when she figured out what he was doing.

"You want me to know that Ken's not just going up against me. That I'm not fighting him alone this time."

He motioned for the waitress. Nodded at someone behind her. He didn't look at Bloom, nor did he reply.

"HE FILED A motion to vacate the decree. The hearing is his chance to show cause to do so. It's also my chance to present my side to the judge. To convince him that there is no just cause for vacating."

Sam heard every word she said, in spite of the raucous laughter and uninhibited conversation going on around them. He generally liked the noise, the feeling of letting go of the responsibility of watching out for others for a few hours with others who understood. And were doing the same.

Off-duty cops weren't in public when they gathered together in that loud and sometimes smoky room at night. They could let go. Be themselves.

Until one of them brought someone who was not part of the brotherhood in to have dinner.

The room was loud. It was nothing compared to what it usually was at nine o'clock at night.

Not that anyone seemed to be complaining. More than the drinking, the letting loose, they had each other's backs...

"Did you hear me?" She'd raised her voice a notch. He nodded.

He filed a motion to vacate the decree. The hearing is his chance to show cause to do so. It's also my chance to present my side to the judge.

To convince him that there is no just cause for vacating, she'd said.

He felt like he'd read her lips. Like he could hear her even when she was silent.

Impatient for the beer he'd ordered, and the wine she probably needed, he looked around for Bots, the woman who'd moved from the commissary kitchen at the station when Thornton and Wager had retired and opened the place.

He'd recommended the pulled pork. She'd ordered hers without the bun. And with coleslaw. His was coming fully dressed with fries.

Bloom's hands left the table. He could tell the way her shoulders and body had moved that she was sitting on them. Or at least on her fingertips.

He'd brought her there to make her feel safe and cared for. Not uncomfortable.

He just didn't know what to do to make the court hearing go her way. He wasn't a lawyer.

"You need to hire an attorney," he said, his words following his thoughts. And then realized how dumb that sounded. She had a divorce attorney.

"I've already talked to her."

Of course she had.

He was beginning to feel like a junior officer trying to play with the big boys.

"She said that it would help if you came with me. If you testified."

He liked the sound of that.

Finally, Bots arrived with their drinks. The soul of discretion, she delivered them with only an under-the-brow look at his companion and an "enjoy" before leaving them alone.

"Kenneth can't be tried in criminal court, but we can present any evidence we have separate and apart from the prosecutor's office in a civil case." Bloom was frowning.

Her testimony had won the criminal case. That and the medical expert's testimony. He'd come up short.

And the expert witness record had been expunged.

Even if they wanted to, there was no way to get such a testimony now, two years later. No time, either.

They could show her medical records...

"Without you it would be just my word against his. In divorce court where women accuse men of horrible things every day. And he's quite convincing..."

"So are you." His gaze was maybe a little too direct, but the point was critical.

She nodded.

"I'll be there, Bloom. You know that. I'll do anything I can."

He wanted to take her hand.

And reached for his beer instead.

THEY'D TAKEN HIS SUV and Bloom would have liked to close her eyes on the way home. To fall asleep out there in no-man's-land, on the move with Sam. She sat up, watching the sleepy streets of a town she loved, not wanting to miss a second of his company.

But only because he was one of the few people in her life who knew what was going on. She hadn't told her friends in LA. A couple of them had been wives of Kenneth's friends, too. And the others…sorority sisters…she wasn't going to drag them into this mess.

Lila knew. And the people at The Lemonade Stand. Because she'd missed her weekly session there—she went as a survivor, not a counselor— and had opted not to put out her guard detail for an hour she could afford to miss.

And people at work knew. Because there was a guard in the building.

She supposed anyone who read the news carefully and figured out dates or looked up records might know. Banyon's cases had been thrown out. It wasn't impossible to figure out which cases those were.

No one had called her about it and none of her clients had mentioned it, thankfully. "You never talk about yourself," she said as he made a turn and took the long way home, driving along the coast road rather than through town.

"I'm the detective on your case. Nothing else to tell." His voice had changed. She detected a note of…defensiveness?

Because of his divorce? Because, due to his guilt, it was a sore spot with him?

Always the counselor, she wanted to know. To help.

You want to help because you care about him.

She did not appreciate the interruption. And was sure that for once her inner voice had it all wrong.

And, anyway, of course she cared. She cared about all of her patients. Only difference was… Sam wasn't her patient.

CHAPTER NINETEEN

As SOON AS they got home, Sam was going to say good-night, and she'd go to her room. He'd do whatever he did out in the house by himself at night. She'd listen to him moving around.

And then, when he went to bed, she'd lie in the dark and think of him lying in the dark, wondering if, even once, he'd lain awake thinking about her, wondering what *she* slept in.

Chances were that he didn't think about her tighty-whities equivalent. He hadn't seen her laundry.

"Thank you for cleaning up, by the way," he said as they drove along the mostly deserted road. "I was planning to do it this weekend."

She'd spent Tuesday evening dusting, cleaning bathrooms and floors. "When, Larson? You're never home during the day. Though you certainly should be. If we don't get a break soon, I should probably move home." Even as she said the words, she knew they weren't her smartest. She needed Sam and his people. At least until they knew who was behind the Gomez warning.

"Don't be ridiculous, Doctor."

Her gaze shot toward him at his use of her title. He'd been different all night. She couldn't figure out how, exactly, and that unsettled her.

"Besides, it's not you. I always live at the office when I'm on a case. Then I might have five days at home in a row when I'm not."

She felt a little better but was still on edge.

"And before you think I noticed all the cleaning, I didn't. Chantel told me about it."

"She helped."

"So she said."

"She tell you you owe her one?"

"Something like that."

Bloom envied them—Sam and Chantel. They hadn't known each other well until recently, and yet, they were part of a whole that made them close. The "brotherhood" that included sisters sometimes, too.

Or maybe it was just Chantel being close to Sam that she envied. She had her own sisterhoods. At The Lemonade Stand. In LA. She didn't need to envy them that part of it...

"You have parents around here, Larson?" It wasn't like her, using his last name like that, even though she'd heard Chantel do it. But so much of what was going on wasn't like her. She needed the distance.

"Nope."

"You're not from here?" Why she'd always assumed he was she didn't know, but...

"I grew up a mile from the beach," he told her. "In a white house with a big deck out back."

"And your parents didn't stay?"

"My mom left us when I was four," he told her. "My father was killed the year after I graduated from the academy."

Her professional instincts were right on task—telling her that he was masking. Hiding from the emotions that should have accompanied those words. And they were being interrupted by a heart that felt his pain for him.

"Killed how?" If he'd been murdered it would explain why Sam was so dedicated to the job—because he hadn't been able to save the single parent who'd raised him.

"In the line of duty."

She watched him in the darkness. "He was a policeman, too?"

"Yes." He signaled a turn into his driveway and waved at the guard at the gate as he drove through.

He was calm. Normal.

"We'll need to let Lucy out," he said as he stopped his SUV next to her Jaguar.

The scene played itself out for her, as though she was her inner voice watching the whole thing. Or someplace outside herself watching.

They were a normal couple, coming home from

a night out. Their dog needed to pee and poop. They had a routine. And they'd sleep. Because that was what nights were for.

Bloom got out of the car. She walked with him to the door and went inside.

But she wasn't going to sleep. She needed... more.

Needed to know how his father had died.

If she knew that, she'd have...something. Something she'd been needing. She'd be...

More.

HE NEVER SHOULD have taken her to dinner. Sam had figured out the error of his ways ten steps inside the door.

From there it had only gotten worse.

While he didn't doubt for one second his ability to keep Bloom Freelander safe from her ex-husband, he was beginning to really disappoint himself. He'd told her about his old man.

How could he do something so asinine?

He could just see the questions swirling around in that psychiatrist mind of hers. She'd want to pick him apart. Make a big deal out of something that happened a long time ago.

When he'd long ago let it go.

Lucy did her business at record speed. Probably wanting the treat she knew was waiting inside for her. He encouraged her to run in the yard for a few extra minutes instead. Bloom was supposed to have headed down the hall to bed, leaving him to his painful penis.

A terminal hard-on was better than delving into things that had happened more than a decade ago. Things that were already laid to rest.

One thing he'd learned over the years was that unless there was something forensically significant to be gained, it was wrong to dig up the dead.

He knew for certain there was nothing—forensically or otherwise—to be gained from bringing his old man's last incident back to life.

Bloom wasn't going to bed. He could see her in the living room. Sitting on the arm of the couch with a bottle of water in her hand. She'd left the door open for him.

In more ways than one.

He wasn't heading into the house until she'd closed the bedroom—and any other—door behind her.

When his phone rang, he was almost relieved. It would be work. Maybe a question on an old case. Or a high-profile one they needed him for, in which case they'd send someone out to sit with Bloom for the night.

Not that he wanted bad news for anyone else, but he hoped it was the latter. He needed to get out of there.

At least for an hour or two.

To focus on the only thing that mattered to him personally. His job. Getting the bad guy. Protecting the community.

"Sam, it's Chantel."

He'd known as soon as he looked at his phone. And felt his jaw tighten even before he said, "What's up?"

"Lila McDonald," she said and he wasn't sure at first why she'd called him. "The managing director of The Lemonade Stand. Someone knocked out one of the guards on the perimeter of the Stand tonight, around dusk. No one saw anything. But one of the residents reports seeing a guard she didn't recognize standing not far from where their normal security detail should have been. She noticed her specifically because she had on a beige uniform. They wear green shirts at The Lemonade Stand."

He stood still, watching Bloom on the couch and willing her to stay there, within his sight.

"The guard she saw was a female? She's certain of it?"

"More than that, Sam. Baker and Oxley were the responding officers and they showed her our picture from last Friday. She's certain it was the same woman."

His mind raced over hundreds of reports— things he'd read over the past few days. "How many of Bloom's clients are from The Lemonade Stand?"

He'd ask her himself. As soon as he got inside.

"More than half," Chantel said.

"Those are the ones we need to focus on. Our perp is there."

"But why use a female guard? How does she play into all of this?"

"I don't know yet. But I will."

"Sam? Everything's under control for tonight. You stay with her. We can start fresh in the morning."

"The other guard, was he hurt?"

"He's a she, and no, she's fine. Better off than Gomez was. She woke up under some trees in a lovely garden, not in a trash bin."

"But drugged."

"Hit from behind. Exactly the same MO."

"It's not Ken." The bastard was focused on screwing Bloom in another arena. Using the court system. His text the night of Gomez's attack had been a coincidence.

"That it's not Freelander is my assumption, as well."

"It's the abuser of one of Bloom's clients who is currently at The Lemonade Stand. Not a past one." Clarity was slow in coming. But it was teasing him.

Bloom had two people after her. Not just one.

"I'll alert Lila to have every one of the Stand's

residents moved to the main house tonight and kept under guard."

Which was the only way either of them would get any sleep.

He looked at Bloom. Still sitting there. Watching him. Everyone was safe.

For now.

SOMETHING WAS WRONG. It wasn't only the late-night phone call that gave Bloom that indication. It was the way Sam had straightened more and more as he'd listened. The way he'd been watching her nonstop.

She sipped from her water bottle. Not really thirsty, but needing something to do.

Nervousness should be descending on her, but it wasn't. Maybe it was the wine.

She had a feeling her lack of fear might be tied to Sam.

He instilled...confidence.

Because he was such a respected detective. And so dedicated to the job.

So why, when she watched him walk toward her, was she picturing him in those tighty-whities?

Because she was avoiding reality, she told herself. Thinking she was really doing well for coming up with the plausible explanation ahead of her inner voice.

Because she was emotionally healthy. In sync with herself.

"We need to talk," Sam said before he was even fully inside the door.

Lucy bounded over to Bloom and put her paws on Bloom's thighs. Burying her face in the red fur, Bloom hugged her. Madge's arms wrapped around her.

No, Lucy's did.

And Bloom wished they were Sam's.

SAM STOOD IN front of the couch. He was going to remain standing as he gave Bloom the latest development, answered her questions, assured himself she was as fine as she could be and then excused them both to bed. His plan was firm.

And then she didn't let go of his dog. Or Lucy didn't let go of Bloom.

He moved toward her, took her hand, sat on the couch and pulled her down next to him.

Then he didn't know what to do with himself. He knew his job. What to relay. Questions to ask. He just wasn't sure what to do with his hands. Or with the rest of his person when he found it sitting so closely beside her.

To jump up—which was what he wanted to do—felt...wrong.

So he sat.

"We need to talk," he said again. And then, giving her no time to react, or comment, relayed his entire conversation with Chantel.

"So what we need to know immediately," he

continued on without pause, "is which of the clients you're currently seeing is staying at The Lemonade Stand."

She opened her mouth and he cut her off.

"Make whatever phone calls you need to make, get whatever permissions you need to get, but we need those names, Bloom. Whoever it is could be in danger. Life and death danger. This guy…he's going after you, after the shelter, and he's serious."

She was shaking. Sitting as close as he was, he could feel her.

Odd, he'd never noticed that reaction when it was herself they were talking about.

"And if you can…it would help me to know your opinion as to who you'd guess might be behind this."

He tripped over his tongue and felt like a complete idiot. He still didn't move.

She shook her head. He took a breath, ready to start in again, and she stopped him. Not with words. Her hand was on his arm.

She could have been touching him elsewhere. Privately elsewhere. Completely, 100 percent inappropriate.

And he shook his head. His mind was on the case. So focused he was already formulating plans, hearing questions in his mind as he interviewed potential suspects. And his body had just grown hard again.

CHAPTER TWENTY

BLOOM COULDN'T GIVE him what he was asking. But she could ask her clients to do so. She could speak with them, in private, by phone or in person, give them her impressions and talk to them about speaking to Sam.

She couldn't force them to do so.

And would not coerce them. Or even suggest that she thought they should. But she could inform them.

Thinking of the twenty-two women she was currently counseling from the Stand, she couldn't think of one who wouldn't meet with Sam.

She was about to tell him so when his phone went off again. It vibrated against her hip. "What's up?" he was saying into his phone, still right beside her.

As close as she was sitting, she couldn't hear the voice on the other end of the line. And Sam was only listening, saying nothing. So she waited and petted Lucy who was on her other side.

"Thanks for letting me know. I'll be in first thing."

Bloom had just about talked herself into believing the phone call was about another case, something completely unrelated to her, and then Sam said, "That was Chantel."

And she knew it wasn't good.

"What's going on?" she asked. He was going to tell her anyway; might as well be proactive.

Because she was going to stand up to anything that confronted her from then on and for the rest of her life.

She'd promised.

And she didn't make promises she couldn't possibly keep.

"Lila McDaniel's car was broken into tonight. The guard who'd been attacked was guarding the back lot at the Stand. Where employees park."

Where Bloom parked. But she didn't say so. What she did say was, "There are security cameras back there."

"They were disabled."

"The ones at my building weren't."

"I'm guessing this guy's getting smarter." Only it wasn't just one guy. And it wasn't all guys.

"So they'll get fingerprints. Or a hair with DNA or something, right?"

"Forensics will go over the car, but real life isn't like on TV, Bloom. There's neither the money nor the facilities to tie up for a vandalized car."

She wanted to lie down and cry. "Is this because of me, too?"

"No!" He took her hand. Held it. And she slid softly back to reality, remembering who she was. A good woman. Intelligent. Capable. Well intentioned.

"This is a sick bastard who, like your ex, is reacting to his loss of control. He's attacking, and we're going to stop him."

"How?"

"He left a note in Lila's car. A warning."

Feeling his warmth seep through her entire body, she held on to his hand, looked into those serious brown eyes and was okay as she asked, "What did it say?"

"That she better learn to mind her own business or more than her car would be hurt."

It wasn't her fault.

It wasn't her fault.

It's not your fault.

"Bloom?"

Sam's voice was different. He was different.

"It's not my fault," she said aloud. "Ken's text… it *was* just a coincidence. Still meant to mess with me, but not because of the attack on Gomez…"

"That's right. Gomez, the other night, it wasn't because of Ken," he told her.

But she could help.

"I need to get to the Stand in the morning. To talk to my girls."

She knew the way out of hell. And had the professional tools to share it with them.

"I'll talk to them, Sam. And then they'll talk to you. I can pretty much guarantee it."

He nodded and the look in his eyes changed.

Which changed everything inside of her.

"Sam?"

"Shhh." His finger touched her lips. And she knew.

It was happening to him, too.

HIS ARM FELT weak as Sam stood and pulled Bloom up behind him. She wanted him. He knew it. Without doubt.

By God, she wanted him.

He wasn't the only one feeling the attraction between them. Wasn't just a workaholic cop harboring unwarranted desires for a beautiful woman.

Lucy looked up at him as she jumped down to join them. He didn't say anything to her. Or to Bloom, either.

He just walked. Down the hall. To his bedroom door. She'd left it closed, as she generally did.

He opened it. Saw her inside, and told her goodnight, closing the door without taking a breath.

BLOOM SPENT THE first half of Wednesday night listing the reasons why she was glad Sam had rejected the opportunity to explore a personal situation between them. Knowing she was lucky that he hadn't taken advantage of her vulnerability.

Respecting him more than ever.

And the second half was spent diagnosing herself. Clearly there was more of a transference thing going on than she'd realized. With Ken back in the picture, she was turning to Sam, her protector, so that she didn't fall back into the fear-based woman she'd been.

She was seeing Sam as her own personal savior.

And…maybe…a replacement for the father figure she'd found in Ken. He'd been fifteen years older than she and she'd realized, sometime shortly after the end of the marriage, that she'd been particularly vulnerable to his charms because of her own lack of a father figure. Her lack of any true parenting guidance.

Sam wasn't as old as Ken. He was maybe only a few years older than she.

But still, there was merit to the theory. Clearly it couldn't be any more than her emotional upheaval prompting her feelings for him. He had one failed marriage under his belt because he was married to the job. He made promises he couldn't keep.

And she'd already been fooled enough.

She slept a little. But woke up feeling ready to tackle whatever the day would bring. She was healthy.

Capable.

And was in control of all of her own choices. Thanks to Sam.

BLOOM HAD REALLY come through. All but one of her clients agreed to speak with law enforcement. Because she was familiar to some of the victims, and knew all of the full-time employees at The Lemonade Stand from prior cases she'd worked, Chantel spent all day Thursday at the Stand conducting interviews. And calling Sam who followed up with investigations of every single abuser, looking for priors, for any kind of police or traffic violation. Over the next two days he spoke to every one of the abusers himself. All but the three who were in lockup.

From that, he had three he liked for the harassment of Bloom and Lila and the taking down of two guards, who did not have alibis for the two nights in question—the previous Friday and Wednesday of that week.

On Friday Bloom called him at work to let him know that she'd spoken with her attorney and due to the situation in Santa Raquel, the court had granted her request for a stay on the show cause hearing scheduled for the next week. They'd been given a month.

It was the first Sam even knew she'd made the motion for the stay—she'd been in her room when he returned to the cottage just after ten Thursday night. But he was more than a little glad her motion had been granted.

Glad beyond what a detective would feel regarding a victim on one of his cases. Glad that she'd been given a reprieve. Glad that they could take care of one dangerous situation before heading into another one.

Glad that she'd taken charge of the situation and had taken care of it. He knew how much that meant to her.

And glad for how far she'd come from the woman he'd known two years before.

The rest of the afternoon was spent investigating his three suspects in Santa Raquel, looking for anything that ruled two out or made one stand out. Looking for a female connection to any of them. A sister, maybe.

Most likely. Someone who'd be willing to commit a crime because she loved him enough to do so. And not a girlfriend, since the targets were those influencing his wife to stay away from him.

Two of the three he liked had sisters who fit the age range. Both had dark hair. Could have been the woman in his grainy picture. Neither had alibis. Both denied ever owning a guard uniform. And Sam didn't get a particular feel either way that either one of them was his perp.

But he didn't feel like they weren't, either.

On Saturday, while Chantel and Bloom shopped

for groceries and whatever else two women shopped for, and to give himself enough of a breather to get his instincts back in check, he went for a long run on the beach. And then turned his focus back to the drug case against Freelander. He'd been granted a month's reprieve to find a way to prove that Freelander had purchased illegal drugs with the intent to harm—a month to ensure that Bloom never had to go to court, to show cause or to ever be in the same room as Kenneth Freelander again.

With nowhere else to turn, he pulled up the list they'd already obtained of Freelander's class rosters for the year before his indictment. And on another screen, pulled up a joint task law enforcement list of known gang members in the LA area. The second list was a hell of a lot longer than the first, but he went through them, one by one, looking for the same name on both lists.

It didn't appear. A headache did.

To go along with the almost continuous ache in a lower part of his body. He hadn't been able to do anything the past couple of days without knowing, in the back of his mind, that Bloom wanted him.

He wasn't going to sleep with her, of course. If he hurt Bloom he'd hate himself for the rest of his life, and he couldn't live with that.

So he started checking first and last names, first names only and then last names only, from Professor Freelander's rosters, against the joint task list of gang members. Thirty-six first names were a hit. Four last names were.

He knew he was really in deep, spinning wheels just to keep from having to face real thoughts, when he set about investigating the students with those four random last names.

Somehow he was going to have to get Bloom Freelander out of his system.

AFTER TWO FULL weeks of living moment to moment, and curtailing most of her activities outside of work so as not to inconvenience those who were giving up their normal daily lives to protect her, Bloom was getting cabin fever.

It wasn't that she had any particular hankering to leave Sam's cottage. To add color to it—okay, yes—but not really to leave. What she needed was to go home. Home to who she was. Home to herself. And she woke up Sunday morning knowing what she had to do.

She knocked on Sam's door—forcing herself not to think of tighty-whities and doing just that—intending to tell Sam that before he went to work, she needed him to pick up some things from her house.

Painting was something she'd done, on a lark, during the first year after her marriage had ended. She hadn't known she could actually paint. She'd just craved the ability to throw color around however she wanted to.

Sara Havens, the full-time licensed professional clinical counselor at The Lemonade Stand, had suggested that she buy a couple of canvases and some paint and see what happened. Kind of an offshoot from the collaging she'd done with Talia Malone, an artist who volunteered at the Stand. The exercise had been suggested as a means of finding her inner self. She'd ended up with an inner voice that was painful in its honesty and some colorful prints on her home and office walls.

It was taking Sam a long time to answer her knock. Maybe he was on the phone. It wasn't until then that it occurred to her that she could have texted him.

But maybe she'd wanted an excuse to knock on his door. Even if only for innocuous business conversation.

She didn't knock again.

CHAPTER TWENTY-ONE

SAM WANTED ALL of the information he could get before going to Bloom, but he had to make certain that her knock on his door hadn't been an emergency.

Ending the call with the officer who'd called him to report a break-in at Bloom's home overnight, he texted her.

On phone. Business. Problem?

And didn't have to wait but a second for her response.

Not at all.

He knew the house was secure. He'd already been all over it that morning. Checked in with both guards on the premises. And Chantel, who was due in less than an hour.

Until he called her and told her what was going on.

"I think I should stay with her today," he told his female counterpart.

"Good. I think I should be the one to go to LA and check up on Freelander," she told him.

He wanted to be the one. But knew she was right. He and Freelander had history. Revisiting it right now would probably not be in Bloom's best interest.

He didn't bother to try to figure out why he thought so. Or why Chantel did, for that matter.

"Keep me posted," he told her and hung up. Only then realizing that without Chantel there, or Bloom at work, he was going to have to shower with her in his home.

Not a good plan.

BLOOM WENT DOWN to the beach path with Lucy.

The grounds were patrolled and safe. Sam had never meant for her to be a hostage.

And she needed some air to clear the clutter from her brain. Make conscious choices rather than reacting to unreliable emotions.

Knocking on Sam's door had been stupid. Plain and simple.

Thank goodness he hadn't answered, saving her from herself once again.

It was time for her to save herself. Past time. She'd thought she'd already passed that point. Permanently.

Lucy started down the path. Bloom looking longingly after her. Pulled her cell out of the pocket of the bright blue cotton capris she'd put on after her shower that morning, and texted Sam.

Heading down to the beach with Lucy. BRB.

Chantel was due in half an hour and she'd be back up by then.

When her phone buzzed, Bloom seriously thought about ignoring it. He was just going to tell her it was fine and she'd look for some kind of hidden message in that, a sign that she wasn't the same as every other victim he'd ever protected.

Some sign that the look in his eyes the other night, the way he'd held her hand and led her down the hall, had meant what she'd known it had meant.

She hadn't dreamed that up.

But she might as well have, for all the difference it made in their relationship. When this was all over, she wasn't going to want him like she did now. Her professional self kept reminding her of that.

Bloom pulled out her phone. She just wasn't the type to ignore a message.

But before she could open it, even start to analyze it, the front door opened and Sam came running out in sweats, a T-shirt and boat shoes.

Bloom froze, too scared even to look around. She shrank into herself, as though if she could make herself small enough she wouldn't be a target for whomever Sam was protecting her against.

She prayed that Lucy was far enough down the path not to hear what was going on. Not to come back up and put herself in the middle of the danger.

"I need you back in the house," Sam said, not even breathless from his sprint.

She didn't argue. He wouldn't have come running after her if it wasn't important.

To allay panic, she spent the whole way back wondering if he wore tighty-whities under his sweats.

And then, when they were safely inside, Lucy, too, she started to shake. They'd all three made it without being shot.

"I'M GOING OVER there with you." Bloom's words brooked no argument.

Sam stood at the kitchen counter, arms crossed over his T-shirt, facing a fully showered and dressed Bloom who stood across the galley kitchen from him, her arms also crossed.

She'd taken the news of the break-in well, hardly reacting at all. But she'd been a pain in his ass ever since.

He didn't want her to see the place until he had a chance to assess the damage.

"I wasn't planning to go," he lied. He was going.

Not because he didn't trust his officers to process the crime scene just fine, but because he needed a feel for the place. To see the damage, not just hear about it.

Sometimes the way something was slashed was more telling than the slice itself.

He just hadn't figured out his plan yet, with Chantel on her way to LA, he had to find someone to stay with Bloom without her feeling like...

"I have a right to go to my own home, Sam."

"Not right now, you don't," he was happy to tell her. "It's a crime scene. You can't go until I release the scene after it's been processed."

He breathed a silent sigh of relief when that quieted her.

"A crime scene?" she said, seconds later. "How much damage was done?"

Hardly any. Which was part of the reason he wanted to see it. He had to know what Freelander had been thinking. To know every nuance of how that man thought.

Or to find out if he'd been looking for something.

And if he had, whether or not he'd found it.

Was it possible the man hadn't disposed of the drugs to a gang in exchange for protection?

Could his intel have been wrong?

"You'll need me to tell you if anything's missing. I'll wear something over my shoes if you need me to. And I won't touch anything."

She was right. Professionally, he needed her there. Which meant that his objection to taking her had been...unprofessional.

"I need to shower," he said, not liking the taste that last thought had left in his mouth. "I'm doing so with my gun on the counter and the door open..."

He started to get hard just saying the words, but knew he'd be fine once under the cold spray.

"Freelander's not the type to show up here unannounced, and we have no evidence that anyone knows where you're staying..."

No indication that anyone had followed them from her office even once over the past two weeks.

"...the grounds are covered. But, humor me, stay away from the doors and windows for the ten minutes it's going to take me." He'd shave in the shower to save time.

She nodded.

"And scream if you even think you hear anything or if Lucy so much as gives a loud sigh."

It was overkill.

Because he felt, so acutely, his broken promise every single time something else happened that had anything to do with Freelander. Because he'd failed professionally.

His attention to her might be more than necessary, his attraction inappropriate. But one thing he knew was that he was not going to fail her again. If anything he was going to keep her so safe she'd feel like a prisoner.

If she didn't already.

"Go shower, Sam. I'll sit anywhere you like and stay put until you're done."

Anywhere he liked?

No. He was not going to screw this up.

"The couch is fine," he said. Turned his back. And prayed for icy water.

FROM THE OUTSIDE the house looked fine. So did Sam. In his coat and tie, he'd returned to the man she knew. The detective she knew she could hold at arm's length. There was a belt and a holster between her and his whities.

And promises he made that he couldn't possibly keep.

Bloom knew exactly why his underwear was on her mind that morning. She was substituting sexual feeling for fear, focusing on whatever it took to take her away from the panic.

"It doesn't look like it was broken into," she said as he turned off the ignition in her driveway, and she knew she was going to have to get out.

Or force him to take her somewhere else while he investigated. Because he certainly wasn't going to let her sit alone in his car in her driveway.

She wanted to see the beach from her back porch. That view had seen her through some of her toughest moments. Bolstering her with hope.

"A back door was left ajar," Sam told her. He hadn't yet opened his door as though he wasn't looking forward to the next minutes, either.

Or maybe he was sensing her hesitation. He'd most likely seen hundreds of crime scenes in his lifetime.

"Why would Kenneth leave the back door open?"

"My guess is someone left in a hurry."

"But no one saw a car. You said no one saw a car. What would have spooked him with enough time to get away in a car without being seen?"

"He could have parked down the beach." True.

Public parking was sparse during the day, but at night...

"He also could have pulled into the garage." She should have changed the automatic door code; she just hadn't thought about it. Not with him in prison. And then her leaving before he got out.

"There's always the possibility it wasn't Freelander."

She knew that. But didn't want to think about that possibility, either. "Whoever warned Lila and me doesn't think we got the message," she said aloud. "And knows where I live?" She was only suppositioning. Not sure which scenario she liked better. Kenneth, or a nameless creep?

"It's possible," he said.

"But you think it's Kenneth?"

"I have a report of the damage."

That didn't answer her question at all.

She didn't tell him so.

A PUNK OUT to give a warning messed things up. The whole warning thing. A few paintings slashed… What kind of warning was that?

Even if they were worth a lot of money—which they could have been, Sam acknowledged as he got his first real look at the colorful framed canvases hanging on the walls partially shredded— they were only paintings. Someone who was angry enough to break into a home was at least going to empty the contents of the refrigerator. He could have done a lot of damage with mustard and ketchup and a few other things that had been left in there.

He'd have slit the sofa, not just paintings.

Emptied drawers and thrown them upside down on the floor. Broken dishes. Mixed things up.

He'd have damaged electronics, if he'd left them there at all…

"It was Kenneth."

Bloom hadn't even walked through the house yet. Now that he had her there, he really needed her to do so but was loath to ask.

Any other victim and he'd talk them through

it. Express his concern and understanding of how difficult it was. But he'd make them do it.

"How do you know?"

She was staring at the desecrated painting over the fireplace, her face expressionless.

Her tone lacked emotion as well as she said, "He called me. From prison. He was allowed to call, you know, as long as I was on his list. I was given the opportunity to refuse to speak with him, but I agreed. I'd hoped that he'd have some epiphanies sitting in that cell. That his knowledge would save him. Instead, it had only given him the psychological means to try to manipulate me in new ways. To remind me how much I loved and needed him..."

Sam's jaw hurt as he grit his teeth together. What had the bastard said to her? And what had she ever done to anyone to deserve such contemptible treatment? After two weeks of living with Bloom in the midst of extreme tension, he knew for certain that she was the kindest person he'd ever met.

Maybe a gift from parents who lived in a simpler world and had borne her into it?

"I kept things professional," Bloom was saying.

Her electric-blue capris and vividly striped shirt didn't belong in this formal setting. Or at least, he didn't want them there.

"I spoke from a therapeutic point of view. Hoping he would understand and just…move…on. At that point I actually hoped maybe we could be friends. Pathetic, huh?"

"I don't think it's pathetic at all." Her need pulled the words out of him.

She continued without looking at him or in any way acknowledging that she'd even heard him.

"He didn't, of course. Understand, that is. Not any of it. No matter what I said, he had a rebuttal that turned the world on its axis and gave an entirely different meaning to the very same words. In the end, I grabbed at a solid piece of evidence that didn't involve words. Or reasoning. Yet was still based in psychological theory.

"I told him about my paintings. About how they'd helped me access mental and emotional health from the inside out…" Her face was still upturned toward the fireplace, her long auburn hair hanging down her back.

Had she just said *her* paintings?

With a chest that felt as though it had been carrying a ton of bricks all morning, he stood there, looking at the walls, and saw the desecration in a new light. Hoping to God he was wrong about what he was thinking.

It was as though he could feel his shoulders shrinking within his coat. And he knew that he couldn't allow that to happen.

"So you think he destroyed the art you two had

purchased together as a way of letting you know what he thinks of the value of art?" He was winging it. But thought his theory held some merit.

She shook her head. "I don't know why he came here last night," she told him. "Maybe he thought I would be here. Maybe he just wanted to talk in person, without lawyers between us. He'd have been told Friday afternoon that my motion to move out the hearing had been granted."

He had to give her top marks for calm. For clear thinking. He was seeing red. And not because of the brightly colored pieces of canvas dangling out from the frame.

"What I do know is why he left. He came in expecting to find me and I wasn't here. That would have upset him. But then he saw that I'd replaced all of his carefully sought after and expensively purchased artwork with my amateur attempts..."

Shit.

CHAPTER TWENTY-TWO

"I NEED YOU to look around. To see if anything's missing." They were the first words Sam had spoken since she'd stopped speaking.

Bloom nodded, thankful for his professionalism and for the space he was giving her to process the event, understand her feelings and then decide for herself what to do about it. Her task was to get through this. Just do. Not feel. In a way, Sam had taught her how to do that. She just had to be the professional she was.

"I'm certain that once he got inside, saw the pictures, he slashed them all to let me know that he wasn't accepting the new me—meaning he wasn't giving up—and then he left. That's why the back door was open. He must have parked down the beach so he went out that way. He always said the beach calmed him. That's why he insisted on living here. So he could come home to the beach every night..."

She was rambling. Professionals didn't ramble.

"He didn't leave in a hurry out of fear of discovery, or because he thought someone was coming.

He left in a hurry because he couldn't stand to be in this house with the paintings."

She didn't want to go in any other rooms. To see what he'd done to the rest of the pictures she'd come to cherish for what they portrayed of her, not for how they'd look to others.

"He couldn't stand what he saw in them," she said, drawing on professional observation, bolstering herself with facts as she entered the hall and saw the painting she'd done of the colorful vase, the one filled with orange and red roses with bright yellow daisies, hanging from its frame in shreds. "He doesn't want to believe that I've healed. That I know what he did to me."

The insight helped her move to the next room. And the next.

Without fail, Ken had taken a sharp object to every single one of her most personal, most intimate truths, damaging them beyond repair.

SHE WAS HOLDING up well. Was more healed than he'd realized. Or was less fragile than he'd feared. Sam wasn't sure which, but, either way, Bloom's mental and emotional health made his job easier.

"I need you to look inside things," he told her. "See if anything's been moved. If anything is missing. Look in your closet, look on shelves. Behind doors, in cupboards you don't use much. Look where you store your Christmas decorations."

Her detachment gave him detachment. Allowed him to do his job as he always did it, with complete focus.

Bloom pulled open drawers with him looking over her shoulder. He didn't care what was in them. He cared if she noticed anything different inside them.

"Can you tell me what you're looking for?" she asked after they'd been through her lingerie drawer.

If she'd turned around, she'd have seen him looking at the wall behind them on that one. He wasn't up to that test.

"If you think he planted a camera or some listening device, you're wrong. That's not..."

"I don't."

"Well, he sure wouldn't have left an explosive device...would he?"

The suddenly pale skin in the placid face threatened his detachment.

"I think he might have been looking for the drugs, Bloom," he told her. "If my source is wrong and he didn't trade them, they might have been hidden here all along. He could have come back for them."

The drugs could have been Freelander's hidden pleasure. Not Bloom at all.

Sam hadn't believed in anything outside his own abilities in a long time, but he almost dared hope that he'd just been given a piece of divine inspiration.

Maybe Freelander wasn't after Bloom at all, just her money and whatever the drugs could bring him.

BLOOM LOOKED EVERYWHERE. Went through everything. It took hours. The house was big and she'd been there a long time. And nothing was out of place. Or had been disturbed. She didn't even have to go into the attic. She'd accidentally painted the entrance shut and the paint seal hadn't been broken.

She also didn't think about Sam seeing into every corner, every cupboard of her life. The detective, not the man, was there, seeing inside every one of her drawers, seeing how she folded her underwear. His phone rang while they were in the laundry room. When she'd finished with her therapy she'd stored her painting things in a corner cupboard that was difficult to access. She hadn't expected to ever need to use them again but had been unable to part with them.

But then, she also hadn't expected Ken to ever get out of prison. Sam Larson had promised her that if she testified she'd never have to deal with Ken again. Her testimony would grant her permanent safety...

"Are you sure?"

Standing with two metal tackle boxes, one filled with paints and the other with brushes, Bloom froze, staring at Sam as he spoke into his phone. There were several small canvases back there, too. She still had to get them.

Sam was staring at her. Eyes open wide.

"Okay. Thanks. Head back."

He hung up.

Took a hold of her arm.

And Bloom didn't want to know.

She'd had enough.

SAM HAD NO idea why he suddenly took the two metal boxes from Bloom's fingers. Had no idea what was in them, or why she held them. Placing them quickly on the counter beside them, he grabbed both of those lifeless hands.

"You okay?" he asked.

She nodded. Smiled. "Of course, why?"

Her fingers were digging into his hands. The grip of someone holding on for dear life.

"Are we done here?" She'd said she'd purposely left the laundry room for last. Maybe because of the metal boxes? "We need to head out."

"Tell me." She wasn't moving.

"Let's get out of here. We can talk later. There's nothing critical." He was lying. Sometimes it was part of a cop's job, to serve the greater good. Right then the greater good was getting Bloom into a different environment.

One that didn't suck the life blood out of her.

"Wait."

She pulled away from him and bent to the opened cupboard behind her, taking out several blank canvases, and he understood. He took them carefully. Grabbed both boxes as well, and followed her out of the house where she'd almost died.

If he had his way, she'd never be back.

"TELL ME."

They were on the coastal road, taking the long way home. Bloom, with her head laid back against the rest on the passenger seat of Sam's SUV, was watching what she could see out the front windshield.

Sort of.

Mostly all she could see was within.

"Kenneth Freelander was not at your house last night."

She sat up, stared at him. "Of course he was. If someone's talked to him, if he's saying differently, he's just lying, point-blank."

"Chantel went to LA this morning, Bloom. She spoke with him."

"He lied to her." Chantel was great. From all accounts an incredible officer of the law, but she wasn't perfect. "I'm a certified genius, Sam. And he fooled me."

"She checked out his alibi. It's rock solid."

"So he's convinced someone else to lie for him. Or to believe his truths. Either way it's the same…"

"We've had extra patrols running by your house on a regular basis. All doors checked fine at midnight. The back door was discovered open at six."

"So when his alibi was asleep, Kenneth left and made it back before she woke up."

Her tone had clearly given her away. His quick glance said volumes. And asked a question, too.

One that his mouth followed up. "He was unfaithful to you, wasn't he?"

"I told you about his erectile dysfunction… sometimes the only thing that worked…was young coeds."

"He slept with his students and you knew it?"

"Not his students." Turning her head away from him, Bloom closed her eyes. "Never his students. Just girls he met in campus bars. And I didn't know about it until the last year or so."

"When you were drugged."

"My theory is that he got lazy about hiding his activities once he was confident that I'd be too dumbed down to do anything about it."

He knew everything else about her. Why not that, as well? He was a professional. Saw and heard all kinds of atrocities. And when this was over, she'd never see him again.

A lump rose to her throat and pressure gathered behind her eyes. The morning was getting to her.

She needed air.

A paintbrush.

Something.

"Ken Freelander spent last night in the emergency room, Bloom."

She sat up. Stared at him.

"The twenty-two-year-old he was with brought him in just before eleven with an accidental laceration due to…well, let's just say things got a little exuberant between them…"

Bloom felt the wave rising within her. She knew, clinically, that it was hysteria based. But knowing didn't stop the burst of laughter from escaping. Again and again. Reverberating around every surface in Sam's sedate, unmarked, law enforcement SUV.

SAM HAD WORK to do. Two abuser suspects with sisters to question about their whereabouts the night before.

He didn't yet have an explanation as to how they'd known to go after Bloom's paintings when they got in her home, but he was confident there was an explanation. One he'd get out of them as soon as he got the guilty party into interrogation.

What he did know was that the attack on her home had been personal. Meant to unnerve her in the darkest, most personal way.

To warn her.

If she didn't back off, if she continued to try to take a man's wife from him, she would pay in a way that hurt her to the core. As he felt he was being hurt.

"I tell a lot of my patients about my painting," she said as he pulled onto the dirt drive that led up to the cottage. It was the first thing she'd said since she'd stopped laughing.

"And they could have told any of their family members or friends…"

He'd already figured that out but was still glad for her confirmation. Glad to know that she was thinking logically. That she was okay.

"Many of them have done paintings of their own," she said now. "Painting and collaging are offered as therapy at The Lemonade Stand."

A buzz of anticipation shot through him. "I'll cross-reference your patient list with those who've done therapy painting."

She nodded silently and Sam wondered what she was thinking. If she was frightened. He didn't ask.

He had to find the guy and stop him. He had to check alibis of the three suspects he liked most. Had to have Chantel access painting therapy records for Bloom's patients who'd given them permission to access their records. And if none of those things turned up their perp, he'd look deeper into Bloom's files and into the lives of her patients who might not be from The Lemonade Stand but might have ties there. And if none of those fit, he'd start looking into former patients. Bloom had only been taking private clients for a couple of years. He was going to find this guy who had a woman front running for him.

And while he worked, he had to protect Bloom. He could investigate from the cottage. Could log into the networks he needed. Use his phone. Send Chantel on initial interviews and to check alibis.

But he couldn't just leave Bloom sitting by herself in his living room, especially after the morning she'd had.

Except...when he came out of the bathroom, she wasn't in his living room. She was out on the porch, facing the ocean, her canvas and the two metal boxes with her. He'd figured, after seeing the blank canvases, that the boxes contained painting supplies. As he came out, she was leaning a canvas against a can that was tied to a porch rail, trying to right it.

If she'd had an easel, she hadn't brought it with her.

"Hold on," he told her, going down the steps two at a time and at his storage shed in record time. He was almost excited as he turned on the light and pulled leftover trim board from the rafters in the shed. He moved to the workbench and turned on the miter saw. Twenty minutes later, after raiding his screw and hinge boxes, he had made a rough, but fully serviceable easel.

He heard Lucy come in as he was finishing, recognizing the sound of her pads on the wood floor. She wasn't alone.

Easel in hand, he spun around.

And was shocked to see tears in Bloom's eyes as she saw what he'd done.

CHAPTER TWENTY-THREE

TIME PASSED WITHOUT Bloom's awareness. She painted. Color to palette, brush to color, color to canvas. She never consciously saw the yard in front of her. She might have heard the waves she knew were down below. Or might have just been hearing them in her mind's ear. Sam brought out an unopened water bottle for her. She opened it and drank. When she turned around he was gone.

Lucy arrived and put her head in Bloom's lap. At some point she left, too.

Bloom wasn't making anything. She wasn't creating. She was…grieving.

When the sun went down behind the cliff above the beach, she blinked. The day was gone?

She hadn't eaten.

Had Sam? Or Lucy?

Putting down the brush, she flexed her fingers, surprised at their ache. She hadn't used the bathroom all day. Had only consumed that single bottle of water.

The canvas caught her attention and she stared at it. She blinked. Stepped back. It wasn't like anything else she'd ever done before. There wasn't any definition. No specific lines.

But looking out at her from those colors was a little girl with not quite red hair, her hand on a dog that was nearly as tall as she was. Colors swirled around them. Bright blues and yellows. Oranges and greens. Some purples.

The hues grew darker as they spread out on the canvas.

Bloom didn't like that part, but had to accept that the darkness was there.

Leaving the canvas to dry, she went inside.

SAM HAD SET up shop on the kitchen table with two laptops and a portable printer. Papers were piled on either side of him, with cords threaded through them on their way to the floor.

He looked up when she came in. Studied her like he was a scientist and she was his specimen. He didn't speak, So she didn't, either. He nodded and went back to work.

Bloom pulled ingredients out of the refrigerator for fettuccine Alfredo with chicken. She chopped onion. Brought sauce ingredients to a slow boil and turned down the heat. Grilled chicken in a pan, then sautéed it in a bit of Worcestershire and vinegar. She gave the tasks her full focus. Creating culinary art. Paid attention to every color. Every scent. To the precise size of the chicken bites as she cut them. The perfect doneness of the fettuccine when it cooked.

If Sam noticed the aromas wafting around him, he didn't indicate it. She poured him a glass of tea. And when it was empty, refilled the glass.

He typed. Scrolled. Studied. Printed. Circled. Highlighted. And typed some more.

Dinner complete, Bloom plated her offering for both of them and put one serving on the table. She took the other with her to the couch. Petting Lucy as the dog joined her.

She'd done well. Dinner was good. And still difficult for her to send down. She did what she could. Chewed and swallowed as many times as she thought her throat and stomach would allow. And then she allowed herself to stop.

Taking her plate to the kitchen, she picked up Sam's empty one as she passed. He didn't seem to notice she'd been there.

She did the dishes and cleaned all of the countertops. Fed Lucy, washed and filled her water bowl. She thought about making brownies. Betty used to make brownies from scratch. Bloom had never learned how.

She tried not to think about the information Sam was perusing so avidly. Tried not to worry. She'd come so far. She wasn't going back. Wasn't going to be that helpless, frightened woman again.

Or the girl who knew that darkness surrounded

her. The tiny little girl who'd somehow understood that someday she was going to have to leave the safety of the life her parents had built for her, filled with all the colors nature had to offer, and venture into the darkness all alone.

But she wasn't alone right now. Sam was there. And she didn't know why.

What drove him to share the darkness with her?

She should go to bed. Lie there and watch mindless television until she drifted off. But a careful assessment told her that sleep was not going to happen anytime soon.

She'd rather be awake all night than take a sleep aid. Not that she had any.

But maybe a glass of wine…

She'd purchased a carton of single-serving sealed bottles the day before. Pinot Grigio. Chantel had done the same. Zinfandel.

Opening the bottle, she pulled out a chair and sat with Sam. He didn't look at her but he wasn't looking at the computer, either.

"I'm not going to sleep. I thought I could help you," she told him. "I have eyes. Can compare lists." She should have been doing so all day.

It wasn't her job. But he wasn't being paid for all of the hours he was spending. Wasn't being compensated for giving up the freedom of his home.

His phone buzzed, something she'd noticed

a time or two before, and he picked it up. Read. Typed, his thick thumbs flying over the tiny screen.

Then he looked at her. "I need to get back to work," he said.

She hadn't noticed him leaving work. But she took his not-at-all-subtle hint and moved over to the couch.

COULD HE BE any more of an ass? Bloom Freelander was more than a victim. She was a respected psychiatrist who spent eighty hours a week helping others. And not only to earn a living. She cared.

He stared at the new list he'd pulled up. Looking for classmates of the ex-father-in-law of one of Bloom's victims. He and his wife were said to be staying with an old high school classmate.

He'd crossed the abuser, the man's son, off his list for a very obvious reason. The kid was deceased.

But in questioning the victim today—the first time she'd been questioned because her abuser couldn't possibly be their perp since he was dead—Chantel had discovered that the young women's in-laws, both in their late thirties, had threatened to take her to court if she didn't move in with them.

It wasn't her they were interested in—to the contrary, they blamed her report of abuse for their eighteen-year-old son's suicide. But they wanted her nine-month-old son. Their grandson.

Bloom and The Lemonade Stand were helping the girl see she had other options and providing those options to her along with the emotional, physical and financial support to pursue them.

Bloom was counseling her pro bono. Because she was kind.

She was a human being who was being forced to live life like a hostage and shouldn't be sitting alone on the eve of the day she'd just had.

She didn't deserve his bad temperament. She didn't deserve any of this.

She'd done as he'd asked. Even in her drug-induced haze she'd found the courage to trust him. And later, the temerity and courage to face down the man who'd brainwashed her, to testify against the man she'd once adored.

He'd promised her safety and freedom.

And while they knew as of that morning that the current happenings in Santa Raquel weren't coming from Freelander, the man was definitely out to get her. Even if only for the money. The pending court hearing proved that.

And he couldn't get that text message Freelander had sent out of his mind. If the man had truly been feeling goodwilled, trying to transport goodwill, why hadn't he followed up with more of the same?

Why had he gone straight to a legal battle over their decree rather than trying to work things out with her?

And who knew what he'd do when the newness of his young coed wore off. Or what he'd do if he didn't get the job for which he'd applied. From what Chantel had told Sam earlier that day, based on off-the-record conversations, the professor job wasn't going to Freelander.

Bloom's hand on Lucy's back seemed to be moving back and forth of its own accord. Other than an occasional sip of wine, she sat on his couch, staring at nothing. She hadn't turned on the TV or put in a movie.

Probably didn't want to bother him.

Why she hadn't gone to her room, he didn't know.

But he cared.

No one should have to be that alone.

And apparently he wasn't as much of an ass as he needed to be. Grabbing one bottle of beer from the refrigerator, Sam uncapped it, tossed the lid and joined Bloom Freelander on his couch.

"I'M SORRY ABOUT your paintings."

Scooting over as much as a sleeping Lucy would allow to make room for Sam, Bloom acknowledged his statement with a nod. "I'm sure their destruction means that I have no further need of them," she said. "They've served their purpose."

Or could continue service without physically hanging in her space.

"Still…it's got to be… I'm sorry…"

"It's fine."

It hurts.

She listened to her inner voice because she had to. She just wasn't going to spend time on what it was saying.

There was nothing she could do about the paintings. And she was not going to waste time and energy on what she couldn't change.

Instead, she was thinking about her caseload in the morning. About the patients on her roster who'd been affected by the recent attacks on her, Lila and The Lemonade Stand. They were vulnerable. Needed her example of how to experience violence without losing their sense of self…

And then she wasn't thinking about them. She was listening to the swish of fabric as Sam raised the beer bottle to his lips. Feeling the heat emanating off him even with the inches between them.

He was such an enigma. That was why he was on her mind so much. His aloneness, his life choices, challenged her professional mind.

"Why do you do it?" She broke the silence between them.

Lucy sighed in her sleep. Stretched her front legs but didn't open her eyes.

"Do what?"

"Work all time. Nonstop."

"I give the hours the job requires."

She sipped from her own bottle. Glanced at him. He was staring into the same nothingness she'd seen for the past several minutes. She couldn't tell, from his brooding expression, what he was thinking.

About the case? Or something else?

"I have it on good authority that you put in twice the hours of a lot of the guys, more than just about anyone else."

"I hadn't heard Chantel had such a loose tongue."

"We're spending more off-duty time with each other than anyone else in our lives," Bloom said. And in Chantel's further defense added, "And she wasn't gossiping about you. She was reassuring me. I was feeling guilty about how much extra time you were putting in on my behalf and she was simply letting me know that you always work this much."

He sipped. Lowered his beer between his legs.

Her gaze followed it of its own accord and rested there for a second. But she would not let those pants fade away in her mind's eye, leaving him only in that underwear covering his bulge.

"You haven't answered my question," she said,

to enforce her mental mandate. She was probably pushing him out of the room. Away from her. And that would be for the better, too. "Why do you work so much?"

Sam's sigh startled her. He wasn't one to give in to such an emotional impulse. As though he were capitulating. Or needing to relax. He wasn't the "take a breather" type.

Holding her own bottle on her thigh, she wanted a sip, but didn't move.

"I talked to the department shrink once." He sipped. She waited. Intensely interested. "But I hated the feeling that everything I said was being analyzed and twisted into some big internal issue or warning."

He was defensive. And that told her that he was holding something in that he didn't want found.

"If you think the fact that you could have an issue or two takes you down a notch, or makes you less capable or reliable, you're wrong." Maybe not what he'd been after from her. "I'd be more concerned if you were as one dimensional as you try to be."

We teach what we most need to learn.

Bloom shook her head as the phrase popped up out of nowhere. Where had she heard that before? And how could it help Sam? What did he need to learn?

He turned his head and looked straight at her.

It was as if he'd shot a laser beam all the way through her. Bloom couldn't look away.

"What if I told you that my father is dead because of me? I bet you'd have a field day with that one." He sounded hoarse. But not weak.

"I'd want to know the circumstances." Her words were little more than a whisper.

Time was open space between them. A cloud that had not been written on. She'd asked a question and he'd brought them here.

"From the first moment I can remember, all I've ever wanted to be was a cop," he told her.

The inclination was natural, given that he was raised by a single parent who was a cop. From what she could tell—and her glimpse into his world in the pub that past week had been a huge insight—as a cop he lived an insular life. It was the only life he'd known.

"My father didn't want that for me."

"He didn't?"

He sipped. Shook his head. "My mother left because she couldn't live with the constant threat of danger. My dad couldn't imagine any other life for himself. But he wanted more for me. Wanted me to have a life without that constant threat."

"Yet he raised you in it." He had to see that he'd been too young to make the choice that had shaped the man he grew to be.

"He did raise me in it." He raised his bottle, as

though in a toast. And then drank. "He raised me to be just like him," he said then. "When I married Stella I told myself it would be different. I told her about the danger. I took her to talk to cops' widows. To the morgue."

"The morgue?"

He shrugged. Grinned. "I was young."

Bloom smiled, too. Shook her head.

"I wanted her to go into the marriage with her eyes open."

And it still failed.

"The thing is, it wasn't her eyes that had been closed. It had been my own. Because the life of a cop—it's not just dangerous—it's all-consuming. There are just times when the job has to come first. When saving someone's life is more important than a birthday party. Even if it's your wife's. Or your own."

"Parties can happen even if they aren't on time."

He looked at her. And didn't say anything for so long she thought they were done.

"I was on patrol with my sergeant."

Bloom laid a hand on Lucy.

"A call came in about two guys holding up a convenience store out by the highway. There was an old man and a young girl inside, and employees whose lives were at risk. I responded to the call per my sergeant's orders as he drove. We were first on the scene. Went inside. He had me take the long way around the shelves to come up from the back of the store while he took the front. As soon as the first perp saw his gun, he put his hands up. My sergeant was already cuffing him as I came up behind the other one—the guy we thought was the leader. I had him on the ground and cuffed without incident."

Bloom's stomach churned. Something went wrong. He wouldn't be telling her this otherwise.

She'd said she'd need to know the circumstances behind his father's death and sensed that she was getting them.

Wanting that man on the floor in cuffs to stay right there until backup arrived and Sam was safe, Bloom held her breath. Had his father heard the call, too? Maybe he died in a car accident on the way to what turned out to be a routine call for his only son?

"My father had heard the call come in. He and his partner were close by…"

It was like he'd read her mind. Or she'd read his…

His next words, "They were second on the scene," brought dread to her heart.

"His partner covered the back of the building while my father came inside to see if we needed any help. That was when a third guy came out of the bathroom. My sergeant was dead on the floor before I knew we had company. I'd have been next except that my father tackled me."

Sam swallowed. His chin quivered as he swallowed again. "He knocked me out of the way of the bullet."

And took the bullet himself.

Bloom didn't need Sam to tell her. She could feel what had happened.

And knew why Sam made all of his personal life choices based on guilt. He was drowning in it.

CHAPTER TWENTY-FOUR

BLOOM TURNED HER HEAD. If she hadn't done that he might have saved himself from another case of the guilts. But she did. And he didn't.

She turned back toward him, her brown eyes filled not only with the compassion and understanding that came with her job, but with…acceptance. She wasn't appalled by the mess he was.

"I want to kiss you." *WTF?* A guy didn't announce that.

"I've been thinking about it, too."

He nodded. Looked at her lips. "You been thinking about it a lot?"

The way she focused completely on him, existed right there in that moment with only him, made him hot. Sexually hot. Uncomfortably hot.

"Yeah." She wasn't acting at all shy about it, either.

His penis was letting him know it wasn't going to lie low for long.

"Yeah, me, too," he said. But he didn't touch her.

He couldn't. For her sake. He'd already broken

one promise to her. He couldn't risk breaking another.

"A kiss isn't a promise," he said out loud.

"That's right."

He still didn't kiss her. Regardless of how strong Bloom was, she was also vulnerable. He was her safety net.

She was afraid. He was her protector.

He wouldn't stop at a kiss. And Bloom would want more than just sex. It was that more that stopped him.

He couldn't give anything more. Not again. His father had made the mistake once. And so had he, thinking he could learn from the old man and do it better.

He hadn't. Because he couldn't.

He stood and held out his hand to her. "We should get some rest," he said and, as he had once before, walked her down the hall to her room.

She didn't go in immediately, as she had before. He opened the door for her. Stood there waiting for her to close it in his face. Needed her to do so.

Had to have the finality so he could get to bed. So he'd be sharp for whatever the next day brought.

"Is it because I'm a victim in one of your cases?" she asked.

Why he wouldn't take things any further between them? He knew what she was asking. And was tempted to let her down easy.

He'd already made a false promise to her. What would one more hurt?

"No." The truth hurt, too.

She reached up, touched her lips to his. And he kissed her. His mouth was open, with his tongue searching. Trembling beneath her soft touch. Drowning in her taste. Weak at the knees, he barely withstood the onslaught.

And then she was gone.

Leaving him wanting more. So much more.

And knowing she'd done the right thing.

AFTER A WEEKEND of running searches and putting out enquiries, Monday morning brought some answers. All three of the men he'd liked the previous week, including the two with sisters who fit the description of his impersonated guard, had alibis for Saturday night.

The in-laws who were now first on his list of suspects still had not been located, but he figured they'd show up soon. Based on his rough profile of them, they weren't going to let their grandson get away from them.

And it looked like he might have a positive hit in Jean Cordoba, a student in Professor Ken Freelander's Effective Thinking class two years before. It appeared that Jean could be related to someone with significant standing in one of LA's eastside gangs.

While it wasn't immediately clear to him whether Jean was male or female, or whether or not the gang leader's relative named Jean was the same one who'd been enrolled at the university, what was clear was that this mysterious Jean appeared to have dropped out of circulation at the same time that Kenneth Freelander was convicted.

And the gang in which the elder Cordoba had so much influence was the same one that had been linked to Freelander in prison.

He might not have his suspect in Santa Raquel nailed yet, but he was closing in on Freelander's drug charge. He could just feel it. So much so that he changed into jeans, a T-shirt and hiking boots. Mussed up his hair so that the too-long strands were messier than usual. Strapped on his off-duty weapon and took a drive to LA late that morning. He didn't find either Jean or Juan Cordoba. But he found a couple of younger gang members.

Ones who didn't make him for a cop.

Ones who didn't know Jean. But they knew Juan. They didn't know where he was, though.

Last they knew he was meeting some rich white dude. A teacher just out of jail. The one kid heard his older brother talking about it.

"You him?" the kid asked, and Sam just shrugged and thanked them for their time.

He walked the few blocks back to the bowling alley where he'd left his car parked.

Freelander had just been handed to him by a kid who couldn't have been more than ten.

BLOOM DIDN'T GET home until almost nine on Monday night. She'd stayed late to meet with The Lemonade Stand clients who weren't scheduled for regular appointments that day. Over and over she listened to them talk about how the violence against Bloom and the Stand was affecting them. Some were angry. Some weakened, thinking they should just give in and go home. Guilt filled the room. And every single one of them was scared.

Over and over she told them what her mind knew. That it wasn't their fault. That whoever was behind the attacks was bullying them. That she and Lila and the people at the Stand were not going to give in. That giving in was the worst thing they could do.

That they were up against one of those times when they had to make a choice. Take control of a life, or give that control up to another.

Not everyone had a good session. But she didn't think she'd lost any of them.

Chantel had called to say that, due to the lateness of the hour, Sam would be meeting her after work to follow her home.

In spite of the way the evening had ended the night before, she was looking forward to seeing him.

And was nervous, too.

SAM DEBATED WITH himself about how much he was going to tell Bloom about Freelander. He'd already shared far more with her than he normally did with victims in his ongoing investigations.

But then he wasn't normally sleeping under the same roof with his victims.

Or trying to make good on a promise he'd made.

Most of his victims weren't geniuses with minds that figured things out whether he told them or not, either.

But, like most of his victims, Bloom was emotionally vulnerable.

Unlike the rest, she didn't seem to know that.

He'd already been home, fed Lucy, had let her out and changed back into his pants, shirt and tie, and jacket. He'd combed his hair. He didn't want his LA street attire to raise questions in the event he opted not to talk about his day.

He didn't want to say anything until he knew for sure. He'd already let her down once, after all.

On the other hand, he wanted her to know that that part of her nightmare—which he was pretty sure was the biggest part to her—was almost over.

There'd still been no sign of the in-laws he was after. But no further appearances by their mysterious female guard imposter, either.

Chantel had shown the photo they had of the guard to the young woman at the Stand whose in-laws wanted her son. She said that with makeup and her hair pulled back it could be her mother-in-law. Maybe. The hair color and size was right. She'd never seen the woman without her hair in her face. Had never seen her with makeup, either. In the end she'd admitted that she'd only ever met her in-laws one time.

She'd been pregnant before they'd ever even known she existed. And they blamed her for ruining their son's life. Even before he'd ended it.

Deciding that was the part he was going to tell her, Sam unlocked the front door, waited until Lucy bounded forward to greet them, a sign that all was well, and then had Bloom precede him in.

"You want some wine?" he asked. He sure as hell needed a beer.

As good as the day had been—as great as it had been—he still hated that he'd worked over ten-year-old gang members.

Bloom hadn't answered him about the wine. She stood, her purse on the table beside her, saying nothing.

And looking drop-dead gorgeous in a slim red skirt and jacket. That colorful silk scarf tied at her neck made him want to just take it off. Run it over her naked skin.

And his.

The workday was done. And her kiss from the

night before clearly was not. He was dismayed at the confirmation.

"I've got some news." Was he bribing her to sit with him? To have something to drink?

"I want the wine, Sam," she told him. "I was already planning on it. I was just trying to decide whether to change out of my suit, as I'd intended when I thought I was drinking alone, or keeping it on. If you have news, I'll keep it on."

"Yes," he said, heading toward the refrigerator. "Definitely keep it on."

His mouth was dry. His penis hard.

They were going to have to talk. About more than the investigations.

WHEN SAM HANDED Bloom the small, still-capped bottle of wine, his fingers brushed against hers.

She couldn't do it. Not that night. Not so soon after the kiss that should never have happened. A reaction, not a choice.

Not as tired as she was.

Not after he'd made it obvious that he needed her to stay fully and professionally dressed. As though he didn't trust himself to handle the temptation of Bloom in more comfortable clothes. Looser clothes. Easier to maneuver beneath clothes.

"You know what, Sam? I think I'm going to take this to my room, after all," she said, looping the strap of her purse over her shoulder. She was making a decision before she could do something stupid like react again.

"We need to talk," he was saying to her back as she headed toward the hall.

"Call me. You have my number." She didn't slow her step. Not even when Lucy jumped down and followed her. She went into the bedroom, closed the door in the dog's face and dropped her purse.

She was shaking.

But she'd made it.

WITH HER PURSE on the floor at her feet, Bloom opened her wine. Took a small sip. She stood up straight and took a deep breath. And then, picking up her purse, moved over to the bed. Wineglass on the nightstand, she reached in her purse for her phone. And she waited.

She wasn't changing until he called her.

Five minutes later she'd taken another small sip or two of wine, but that was all. She hadn't moved from the side of the bed.

And she hadn't spoken to Sam.

What was it he'd had to tell her? Something about her case, obviously. She'd been rash. Less than adultlike, running away from him like that.

But if she'd stayed...

She jumped when a knock sounded on her door. She stared at it. At the handle, as though expecting it to move. She knew it wouldn't. He would never invade her privacy that way. But she was fascinated with that old gold handle.

"Bloom?"

She had to answer him. He was supposed to be protecting her. He'd be worried if she didn't answer…

And she was acting like she didn't trust herself. Like she doubted her ability to take care of herself.

After standing, Bloom crossed the carpet and opened the door.

BEER BOTTLE IN hand for…false courage, he guessed, Sam forced himself to look at the woman who was driving him nuts. "We need to talk."

She didn't let go of the door. She held it with both hands. "Okay."

"If you need me to leave…need to arrange to have Chantel move in…"

"Of course I don't," she said so quickly he didn't have time to tamp down the pleasure that surged through him. Or the relief.

And their problems were only beginning. "So…I imagined the way you ran from me back there?" He motioned down the hall with his bottle.

"No." He knew he hadn't. Just as he'd known she'd be honest with him. Bloom was as black-and-white as they came.

A self-honesty, he knew, born from having her

faith in herself, in her ability to discern, obliterated by a man who'd used her love for him against her in the cruelest way possible.

He swallowed. He had to be honest with her. More than anything, deception would hurt her.

"I have a burning desire to have sex with you." For come-on lines it might have worked in a whorehouse. He wasn't sure. He'd only ever been in one to make arrests.

"Okay." Bloom hadn't even blinked.

CHAPTER TWENTY-FIVE

"OKAY?" SAM NODDED as he repeated the word, feeling…not good. What in hell did "okay" mean? "Okay, I can have sex with you? Or it's okay that I want to? Okay, it's out in the open now? Okay, you heard me? Okay, am I done yet so you can close the door and get back to whatever it was you were doing?"

And what had she been doing? She was still dressed, down to the two-inch pumps she'd worn to work that morning. Had anyone ever told her what those shoes did to her calves? How they tightened the muscles and made him want to run his hands along them?

Great…he was almost forty years old and developing a calf fetish. Wouldn't Dad be proud of him now.

"Are you done?"

Shifting his weight from foot to foot, Sam wondered how he'd gone from a sane and in control detective to swirling in a funnel cloud in the space of fifteen minutes. He also wondered how in the hell to get out in one piece.

With her in one piece.

The case in one piece.

And no more guilt on his shoulders.

He had to be honest with her. He'd made a promise he hadn't kept. To an abused woman who'd fought hard to get her life back.

"No, I'm not done," he said, calmer now. "Although I do apologize for..." What? Speaking with the passion she aroused in him? Being honest enough to let her know how much she was getting to him?

Other than his ex-wife, he'd never had a woman living under his roof before...

"Do you mind if I sit down?" she asked him. "My feet are killing me." As though unaware of the danger, Bloom walked into the room, kicked off her shoes and sat on the edge of her bed.

His bed. He'd bought that mattress. Those sheets. And the comforter, too, though he'd never slept on it. He'd washed it once. The day he'd taken it out of the...the day he'd brought her to... Now he couldn't think straight.

"The case first," he said, leaning his shoulder on the doorway. He wanted to finish the beer he'd yet to start. Determined it would be best to wait until he was through there.

Bloom listened without interruption as he told her about her young patient's feeling that their female guard imposter could be her mother-in-law.

The rest, the part about the girl only ever having seen the couple one time, she'd already known. "And you knew they'd only been married a few weeks?" he asked.

She confirmed that, too.

"He'd been hitting her before they got married."

Bloom couldn't say either way. But he knew he was right. Though the girl had never called the police, he was now in possession of the medical records that showed more than a year's worth of "accidents."

"He started hitting her when she got pregnant," he said now. "And she stayed with him because she had nowhere else to go. She was young and pregnant and..." A foster kid. He got the picture.

"We'll get them, Bloom. She and her baby will be safe."

He could have bitten off his tongue the second he heard the words. It didn't take her silent nod to tell him he'd just made another promise that came with no guarantee. When had he started thinking he was the man who could leap tall buildings in a single bound?

"My experience with this sort of thing tells me that we have an excellent chance of bringing them in and closing this case quite soon."

As difficult as the words were, they were worth far more than the effort it had taken to say them when she smiled.

"Thank you."

He thought about Freelander. About ten-year-old boys.

And didn't want to get her hopes up. He was sure. But he still only had the word of gang members. And a class roster. When he had proof, he'd tell her what he knew.

"So…I'm struggling with this whole sex thing," he said.

"I know."

She knew. The response raised about the same reaction in him as her "okay." Of course she knew. He'd just told her less than five minutes ago.

"But you don't want me to move out."

"Of course not. This is your home."

"You're not leaving…"

She held up a hand. "I have no intention of leaving, Sam. I'm not stupid. My house was just broken into. They've been to my office. For all we know, they know about this place, too, but at least here I'm…protected."

By him. And the fact that his house was a mile up from the road, behind an unscaleable iron fence, with two armed guards on the premises.

"So…what do you suggest we do?" She was the counselor. And, incidentally, the one who'd made everything so much worse when she'd kissed him the night before.

"Talk," she said, patting the bed beside her. "We talk."

He looked at her. At his bed. And didn't feel like talking. At all.

But he pushed away from the doorjamb and moved slowly toward her. Rested his ass several inches up the bed from her and dangled his beer bottle between his knees.

"What I know is that the best way to deal with a difficult situation is to confront it."

She wanted him to confront it. He'd confront it, all right. Beneath a cold shower. Only that wasn't working. Not for long enough.

"It's a little...tricky...for me because I have to deal with the situation myself. I can't put myself in your shoes or try to imagine what you might or might not do."

Wait a minute. Wait just a damned minute. "You're in the same boat?" he asked her.

His loafers were fascinating. He couldn't look away from the stitching on the toes. Didn't trust himself to catch a glimpse of her in his peripheral vision.

So much for the tough cop he'd been most of his life.

This woman practically had him on his knees. Using his own...weapon...against him.

No. That wasn't right. She wasn't using anything. And she wasn't against him. She was in the boat with him.

"So…we're agreed that we both have a supreme desire to see the other naked."

The words were as erotic as his late-night thoughts had been. Only worse because she was actually present. Hearing them with him.

"Yes."

Oh, God. He sure as hell hoped she knew what she was doing with this whole confronting thing. So far, for him, it wasn't helping matters any.

"And I think it's pretty clear that we both know that for us to actually see each other naked, or in any way engage in a physical encounter, would not be good." Her running act earlier had confirmed that she shared his opinion.

"Correct. It would absolutely be wrong."

Right. So, he was glad they'd had this talk, and…

"It would help if we talk about the reasons why it's wrong," she said before he could get out of there. "Addressing them will help to solidify them in our minds. Make them more real. If we understand them, and truly agree that they're valid, their presence will build a wall between desire and action."

He wasn't so sure about that. But she was the professional on this one. And sounded a hell of lot more in control that he felt.

If not for the way her hands were shaking, he'd think she wasn't affected at all.

"I'll go first," he offered. "And state the obvious. I can't promise you more than a one-night stand, and you aren't a one-night stand type of woman."

"No, I'm not. And it is clear that, with you, the job comes first."

"I've already made you a promise I couldn't possibly keep. If I have sex with you, knowing that you need more than just a night of sex, I'm making another promise I can't keep. And I can't live with that." It might have come out better if he'd actually had some of the beer he'd opened.

But he was getting the hang of this. Was on a roll.

"And you have…daddy issues."

She stiffened. Noticeably so. Maybe there was a limit to the amount of honesty required in this discussion. But if he pissed her off, and she wouldn't let him near her…that plan could work, too.

He took a sip of his beer. Getting into the spirit of things. "I don't mean that as any kind of slur on your father, Bloom," he clarified before he went on. Just in case.

"I know that. You're not the type of guy who'd go for the kill with innuendo."

No, he just pulled his revolver out of his holster and shot. He'd killed a man, once. Before that man had shot the child he'd been holding hostage.

"But you do seem to have a thing for older men," he told her. "Freelander's fifteen years older than you are."

"I'm not denying your assertion," she said, picking at the foiled label wrapped around the top of her bottle. "I've already come to see the truth of that for myself. I know that my subconscious need to feel the safety a child feels from a parent, that unconditional and protective love, made me vulnerable to Kenneth's manipulation."

"And I'm older than you and currently in a position of authority in your life." That was just a fact.

"Okay, but I didn't know that when I first started to feel…"

She broke off just when things were getting interesting. But if she thought it was for the best that she stop, it probably was.

"My strong reactions to you are most likely a simple case of transference mixed with a bit of childish hero worship," she said. "It's not uncommon for a patient to think he or she is falling in love with his or her therapist, for example. Or for someone who is being protected to fall in love with his or her protector."

Whoa. They weren't talking about love here. This was a sex thing. Pure and simple.

"And the same holds true for sexual attraction," she was saying, as if she'd read his mind. He started to breathe again.

"I can see that," he said. He'd add her point to his list of "why nots."

"You're an adrenaline junkie," she said next. "I crave peace."

He didn't have a thing against peace. But a world with crime and criminals wasn't a peaceful one…

"I can't disagree with you there."

"I also feel, as of now, that my life is better lived without a man in it. I actually didn't think I was capable of feeling sexual desire at all," she said. He looked at her then, against his better judgment. Because her tone had been so…uncharacteristically filled with emotion. "After the things Ken made me do…it wasn't just the actual actions, it was being forced to do them… Sometimes the result of that kind of abuse is…a woman's inability to feel sexual desire."

"You really thought he'd stolen your ability to know sexual pleasure ever again?"

She nodded. "But it was okay," she told him, meeting his gaze. He wondered if she knew how wide-eyed and innocent she looked to him. How naive. This woman who was ten times smarter than he was.

And had a way of making him feel so smart.

"I don't trust myself enough to enter an intimate relationship, anyway," she said. "I don't know that I'll ever be ready. I don't know that I'll ever want to give up control of self to another... ever...again." The wine bottle slipped and she almost dropped it.

He took it and set it on the nightstand beside his beer bottle. "Isn't a healthy relationship one in which neither party gives up self, but rather, both selves contribute to a third whole?" Or something like that. His ex-wife had espoused marital counseling tips at him so often he pretty much knew them all.

He'd listened the first couple of times they'd gone to counseling, too. Hoping he could somehow make it all work. Could find a way to be as committed to her as he was to his job.

"Of course," she told him. Then added, "But not everyone starts out whole," she told him. "I have a tendency to give up self in order to please."

"But if you're with the right guy, wouldn't that mean he'd have a tendency to demand autonomy from you even while he's loving you?"

Why in the hell was he fighting her on this? Like he was trying to convince her to go start a relationship with someone else.

Maybe he was. Because he wanted her happy. And safe from him.

"In a perfect world," Bloom said, confidence

fueling her voice again. "Anyway, I think we have a list solid enough to build a fortress between us."

She didn't need to sound quite so cheerful about it. But… "I agree." He felt as certain as he had all along that he was wrong for her. That he couldn't sleep with her.

"I'm sorry I can't sleep with you," she told him.

Not nearly as sorry as he was. He didn't tell her so. Because he wasn't feeling anywhere near as together as she sounded.

"But at least something good's come out of all of this."

He looked for it. Couldn't find it. "What?"

"I'm not as damaged as I thought. I know I can feel sexual desire." She was smiling. A little crookedly. And the twitch at the corner of her mouth finally gave her away to him.

She wasn't any more okay than he was. She was just far more skilled at pushing aside her own feelings while she tended to others. Her cheerfulness was for his benefit.

If he was going to be a friend to her…and he wanted—badly—to be that, at least, it would require her autonomy.

"Tell me what you were just thinking," he said. "Honestly, not the version you're giving so that this is easier on me…"

"I'm not…" She stopped. "Yes, I am."

He waited.

"I was thinking that…I shouldn't get too excited about feeling sexual desire. Not until I know I can maintain the feeling through sexual interaction and actually experience an orgasm."

Her entire being changed. Her expression filled with he didn't know what. While his body surged with a desire so intense it knocked all thought from his mind.

"So I was thinking, you're safe. You want sex with me, but don't want a relationship, and I just want to know whether or not I'm capable of a normal sexual encounter. We could both get what we want with neither of us being in danger of hurting the other. Or taking advantage of the other."

"Are you saying you want to have sex? With me?"

He was probably completely off base. Could even be talking with his penis. But she was all about honesty and he had never been more truthfully certain that he wanted to help her in any way he could.

"We know there can't possibly be anything between us. And…you've got something else that I likely wouldn't find with anyone else I might have a one-night stand with." Her statement sent shock waves through him. And curiosity.

"What's that?"

"I trust you. I admire you. And it can't get any safer than you in terms of experimenting," she

continued, and took a breath as though to ex-
pound further.

He wanted to hear her out. But she didn't get
a chance to speak again. He'd shoved his tongue
in her mouth.

CHAPTER TWENTY-SIX

BLOOM MADE A conscious decision to have sex with Sam Larson. And she completely trusted that they both really just wanted to have sex one time—not start a relationship.

Like a man picking a woman up in a bar for a one-night fling, only she was the one who was doing the picking up.

Sort of.

When Sam kissed her, she kissed him back. Using her tongue as she'd been taught to use it. Kissing, having sex, was a no-brainer to her in terms of what to do with body parts.

And because this was just an experiment, not a relationship, there was no reason for conversation. She noted when he broke away from her long enough to take a condom out of his wallet and toss it on the nightstand. She noted his sporadic breathing and…

Mmm. His lips were… His tongue was…

What was he…

His tongue was soft against hers. It was caressing hers. Gently. His whole mouth was…gentle.

And the curious butterflies of pleasure flittered down between her legs.

The man could kiss.

And she wanted more.

She followed his lead. Let him take her. She didn't have to worry about his pleasure, about making it good for him. This was an experiment. To prove something to her.

Her arms tingled. Her breasts ached. She lost her balance and braced her hands against his chest.

The thump of Sam's heartbeat righted her for a moment. Gave her something familiar and cerebral to focus on. The rate was elevated.

He was enjoying this, too?

The thought startled her and she broke away from his mouth to look into his eyes. They weren't the same. They were…softer…which made no sense. Deeper, like he wasn't only seeing through them, he was helping her see. She wanted to see. As deep as it could go.

"You okay?" His voice wasn't the same, either. It was hoarse and moist and…

She looked for words. Came up blank. And nodded.

"You want to go on?"

"Oh, yes."

Was he in doubt? She knew what to do about

that, how to show him that she wanted to pleasure him…

Loosening his tie a bit more than he already had sometime before they'd arrived home that night, she left it on, unbuttoning his shirt, opening it to reveal a chest full of dark, sexy hair. And his nipples.

Thrilling at the hair—Kenneth hadn't had much—she put off her own pleasure to zone in on his nipples. Teasing them with her fingers. And then her tongue. He groaned and she felt his appreciation all the way to her core.

To…her feminine core.

What was going on? She continued kissing him in a way she knew men liked. And because this was about her, she also ran her fingers through the hair on his chest. It was a curious mixture of soft and coarse. She buried her nose in it, running her lips across it, fascinated by how it tickled and enticed at the same time.

He pushed at her jacket, and understanding what he wanted, she helped him slide it off, returning to her task—and her delight—as soon as her arms were free. He unbuttoned her shirt. She knew he wanted her breasts. Men liked breasts. She was happy to provide his pleasure. The squeezing and fondling.

She was glad to have Sam's hands there, to have him know her that…intimately.

The thought stopped her until she realized that she only wanted Sam there because he'd saved her from Ken. It was a symbolic thing. Nothing more.

Her bra had a front closure and he handled it with skill. Not surprising, considering how gorgeous the man was, that he'd had a lot of experience with women's underthings. Burying her fingers in his chest hair, distracting herself, she still felt his fingers on her breasts. Covering them, as though memorizing their shape. Gentle caresses on her sensitive flesh with the tips of his fingers distracted her from his chest. And when, with one finger of each hand, he brushed her nipples, back and forth, back and forth, Bloom fell over onto her back, lying flat out beneath him on his bed.

She'd never felt so damned good in her life.

SAM HAD HAD his share of "wham bam thank you ma'ams." Probably more than his share. He'd always left his ladies satisfied, but he'd never been so compelled to know every inch of them.

To touch every inch. With reverence.

He was hard to the point of pain. He needed to sink himself in and find relief. But he had so much to do first.

This one-time thing was the only chance he was going to get. He had to make the most of it. Know everything. Get it all. Give it all.

He had one time to show her how great sex could be for her.

Her touch was at once skilled and naive. Schooled and completely innocent. Her body curved and inviting. All woman. Luscious. But it was those brown eyes that drove him.

He might question his sanity later, but as he lay beside a half-clad Bloom, Sam kept looking into those brown eyes. Kept seeking them out. They were his guide.

And his salvation.

HER SKIRT WAS GONE. So were her panties. She'd lost track of them. Of time. Still with her blouse hanging off her shoulders, and her bra bunched at her back, Bloom rolled over. She wanted her naked detective beneath her so she could taste him like a man wanted to be tasted. She started at his chest, because she couldn't seem to get enough of it, and then started downward.

Pausing at his stomach, she found almost as much pleasure there as she had at his chest. It was just…fine. So strong and masculine and…Sam. It protected his vital organs.

And he was vital.

Vital.

She paused, even while sexual vibrations pulsed through her.

He wasn't vital. The experiment was.

The heat pumping through her blood hadn't cooled yet. But she kept putting off the inevitable. Every time she felt like he might mount her, enter her, she moved. His fingers had lightly explored her body, but when they'd started to do more…she'd moved.

She didn't want the deliciousness to end.

Not the moment. Or the feeling.

What if she couldn't get there? What if this anticipation was all there was for her?

Buying herself some more time, she moved lower, knowing exactly what to do. How to do it. The tip of him lay just beneath his belly button. She should see the velvety softness. Could practically taste…

"Bloom?" With the hoarseness still clouding his voice, Sam pulled her up. "This is just you and me. You don't have to perform."

How had he known? And why was she burning up even more? Why hadn't she just gone cold?

The moment could have been awkward, but it didn't get that far. Sam was kissing her again. Full mouth, nothing-held-back kisses that went much further than mouth to mouth. She could feel him, the man who'd just honored her in a way she hadn't even known to want, and let him feel her, too.

"I want you," she said. "Inside me." The words were foreign to her and felt so natural.

"Not yet," he told her. "Trust me."

She did trust him. And so when he told her to lie flat and open her legs, she did so. "This is my treat." His breath sent shivers all over her as he started at one breast, licking, tasting, kissing and nipping, moving up to her nipple, across to the other breast.

She was wet. Not just from his mouth. And she didn't care. Her hips moved of their own accord. She was on a glorious journey and her job was to ride it out. He moved to her stomach and she liked him there, too. Liked having him tend to the protection of her vital organs.

An odd thought. And yet, it meant so much to her.

But when he dipped lower, when his chin brushed the top of her pelvis, she started to panic. She pulled at his shoulders, feeling weak and in-effective as he continued on his path.

"Sam..." Her entire body was trembling. Her voice sounded frightened, tremulous, even to her own ears. But he didn't stop.

He just continued on down, stroking her with his fingers, with his tongue. Her body arched, reaching for him, reaching for more. She didn't know herself and didn't care. With her fingers clutching the comforter, she let Sam do whatever he wanted.

A crescendo rose inside her. With no warning,

no time to think or process, she cried out. And then cried again as everything just…exploded. Wave after wave after wave of the most exquisite pleasure. More than she'd ever imagined. And even as she rode those waves, Sam quickly sheathed himself, moved up her body, positioned himself between her legs and pushed himself home.

Her body pulsed around him, taking him and letting him go, and a new, unbelievable swell happened, from deeper inside her. Her muscles convulsed with it. She was dizzy and euphoric and never wanted it to stop.

Sam groaned, once, twice, he tensed and trembled and she felt the heat as he emptied himself inside her.

They were done.

HE HADN'T MEANT to fall asleep. But then, he hadn't meant to have sex with her, either. Sam woke sometime during the night. The bedroom door was open and Lucy had jumped up on his feet. They were where she normally slept when the room was theirs.

Bloom lay with her back to him, facing the opposite wall.

He could stay. Who was to say he'd woken up?

He could even cuddle up behind her. His exwife used to cuddle him in his sleep.

Wife. Which spelled relationship with a big *R*.

As quietly as possible, moving as little as necessary, he slid from off the top of the rumpled bed. Seeming to understand the criticalness of the situation, Lucy jumped down as well, watching him.

He made it halfway across the room without looking back. When he did, he saw the naked back and perfectly rounded bottom of the most incredible woman he'd ever met.

He saw her shiver.

He couldn't just leave her that way.

Quietly, carefully, Sam crept back. He lifted the king comforter from Lucy's side of the bed, carried it over and laid it atop a still-sleeping Bloom.

She didn't move. Her deep sleep spoke of extreme exhaustion.

Due, in part at least, to the incredible sex they'd shared.

No matter what else they had going on with the investigations, the destruction and the damage, the court case and an insecure future, one thing was for certain.

Her experiment had been a success.

BLOOM'S SECOND APPOINTMENT Tuesday morning was with Heather Ramirez, the young mother whose husband beat her for the last time on the night she turned him in and he committed suicide. That was the night that he'd also turned his anger on their baby boy for the first time, forcibly yanking him from his mother's breast and throwing him on the couch.

Tuesday's session was unscheduled. Heather had phoned the service that handled Bloom's calls when she wasn't in the office and booked the first available appointment.

While she'd thought she'd have the hour after her seven o'clock to prepare for the rest of the day, Bloom felt it was probably for the best that she just stay busy.

She was a little shaky that morning. Due to the night before.

She wasn't worried about her and Sam. Afraid that they'd gone too far or made a mistake. They'd done what they set out to do. And the morning had been just like any other. She'd only seen him as they left the house for him to follow her to work.

He'd asked her if she was okay, she'd said she was fine. Then they got in their respective cars and drove off.

She was great with all of that. Happy about it. She just hadn't counted on the aftermath of the hormone surge, the adrenaline surge, the endorphin surge that had accompanied the first orgasm she'd ever had. And the second one, too. The dissipation of said hormones was causing her a bit of…depression.

So she would work harder than ever. Helping others took the focus off herself. Put life back into perspective. She was a very, very lucky woman.

In charge of life.

Able to choose whatever she wanted to choose for her course to the future.

She had the money to buy what she wanted, too.

And lived in paradise.

Sam had called during her first appointment. And then he'd texted to tell her to call him as soon as possible.

Heather was waiting when she showed out Donna Graph, her regular Tuesday, 7:00 a.m. patient. The girl's face was tear-streaked. Sara Havens, the full-time counselor at the Stand was with her. Heather was staying at the Stand. Someone there watched her baby son when Heather had her sessions with Bloom. And whoever was free drove her over.

Sara wasn't usually free. Bloom hoped the baby was at the Stand.

Bloom invited them both in, but Sara, who'd counseled Bloom and didn't counsel Heather, opted to stay in the waiting area.

In the two minutes she'd been gone, Sam had called again. She didn't have time to talk to him, but sent a quick text.

Am I in immediate danger?

His response was quick. No.

She put the phone down, uneasy.

It could just be a coincidence that Sam was trying to reach her and the victim whose in-laws he thought were responsible for the recent threats against her and the Stand was sitting on her sofa crying softly.

Sam didn't believe in coincidences.

She wished he was there, too.

Which was ridiculous. She liked him, but she didn't *need* him. She didn't need anybody.

And liked it that way.

Liar, liar, pants on fire.

What in the hell… She tuned out her inner voice to tend to the matter at hand. It was important.

Bloom sat beside Heather on the couch. She didn't touch the girl. But she stayed close. Human contact was often a healer in itself.

"Can you tell me about it?" she asked. If the in-laws had that baby…

She had to get Heather to talk. To get Sam whatever information he might need…

When the teenager looked up at her Bloom's stomach felt like lead. Once a pretty blonde, Heather looked…horrible. Pale. Sick.

"I killed them."

Whatever she'd been expecting it wasn't that.

"What?"

"They went to court yesterday, to file for custody of my baby," she said. "They have more money than I do. They have a home. I don't even have a job yet. I quit high school to have him, thinking my husband would support us, and I can't even get insurance money because he killed himself and…"

Her mouth was thick with saliva as she spoke, her eyes blurred with tears.

Bloom also noticed for the first time that Heather's hands were dirty. Like she'd been playing in the dirt.

"I've never had anyone, Dr. Freelander. All my life I've been alone, and then I met Omar and he was so sweet to me. When I got pregnant and he wanted to marry me…I finally started to believe that I could be like everyone else. That I could have a family of my own. But his parents hated me. They said I got pregnant deliberately to trap him. They didn't want him to quit college to work. They didn't want him to marry me. They were on him all the time. Every day. It wasn't his fault that he was taking it out on me. Who else did he have? I got that. But when he threw our baby…

"Do you know what could have happened if the baby hadn't landed on the cushion? His neck could have broken… He could have died."

"Tell me what happened with your in-laws." Bloom was calm. In control. Caring for the young girl, and aware of her professional responsibilities, as well. Anything Heather told her would be in complete confidence.

"I know the police were looking for them. I

was, too," Heather said, her tears subsiding for a moment. "I was scared it was them threatening you and Ms. McDaniel and hurting those guards after the detective showed me that photo, but it wasn't them. I found out they were in Los Angeles, staying with friends while they saw a lawyer and filed papers to take my son away from me. They'd left their cell phones at home and didn't want anyone to know what they were doing until they knew for sure they could and should do it. Their friend is some kind of counselor, I guess. Mrs. Ramirez called me last night and told me what they were doing. She wanted me to understand, she said, and said that if I'd just cooperate and let them raise my baby, they'd let me see him whenever I wanted. She told me all the things they could do for him that I couldn't. And said what a better life he'd have with them, and I knew that when they told the judge those things I was going to lose my baby."

"So what did you do?"

Heather was there because she needed to talk. She'd have run if that had been her intention.

"I told Mrs. Ramirez I'd come over to talk but I wasn't bringing the baby with me. Then I called Maddie, you know, the child care worker at the Stand, and asked her to stay with him. I went to the Ramirezes'. They were being all nice because they thought I was going to give them my baby. I asked if I could see Omar's room. I knew he used to have a gun there and I told myself if it was still there, it was a sign that I should use it."

Bloom felt sick. Physically nauseous. Despair was more lethal than anthrax.

"The gun was there. So I used it."

CHAPTER TWENTY-SEVEN

SAM REALLY HATED it when things didn't go according to his plan. Almost as much as he hated it when his hunch was wrong.

The Ramirezes weren't his perps in Santa Raquel. They hadn't taken Gomez down, hadn't knocked out the guard at The Lemonade Stand, vandalized Lila McDaniel's car or broken into Bloom's house and slashed her paintings.

They'd been in LA, seeking counsel, both legal and otherwise. And then they'd filed for custody of their grandson. They'd been upright citizens, trying to deal with a devastating situation in the best way possible.

He'd liked them for criminals.

And now they were dead.

He wasn't lead on the case. He wasn't really on the case at all, though he'd been called.

Forensics would process the scene.

But the suspect had confessed and was in custody. Her young son would be put in the system. He was young enough that his chances of adoption were good.

Sam had one hell of a headache, from lack of sleep, he was telling himself. He was bothered that Bloom had had a murderer in her office that day—and bothered that she would have been upset by the experience, too.

Mostly, he was angry that he had no leads on who had attacked two armed guards, slashed paintings and vandalized a car.

What was he missing?

He spent the rest of Tuesday and into the evening looking. He'd have stayed at his desk all night if not for the fact that Chantel expected him at the cottage to relieve her at eleven.

At ten to eleven he shut down his system and went home.

He greeted an exuberant Lucy, and spent a few minutes in the yard with her just because it felt good to do so. Felt normal. He thought about a beer and decided against it. Thought about throwing in a load of laundry. Decided against that, too, and went to bed.

He didn't so much as look at the closed bedroom door across the hall. Other than a brief greeting at their cars that morning, he hadn't spoken to Bloom since the night before. They'd texted.

When Heather Ramirez had been ready to turn herself in, Bloom had called Chantel.

He knew that she was living by their agreement the night before. They'd conducted an experiment purely for her personal knowledge base. She was showing him that nothing had changed between them.

And expected him to show her the same.

Only problem was, as he lay on the top of his covers in sweats and T-shirt, hard as hell and aching in every bone in his body, he knew that he was lying.

Somehow, in the space of a few hours, everything had changed.

It was up to him to see that it changed back.

BLOOM WASN'T CHANGING her mind. Not even thinking about it. She didn't want to change her mind. She and Sam had conducted an experiment. They had not started a relationship. She didn't want a relationship with him.

She just wanted to watch the movie one more time.

To make sure that she caught every aspect of it. Learned fully from it. She wanted to know if it had been a fluke, how much she'd liked sex with him the first time around. The first time she'd ever liked sex.

She listened as Sam settled in for the night.

And then she got up.

Her choice was well considered. She'd spent all evening on it. And had counter choices ready depending on which of the various responses she'd anticipated actually happened.

And a wild card abort plan, too, in the eventuality that she received an unanticipated response.

She concentrated on the plan, the thoughts, rather than on the hormonal cocktail shooting through her veins as she crossed the hall.

Sam slept with his door open so he could hear her or anyone in the rest of the house. She'd known that from the first night. Because he'd prepared her in the event she wanted to make a kitchen run in the middle of the night.

He'd neglected to say that he slept fully dressed— albeit in more comfortable clothes than the pants and tie he'd had on the night before.

Thoughts of that tie sent another ripple of cocktail through her. He'd worn that tie all night.

It had given her the ability to look at him in a whole new light every single time she saw him dressed for work.

And that way of thinking had no valid point. Or purpose.

Lucy lifted her head as Bloom drew close to the bed. Sam didn't. But he was watching her with his eyes wide open.

Of course he would be.

He was there to protect her from intruders. What good would he be if he didn't know someone was intruding on his own bed?

She lay down. Lucy jumped off the bed.

"This doesn't change anything," she whispered.

He didn't. "Understood."

She found out that the movie was even better the second time around. There were things she'd missed...

Bloom lost herself in the ecstasy. For one more hour.

Then she went back to bed.

As SOON AS Sam followed Bloom to work Monday morning, saw her safely inside with Gomez at the door, he entered the freeway and headed to LA.

Chantel was going to be looking over all of their Santa Raquel files, The Lemonade Stand files, comparing histories to those from Bloom's client files. She was looking again at the three abusers who'd appeared to have alibis. He'd missed something.

Probably because he'd been so tuned into Freelander.

The first place Sam went, without calling beforehand, was the state prison. He shown his identity and named the man he wanted to visit. Because he was who he was, his request was granted. As he'd known it would be.

"I swear to you, Detective," Shaq Dunning said. "I told you the truth." Dunning, a man who'd been present when a drug deal went bad resulting in the deaths of two men, was in prison for life. He hadn't committed murder, but he'd been selling the drugs. To pay for his infant daughter's heart surgery. After the surgery, Sam had helped relocate Mrs. Dunning and her two young children to Santa Raquel. He watched out for them as necessary in exchange for Dunning's inside information—as necessary.

"You better not be jerking me, Dunning," he said now, more serious than he'd ever been. "If what you told me about Freelander unloading those drugs is false…"

"No, sir, it's true. You know I'd give you names if I could, but I do that and I'll be dead in here by tonight."

"And you're certain he threatened to go after his wife when he got out?"

"Yes, sir. It's all the bastard talked about. Getting her back or making her pay. One or the other. Some days it was hard to figure out which he wanted worse."

Sam wanted to ask if Cordoba was a name Dunning recognized. He wanted to name the gang. But he wasn't going to have another man's death on his conscience. Not when, if he did his job right, he could get the answer without Dunning.

And in the meantime, he'd just continue to do what he was doing. Going after Freelander. And keeping Bloom safe.

The other…her little experiment…well, they'd wrapped that one up. Parts of him wished it had taken a little longer.

SAM WAS HALFWAY to his car when he turned around, gave up his gun one more time and headed back inside. To records. He wanted to know if Freelander had had any visits while he was in prison. Any regular visitors.

Bloom had said she'd only spoken with him once. But there could have been someone else. He should have thought of it before.

Maybe would have if he'd known about Freelander's penchant for young coeds earlier than the previous week. The professor had been so obsessed with Bloom and, from the sounds of things had, spent all of his free time with her, that Sam hadn't even thought to see if there'd been someone else in the man's life during the time he'd been married to Bloom—some other reason he was keeping his wife on medication that would slow down her reasoning abilities.

The man's attorney had visited him. Which was to be expected. And every single week he'd been inside, he'd had one other visitor. A woman. By the name of…Barb Miller?

Of course, there were many Barb Millers in the world. But the name didn't ring true to Sam.

It was the type of name someone would choose if they didn't want to be found out.

With instincts back on track, talking loud and clear, he collected his gear and headed out into the California sunshine.

CORDOBA WAS THE next man on his list of people to visit during his day in the city. Back in the East Side, he parked a few blocks from the bowling alley, in the parking lot of a doctor's office. And walked to a bar he knew was a regular hangout for members of the East Side gang.

He wasn't all that surprised when Juan Cordoba stood up as soon as he walked in the door. Introduced himself and invited Sam to have a seat.

The kids would have told the man a white dude was asking for him. Probably told him they thought he was the professor, too.

Sam had counted on that part. He was more interested in knowing what Cordoba was going to do now.

Not kill him. He knew that much. The boys wouldn't want the death of a cop on their hands. Not good for business. They'd know that other cops would know where he was. And with who.

And they did. Everyone on his floor knew where he was and why. And officers in the LA neighborhood he was sitting in knew, too. It was how the game was played and everyone knew the rules.

Except maybe the ten-year-old kids he'd lucked upon the other day.

"You been asking for me," Cordoba said.

"It's not really you I want." Sam stared the man in the eye. He did want him. For the drugs. But he wasn't going to get ahead of himself again.

One thing at a time. He'd worn his regular pants and tie, figuring his target already knew by now that he was a cop, and sat back, so the gun beneath his jacket and the badge clipped to his belt were in plain view.

"Who you want?"

"A relative of yours. Jean?" He pronounced it as though it was a girl's name. He was going on a hunch. But he really wanted Jean Cordoba to be Barb Miller.

In the worst way.

"My sister? What you want with her?"

"Just to talk to her," Sam said. He stood. Pulled a card out of his wallet.

"What you think she did?"

"It's not what she did, it's who she knows. Have her call me."

He dropped his card on the table and walked out. But not before he'd seen a younger man, maybe sixteen or seventeen, slink back into the corner as he passed. Another gang member, he was certain. Someone on the side. Just in case.

Sam wanted to know why.

But didn't stick around to ask. He'd already outworn his welcome for one day.

AFTER STOPPING AT the university to ask around, Sam considered a visit to Freelander, just to give the guy a very serious warning—along the lines of, if he thought he was going to get at Bloom he was going to die trying—but he thought better of it.

As soon as he did something asinine like that, Freelander would be the victim. And Bloom would pay the price.

He was halfway back to Santa Raquel, thinking about dinner and a beer at the pub, when his phone rang. He didn't recognize the number—a good sign.

It was Jean Cordoba. She was willing to talk to him. But only if he could get to her within the next hour. She was on a break from work—a free clinic not far from the bar he'd been at earlier. He was supposed to meet her at the back door of the clinic and she'd show him into the break room.

Putting on his lights as he did an illegal U-turn, Sam sped back to the East Side of LA to meet with a senior psychology student turned nurse's aide.

CHAPTER TWENTY-EIGHT

BLOOM LEFT WORK just before five that evening. Her six o'clock had cancelled and she was tired. Days were longer now as the sun set later and she needed some time down at the beach in order to process the day before—the eighteen-year-old she hadn't helped enough.

She'd run from the situation the night before—straight to Sam's bed. She couldn't keep running.

Chantel was waiting for her as she wished Gomez a good night and left the building. And the female detective also waited while Bloom changed out of her suit into sweats and tennis shoes for a trek down to the beach. Chantel, still in uniform with the black boots she always seemed to wear—what was it with Santa Raquel cops and their footwear?—seemed eager enough to accompany her down the hill.

Lucy was ecstatic about her adventure and bounded down in front of them, as though showing them the way. Bloom had intended to walk—as far as the cliff face would allow before it swung around to meet the ocean and block off beach ac-

cess. Instead, she sat where she and Sam had sat
the night they'd come down.

Chantel dropped down beside her.

"Rough couple of days, huh?"

They'd talked some the night before. Chantel had been open to conversation. Bloom hadn't been.

"I just keep thinking there's more I could have done for Heather," she said now. "I was counseling her. I keep trying to figure out what I missed."

"Who says you missed anything? Maybe it's just like she said, the thought of losing her son was her cracking point."

"She didn't know she was going to lose him."

"She believed she would, and that's what mattered here." Chantel's pragmatism made everything sound so…plausible.

And right.

"I read through her file again today," Bloom confessed. "Looking for anything I might have missed. Any sign that she was in dangerous emotional territory—beyond what any young girl who'd been abused and was living in a shelter would be."

"I think the key is all of those things you listed. Heather had a rough life. Everything stacked up against her. And none of those circumstances were things you could have prevented."

"Of course not, but—"

"You remind me of Sam."

Bloom's heart, which had been open, filled with compassion for the teenager who was going to be spending the rest of her life in prison, was now suddenly closed up tight.

"How so?" She and Sam were good. They had their understandings. And would move on with their lives—separate and apart—just fine. He'd had his life right where he wanted it before Kenneth's release from prison. So had she. Those lives were waiting for both of them as soon as all of this was over.

"He blames himself for his father's death and yet there was nothing he could have done to prevent it. His sergeant was caught unaware, too. It was circumstances. Sam did his job exactly right and yet tragedy happened."

That was different.

How so?

The intrusion of her inner voice was only confusing her. Not helping.

"It's like both of you, as nice and hardworking and ethical as you are, are also filled with this huge sense of self."

The skin around her hairline grew tight. It wasn't like Chantel to be mean. What was going on?

"Don't get me wrong," the other woman continued, her voice slightly raised over the sound of the waves.

Bloom watched Lucy pouncing on the beach. After sand crabs Sam had said.

"I am really fond of both of you. Well, I respect you both a great deal, and have grown really fond of you," she clarified, and Bloom felt a measure of peace return.

For a second there her feelings had been hurt. It wasn't like her to be so sensitive.

But then having a patient turn to murder while under her care wasn't like her, either.

Neither was being truly intimate with another person.

She just needed to get home. Back to the life she'd built. The one that served her purposes. The one where she was happy.

"All I'm saying is that you both take on too much responsibility. How can all of the things that transpired against Heather, how can her emotional makeup, be your responsibility? All you could do to affect that situation was try to give her ways to deal with the cards she'd been dealt. You tried. You worked with her. You did your job well. And then it's out of your hands."

Peace was a wonderful thing. Over the past two years, Bloom had grown to recognize it and love it.

"Thank you," she said softly, not sure Chantel had even heard her over the sound of the surf.

The detective reached over, squeezed Bloom's fingers, and Bloom knew she'd heard.

EVEN IN LOOSE-FITTING scrubs with her hair tied back, the young woman was exceptional to look at. The combination of loosely contained blond hair, blue eyes and dark skin was quite striking. As was the perfect shape of her young body, the grace with which she moved.

Juan Cordoba had dark hair, dark eyes. "You don't look much like your brother," Sam said as they settled in a conference room down a quiet hallway filled with what looked like labs in the back of the clinic.

"I got permission to use this room so we won't be disturbed," the woman said, closing the door and motioning Sam toward the table.

"And Juan's my half brother," she told him, taking a seat across from him and folding her hands on the table. "We have different mothers."

He wondered if they'd been raised together. Were close enough for the sister to arrange a drug deal for her brother. For the sister to have ties to the East Side gang her brother ran.

Or if Sam was heading toward another dead end.

"Juan said you wanted to speak with me."

"That's right. It didn't take him long to find you. You two close?"

"He watches out for me," was all she said. But Sam started to feel better. Enough so that he listened to his instincts and took a chance.

"Tell me about you and Kenneth Freelander."

He had to hand it to her. She showed no fear. No fidgeting. She just looked...sad.

"What do you want to know?"

I was right. I've got him. Sam didn't let his relief get away with him. Didn't take his piercing stare away from his subject even for a split second.

"When your affair began, for starters. How long it lasted." Reading her, he played to the sadness.

"Kenneth and I didn't have an *affair*. We were going to be married."

"You were lovers up until two years ago, when he was sent to prison. Lovers while he was still teaching, right? That's how the two of you met. In class." He was winging it. But it made too much sense to be wrong. He'd been over every step Freelander took on that campus and Bloom had filled in the blanks for their time together at home. Jean had to be the gang connection...

"I met him at a lecture he was giving," the woman said. "Some guys were bothering me and he told them to get lost. We fell in love my junior year. He's the one who told me to take his class. So we could see each other every day. Have more excuses to be seen together. He said he loved me and wanted to marry me."

She could be faking the hurt in her voice, but he didn't think so. And he wondered how Juan felt about Freelander breaking his little sister's heart.

Or if she'd been a necessary casualty for a bigger, more profitable cause. If maybe Freelander, whose medical license was legal now that the revocation of it had been revoked, was still providing drugs to Cordoba and his guys...

He couldn't get ahead of himself.

"You do realize he was already married, right?" he asked.

"He was going to divorce her. He was just waiting for the right time..."

Waiting for Bloom to be so drugged she wouldn't fight him? Sam didn't think so. Freelander had just been playing the girl. Like he played everyone...

"You said you *were* going to be married. What changed?"

She shrugged.

"Did you change your mind when he went to prison?"

Her gaze shot up. "Of course not! I loved him."

What was it about the bastard that earned such loyalty? From Bloom. Jean. And who knew how many others?

"Why did you choose the name Barb Miller?"

If he had to, he could pull prison videos to verify that he had his woman. But it would take a subpoena. And time.

Her chin jutted forward. "You don't know that was me."

She'd just told him it was with that statement. "What was you?"

Her hands flew up and landed with a splat on the table. "Okay, so I used a different name when I went to see him. I didn't know who all heard about that sign-in sheet and I didn't want Juan to..."

She broke off. "Your brother didn't know you were still seeing Freelander?"

"He didn't know I ever saw him. He wouldn't be into me and an old man. I didn't want him to find out."

"You introduced Freelander to Juan without telling your brother you were seeing him?"

"I didn't introduce them."

"But the professor knew who your brother was. That he heads up the East Side gang."

"No way. And Juan's not like that, anyway. He has some guys, but..."

Either she was lying or she didn't know her brother very well. Sam wasn't sure how much time she had. He could come back to that.

"What do you know about Freelander's feelings for his ex-wife?"

"I know he wanted her to pay for putting him in prison for something he didn't do."

"Pay how?"

"He was going to…you know…show her that she couldn't get away with what she did."

"Show her how?"

She shrugged. "He used to…you know…talk about how he knew just how to play with her head. He'd keep at her, scaring her, making her worry, until she'd admit what she did. Then he was going to take back all of his money and marry me."

"So what happened?"

She shrugged.

"I'll tell you what happened. He got out of prison and found himself another coed, didn't he?"

"He didn't even come see me!" She sat upright, her face red with anger. "All that time I visited him and I'm sitting here waiting for a phone call that he's free. I'm thinking he's still in prison that he got held up or something…"

"How'd you find out he was at that hotel with a couple of beauties?"

Her face dropped. "He was what?"

"You didn't know?"

"Hell, no, I didn't know. All I know is that he didn't call, and then a couple of days later he finally did. To tell me he's met someone else. Some girl who goes to Cal State…"

If Jean had still held any loyalty at all for Freelander, it had just switched to Sam.

"Do you know if he's acted on any of those plans to go after his ex-wife?" he asked while his having her was still fresh.

"Yeah. I know he did."

Bingo.

"Tell me about it."

She shrugged. "He had this plan to intimidate her. To show up at her work. Her house. Things like that. He was going to have some guys mess up a car at that shelter that turned her against him in the first place. He was not happy with them. Said if she didn't have them feeding her shit and giving her a false sense of strength she'd still be his."

"What guys?"

She looked away. Stared down at her fingers. "I don't know. Someone he met in prison knew someone was all he said…"

She was hiding something. Protecting her brother? Sam wasn't sure.

"You said you *knew* he'd done something…"

"I…kinda…followed him one night last week. I thought he was going to see this new bitch and I wanted to know who she was…but instead he drives to Santa Raquel. He goes to his old house. I'm thinking he lied to me about ditching his wife, too, so I follow him in. No one's home and I think he's going to leave, but he lets out this, like, growl sound and goes berserk. He takes out a knife from the kitchen and starts slashing all of the paintings in the place. Made no sense to me. But it sure cured me of wanting to be with him."

She still wasn't looking at him. And Sam had a feeling the woman still cared about Freelander.

Funny how the heart didn't always follow what the head knew it should...

A thought for another time.

Or not.

"You saw him slash the paintings."

"Yeah. I was hiding in the laundry room and could see through the crack where the hinges go."

"What did he do with the knife when he was through?"

"Put it back in the drawer."

Slashed paintings hadn't been enough to warrant forensic testing of possible weapons. But if he knew where the weapon was, he could get an order for tests.

Freelander, you're mine.

He'd lock the bastard up for breaking and entering and destruction of property, and go from there.

He wasn't stopping until he'd kept his promise to Bloom. She was never going to have to worry about her ex-husband again.

Jean's thumb rapidly moved back and forth on the table. "You know anything about a security guard or cop uniform?" he asked, on another hunch. Did Jean know more than she was saying?

Had she been in that house to help Freelander, not to spy on him? And had she been with him other times, too? Like at Bloom's office?

"I know while Ken was in prison he got this uniform fetish," she said. "He kept talking to me about how he'd lie awake at night and fantasize about me in one of the guard's uniforms."

"And you didn't think that was..." He stopped. It wasn't for him to judge.

"I thought it was a sign that he really loved me," Jean said, looking him in the eye again. "He was fantasizing about me. And wished that I was the one in charge of him. So to speak."

"So you bought a uniform and..."

"Noooo. I didn't." Jean was upset. "He said that when he heard he was getting out, to celebrate he ordered one out of some catalog. He said that it was going to be his coming home present to me."

"But you never got it."

"No. But I'll bet his new girl did. And more power to her, as far as I'm concerned. I want nothing to do with the jerk."

There was a ring of truth in what she said.

"Seriously, Detective," she added, hands calm now as she sat up. "I'm lucky that I saw what he was before I was married to him. I'm getting my life together now. Going back to finish my degree and go to grad school. I want nothing more to do with Ken Freelander."

"Would you be willing to testify against him?" He was serious. And testing her, too.

"About what?"

"The break-in at his ex-wife's home in Santa Raquel. His statements to you that he was going to get back at her. The slashed paintings."

"Absolutely."

No hesitation.

"So you really were hiding that night? He didn't know you were there?"

"Do you think I'd be sitting here talking to you right now if I was working with him? I was hiding, Detective. I was so afraid of him finding me that I stayed for a long time after he left, just sitting there behind the laundry room door. I didn't want him to find me there. Then, when I finally decided it was safe to leave, I was creeping out the back, and I see this flashlight, like someone's coming around the house. I bolted so fast I left the back door open..."

Sam believed her. The flashlight had most likely been that of an officer doing a check on the place as ordered.

"And you're sure your brother has never met him."

"I didn't say that. I said Juan didn't know we were seeing each other. He knew about him, yeah.

I told him about this professor who stood up for me when some guys were giving me a hard time. And he knew the same professor helped me out once when I was struggling in class. Helped me get my grade up. Juan did go see him after he got out and I found out he was seeing someone else. I lied to Juan about him, told him that Freelander was bothering me. I just wanted to scare him. Anyway, I know Juan told him to stay away from me."

"Did your brother hurt him?"

"No. I told you. Juan's not that way."

"How do you know your brother saw Freelander?"

"He told me."

Before or after Sam had told Juan Cordoba he was looking for his sister? How much of what she'd told him had been coached by Juan?

Sam wasn't sure it mattered. She'd given him enough to arrest Freelander and had agreed to testify.

"I don't suppose you know anything about Freelander giving your brother a stash of drugs in exchange for protection in prison?"

"Absolutely not. My brother doesn't have anything to do with drugs."

He didn't believe her about that but hadn't expected her to tell him if she did know. What he expected was that she'd go back and tell her brother that he'd pieced together the truth.

As far as the drugs went, he could wait a day or two to see what happened.

CHAPTER TWENTY-NINE

BLOOM AND CHANTEL sat on the beach for more than an hour. Sometimes talking. Sometimes not. They laughed at Lucy's antics. Watched the tide come in. Talked about how picturesque the sunset was.

Bloom kept waiting for Chantel to mention Sam. As though the detective could somehow know that he and Bloom had had sex.

Twice.

To Bloom, the air in the cottage was different enough that Chantel would have picked up on the change.

Eventually Lucy tired and came to lie down next to Bloom. With a hand on the dog's back she started to feel…better.

"I guess I should ask about the investigation," she said now. "Since Heather's in-laws are no longer suspects…"

Detectives didn't report to their victims every step of the way. They briefed them if necessary. And Bloom had been too focused on other things to worry about what she could neither affect nor control.

You want to know what Sam's doing.

Okay. Yes. He'd been up as late as she had the night before. She hated to think of him out chasing bad guys while he was tired.

And...

"Sam's been in LA all day, following up on some things there," Chantel said. "But I found an old classmate of one of the previous suspects who admitted that he'd heard his friend say that if people didn't quit messing with his wife's head, he'd make them stop. I'll fill Sam in in the morning."

Bloom wouldn't be speaking with him in the morning. She never did.

And wanted it that way.

SAM FELT LIKE he could run ten miles and then swim another ten as he turned his SUV onto the dirt road and then on through the gate. He was early by a couple of hours, but he'd called to let Chantel know that he was coming.

The detective was good at her job and he didn't want to risk a bullet hole through his windshield. He'd told Chantel that he'd speak with her and Bloom together when he got there. Chantel would be thrilled to know that her evenings would once again belong to her fiancé and the new life they were building together.

He'd wanted to call Bloom, but knew that he could not. They weren't…friends. He handled things professionally. As they'd agreed.

But his eagerness wasn't exactly professional as he stopped the car and thought of the news he had to give her.

Right until his gaze landed on her car in the drive and he realized that there was no longer any reason for it to be there.

For Bloom to be there.

He'd thought there'd be nothing that could take away his pleasure at seeing Freelander back behind bars.

He'd miscalculated.

"I CAN'T BELIEVE IT." Bloom stood behind the couch, holding it with both hands, as she looked from Sam to Chantel. Chantel had been standing by the kitchen table, having checked to make sure it was Sam's car in the yard, when he came in. He'd come to stand straight in front of where she'd been sitting on the couch.

And when he'd made his announcement, when he'd told her Ken was in jail, she'd jumped up so fast Lucy had jumped down, startled.

"You found the drugs?" Chantel asked him. And with refreshed hope in her heart, Bloom's gaze swung to him, as well.

"Not yet," he told them, rubbing his hands together. "I'm still working on that. Another day or two at most, I'd guess," he said. "Cordoba went out of his way to give him up to me on harassing Bloom, though, which tells me that he's trying to hide more than one gift of drugs from two years ago."

"You think Freelander's still in their pocket?"

"I do."

"Why?" The detectives seemed to understand something that she did not.

"Whether he's got his medical license back yet or not, he will have it back since all charges against him no longer exist, at least until the medical board pursues an investigation on their own. And as things stood, with the conviction thrown out, it's not likely that they'd be able to do anything. They have no proof of wrongdoing—"

She knew all of that.

"—which means that he can still write scripts," Chantel said.

"You'd be surprised how many members of a neighborhood suddenly develop ailments that require prescriptions when they have a doctor who will write them just because he's told to do so..."

Oh, Kenneth, what have you done?

And why didn't she care more? She'd been married to the man for ten years.

"But you said you don't have him on the drugs."

Bloom, all caught up with them now, wasn't sure why he seemed so celebratory.

"I've got him on breaking and entering with the intent to harm, and on property damage," he said. "That'll be enough to hold him until I can put the rest of it together. He's off the streets, Bloom. It's over."

He was so happy. She was, too.

But...over?

Over.

It was what she'd wanted. More than anything.

What she still wanted.

Something he'd just said dawned on her.

"You got him for breaking and entering and property damage? Kenneth broke into our house? He ruined my paintings, after all?" She'd *known* it. Standing there that day, she could feel him there. Feel his anger.

And she hadn't buckled.

"What about the back door being left open?" Chantel asked.

Bloom listened while Sam told them about his meeting with Jean Cordoba that afternoon. Heard about the affair her husband had been having, about another young coed who he'd promised to marry. Heard about Barb Miller and two years' worth of weekly prison visits. Heard about Ken's latest sexual fetish—guard uniforms.

"So she was the female guard impersonator?" she asked.

At the same time Chantel said, "So she was his connection to the gang. She arranged for him to unload the drugs."

"I don't think she knew about the drugs," Sam said. "She says she didn't and I think I believe her. She was definitely Freelander's connection to the gang. I'm certain the arrangement with her brother was made through her. I'm just not sure she knew what was going on. She thinks her brother warned Freelander off her. Cordoba thinks Freelander is far too old for his sister. But instead of Cordoba warning him off, I think that meeting was to make a business deal."

A deal Kenneth had been stupid enough to take. And was going to pay for for the rest of his life.

"If you do get the proof of drug activity, will Jean be charged, too? Even if she didn't know about it?"

"As of right now, Jean's not being charged with anything," Sam said. And Bloom wondered if he'd somehow been hoodwinked by the young woman, as well.

For a second there, she was jealous.

But only for a second.

"You said that he ordered her a guard uniform. Isn't she going to be charged for knocking out

Gomez? And the guard at the Stand? For vandalizing Lila's car?"

Had he cut some kind of deal with the girl? Letting her off scot-free?

"She didn't do those things," Sam said. He'd come around the couch, taken her hands and pulled her around to sit again, beside him.

"What do you mean she didn't do them?" Chantel didn't sound any happier than Bloom felt about Sam's seemingly light treatment of the woman who'd had them all in a panic.

"Freelander never gave her the uniform he'd ordered. But when we went to talk to his new girlfriend, we saw it draped across a chair in her bedroom."

Oh.

"I take it she's in custody, too?"

"Yes she is. Though she claims she was never at Bloom's office or at The Lemonade Stand. Or even in Santa Raquel. She says the uniform was only for sex play."

"But Kenneth admitted to being there?"

"No. He says he didn't do any of it, either. He says he may have been in Santa Raquel. And might have tried to see you at your home. And that's all. But Jean's already given a written statement. We have him ordering the guard uniform. And as soon as the knives in your kitchen drawer are tested, when they turn up fiber residue from the slashed canvas, as well as his DNA on the handle, we'll have them as proof of the weapon he used to slash your paintings."

"Did you give him a chance to deal on the drug charge if he gave up the East Side gang?" Chantel asked, still standing by the front door—her bag on her shoulder now.

"I did."

"He didn't budge?"

"He wasn't saying any more without his lawyer. But I don't expect him to try to make a deal. He's in a no-win situation. If he talks, he's still going to do some time, and with East Side enemies on the inside, he'll never make it out."

Bloom was sorry for him.

But glad to know that he didn't win.

She was also weak with relief.

She was free.

SAM GOT UP to lock the door behind Chantel. And then wished he hadn't moved from Bloom's side. How did he get back there without looking like he was trying to get physically close to her?

She looked so alone, sitting there. And a little lost. Like she needed a hug or something.

Not in his department.

He'd been inside her the night before and now he couldn't even give her a hug.

He wasn't cut out for this stuff.

But he wasn't married to his job, either.

The bald truth was as clear as anything had ever been as he stood there, needing to comfort her, to hold her. Maybe the sex had done this to him.

But he'd had to close the case—make the arrest, at least—before he could allow himself to know what was there.

Not for the job. Not to have another case number on his list of accomplishments. But so that he could keep his word to Bloom.

She drove him.

Not the job.

"I know it's after nine, and kind of late, but... I'd like to go home."

She was standing now, too. Not still, like he was. She was moving around his home, collecting things. A water bottle on the coffee table. The tablet she'd had on her lap when he'd first come in. A sweater over the back of one of the kitchen chairs. She looked toward the laundry room.

He'd stored her suitcases in the closet in there.

"You can come back for your things," he said, suddenly in action, too. Even as he knew he was clutching at air.

She looked at him and for a second there he had hope. She'd remember the sex. Know that there was something behind it.

"You're probably right," she said. "I'll just get my cosmetic bag..."

She was down the hall and back in less than five minutes, an overnight satchel he'd forgotten about over her shoulder. She'd said she'd keep the satchel in her room…

"Ready?" He pushed himself off the wall, grabbed his keys.

"You don't have to follow me, Sam," she said. "Remember? It's over. I'm safe."

"Humor me," he told her. "Let me check out the house."

The excuse was lame. And then he remembered.

"I need to get all of the knives out of the drawers in the kitchen and have them put into evidence before you're back in there." He thought about telling her that the soonest he could get someone there would be morning.

He could have her for one more night. And hope that she'd come to him again.

If he wanted to be a liar he could.

If he wanted to trick and manipulate her.

But they'd had an agreement. No personal relationship. No expectation.

She trusted him.

He couldn't betray that trust.

"Let me make a phone call and have someone meet us there with an evidence bag. We'll be in and out in no time."

She nodded. Looked relieved. "Thanks, Sam. For everything."

Her gaze was warm. Personal.

And he somehow knew that she was saying goodbye.

CHAPTER THIRTY

IT WAS AFTER eleven by the time Bloom was finally alone. Sam had stayed while a forensic officer got what he needed from her kitchen. The two had just left together, backing down the driveway one after the other.

She watched from the living room window. Saw their taillights go down the street and then around the corner.

Only then did she turn around and take a deep breath.

She was free.

BLOOM'S SECOND NIGHT at home, she was very busy. First thing she did was unload the painting she'd done at Sam's house from the back of her trunk. She hung it over her fireplace. He'd made arrangements for her to access his house on her own, after work, to collect her things. She didn't know where he'd gone, but wherever it was, he'd taken Lucy with him.

She missed seeing the girl.

Sam had left her bags outside her closed bedroom door and she'd had them filled and ready to go in under twenty minutes.

She'd taken another extra twenty or so, standing inside his bedroom. Remembering. Telling herself she was storing moments to draw on later if she ever doubted her capacity for intimacy in the future. If her mind ever played with her and tried to tell her that Kenneth's lies about her—that she was a frigid bitch—were true.

Then she'd made a deliberate about-turn, paused in the doorway long enough to look back at the bed, and with a whispered, "Thank you, Sam," was out of there, down the steps and inside her Jaguar.

Ken's violence hadn't stopped her. She was still there. Painting new stories. Replacing the ones he'd destroyed. He hadn't won. She had.

When she had returned home, it occurred to her that she could have brought other paintings from the office to fill some of the other vacancies left on the walls after officers had carried the slashed paintings away as evidence. She decided, instead, that she'd paint new ones.

The old ones were the story of healing from Ken's abuse. The new ones would be about her true, healed self, living life to the fullest.

She had new things to say.

She wasn't sure what, yet, but things were different now.

Ken was in jail and she was still standing. Free. Without anyone telling her what to do.

She was older. More mature.

And thought a glass of wine sounded good. So she opened a new bottle from the rack in the garage and poured herself some in one of the crystal wineglasses she'd purchased the day her divorce had been finalized.

She took the glass out to the deck and, watching families and couples out on the beach, walking, sitting, enjoying the evening, she drank every drop.

FREELANDER CONTINUED TO eschew his innocence. No wonder, he had his expensive attorney sitting right beside him. The professor wanted out on bail. Sam was able to hold him at least until forensics came back on the knife. Use of a deadly weapon carried different charges.

Sam was giving Cordoba one more day to make a move. Then he was going to LA for a real confrontation. One way or the other, he was getting what he needed.

FRIDAY NIGHT WAS Bloom's third night of freedom. She worked late. Stopped at the grocery store. She was in no hurry to get home. The wine, the deck, the people-watching would wait.

It wasn't like she had a dog waiting for her.

The wine was as good as she thought it would be when she got to it. The people were there—on the beach. The evening breeze was nice and the tail end of the sunset was spectacular.

Maybe getting a dog wouldn't be a bad idea. She would call animal rescue in the morning, just to see what they had.

And maybe she should think about moving. Get a smaller place.

One without memories of Ken.

Memories of Sam will still be there.

"That's the point. I learned a lot about myself through him. I am grateful to him," she said softly. Affirming out loud to give the thoughts more substance. More power. To put them out into the universe as a statement of intention.

You learned how to get out of hiding.

Now that was just the wine talking. How could she possibly have learned how to get out of hiding when she'd been *in* hiding?

Unless she was glad she'd been able to leave Sam behind and come home again. She tested the thought out in her mind.

Daring that inner voice to pipe in again.

If it did, she was cutting it off from any more wine that night.

Which would be a shame since she really needed another half glass.

Needed?

Yeah, she'd caught that one herself without any internal help. Thank you. She'd meant *wanted*.

A man was walking down the beach. She'd noticed him because of his dog. A black Lab. About the size of Lucy.

She meant Madge.

He threw a stick into the ocean. The dog dove in after it and brought it back to him. They walked together side by side. And a few minutes later, the man threw the stick again.

He reminded her of Sam, but shorter and stockier. Maybe a little younger, too.

But the way he tended to his dog…like it was a real person…

Like Madge had been to her. Parents and sibling rolled into one.

And she hadn't even been able to be there when Madge got sick. When they'd had to put her down.

She'd begged to be allowed to come home.

"It's just a dog," she'd been told.

Sam knew dogs weren't just dogs.

For such an arrogant, hard-nosed, married-to-his-job cop, he sure was sensitive.

And gentle. So…gentle.

But strong. A mirage of pictures of Sam flashed before her mind's eye as she watched the man and dog continue down the beach toward her property. They'd be passing her soon. And then be gone.

As Sam was.

A pang of loneliness stabbed her. Because of the dog. Because of Madge.

You have a second chance.

She wanted to tell that inner voice to shut the hell up. But she'd worked too hard, too sincerely.

And she knew. She wasn't healed yet. She hadn't recovered. She'd gone into hiding.

And sex with Sam had brought her out.

She hadn't known, going in, that the feelings he'd arouse in her weren't just physical. Couldn't possibly have known that to all the physical pleasure he'd given her, a key to her heart had been attached.

She'd never been given sexual pleasure before him.

She'd loved, though, once. Deeply. Unconditionally. She'd felt safe and secure and filled with joy.

Anytime she was with Madge.

She'd loved fiercely, as a little girl loves.

And now she was all grown up.

Madge had led her to Lucy who'd led her to Sam. In a heart sense. She understood. Intellectually she got it.

But as her heart opened up, as the pain of Madge's loss, of being stripped from everything she knew as a small child, of a lifetime of fear and insecurity, of not fitting in, of loneliness started to engulf her, Bloom wasn't sure she had what it took to accept the bad so she could embrace the good.

She had what it took to stand up. Brush herself off. To take care of herself. So that she could use her gifts to help others.

SAM HAD THE entire weekend off. Saturday morning, dressed in his coat and tie with his off-duty weapon strapped to the belt of his dress pants, he got in his car and drove to LA.

Juan Cordoba was waiting for him. He'd known he would be. The message he'd left for the other man had been curt and to the point.

Meet me or you'll wish you had.

"Hey, man," Cordoba greeted as Sam walked into the bar where they'd first met. Before noon on a Saturday the place was empty.

Which was just fine with him.

Cordoba could have ten guys waiting around corners and behind things. He didn't much care. If they killed him they'd all go down.

At least he'd let them think half the police force knew he was there; in truth, no one did.

Freelander was going to be able to make bail unless Sam found a charge that carried more weight than breaking and entering. Especially when the crime had been committed in a marital home that was included as part of a show cause hearing that had been postponed by the defendant's ex.

"I'm here to deal, Juan," he said, his tone easy as he took a seat at the high-top table across from the other man.

"I got no deal with you."

"A smart man would listen before he made a statement like that." His tone didn't change.

"I'm listening."

"I've got Freelander in custody."

"I heard. My baby sister come crying to me about it. Seems she had a call from the guy. Turns out she's in love with him and now she's not sure she wants to testify against him."

Cordoba was not making Sam happy.

"What'd you tell her?"

"That she had to do the right thing."

The man looked him straight in the eye as he spoke. And Sam relaxed. He'd read Cordoba right.

"So here's the thing. I know Freelander used his connection with your sister to unload drugs to members of the East Side gang two years ago in exchange for protection in the event that he ever went to prison."

"That's news to me."

"I thought you were a smart man."

Cordoba bowed his head and then faced Sam again. "I'm listening."

Good. He still had his interest, which meant that Cordoba knew about those drugs.

"I'm a Santa Raquel cop," he said. "I got no

jurisdiction here." This wasn't about the job anymore. It was about Bloom. About keeping his word to her. Keeping her safe.

Juan nodded. Leaned forward, his arms on the round table between them.

"I don't care what you guys have going on here. I see before me a good guy who's telling his sister to do the right thing."

"That's right. I'm a good guy."

"But I know about those drugs," he said again. "And sooner or later, I'm going to find a hospital record of someone who OD'd on them. Or find a mama whose kid lost his way because of them. Or find someone who's in more trouble than the drugs would bring who's willing to rat in exchange for favors. If I don't break Freelander first, which is a definite possibility. And then it not only becomes your problem, it becomes your baby sister's problem because she'd be an accessory..."

Cordoba didn't look as happy now.

"But as I say, this isn't my jurisdiction. And I have no reason to call anyone here and tell them what I don't see."

"What do you want?"

"Proof that puts Freelander away permanently." They wanted the same thing. Which was why this was going to work.

Cordoba looked over Sam's shoulder. Sam braced

himself. He could have called it wrong. He could take a bullet to his back.

But he knew he wouldn't.

"Did Freelander come to you offering you the drugs in exchange for protection?"

"It might not have happened exactly like that."

The room was deadly silent.

"How might it have happened?"

"He might have tried to sell some scripts to some people I know and they might not have wanted to pay for them. They might have offered to take them off his hands, though. You know, just to dispose of them properly."

"To flush them down the toilet?"

"Something like that."

Cordoba had brokered the deal. Sam knew it.

"I need proof. Witnesses. Something. And I need it fast."

"What do I get?"

"You get to go about your business as usual. If you testify you get my backing that you disposed of the drugs."

He was implicating himself.

But only if he went through with a lie to authorities.

Which he wouldn't do.

"You get Freelander away from your sister for good," he said then, knowing the ace he really held. Everyone had a vulnerable spot. Cordoba's was Jean. The girl who made good.

"This witness…can you guarantee, if he's a juvie and ain't got no record, that he'll get immunity?"

Sam nodded. Didn't promise.

Silence fell. Sam let it lie there.

"I'll get you your witness," Juan finally said. "And to show my good faith in your honor, I'll do one better…"

Because Cordoba wanted Freelander gone as badly as Sam did. Freelander's phone call to Jean must have really gotten to her.

"What's that?"

"I'll give you an out of work doctor-type who been writing scripts for some of my people, telling them they're sick when they ain't." The street talk came out in full force.

"You got any of those prescriptions that haven't yet been filled?"

"I can get my hands on a pad of them."

"Would that pad have Freelander's fingerprints all over it?"

"On every page. He signed them all."

"And you've come to me about it because I came to you looking for your sister and you're tired of this doctor trying to mess up your neighborhood, right?"

"That's right." Cordoba met him stare for stare.

"Good."

"We have a deal?"

Sam stood. Shook on it.

And noticed the little square photo frame hanging from Juan's neck.

The photo was a girl. Side view. The point of the chin bone looked familiar...

"Who is that?"

"My sister, Jean," he said. "I raised her since she was born."

He wanted to care about Juan's troubles. About having a little sister you had to protect. But he kept staring at that photo.

"Her hair's dark in that picture."

"Of course it's dark. Look at me."

He pictured the nurse's aide. The blond hair that had been parted down the middle. It had looked natural. But...

"When I saw her the other day it was blond."

"She admits to me today that when Freelander got out and took up with one of his own kind she had some fool idea that if she dyed her hair right and got some of those lenses that change eye color he'd look her way again."

The photo he'd passed around. The woman who'd posed as a guard in Bloom's office...same profile. Same point to the chin.

"Jean, is she your half sister?" The man was wearing her picture around his neck.

"No, man! She my full blood sister. She all I got left in the world."

Jean had lied to him. Which, to Sam, meant she had something to hide.

"Get me that pad," he said, hardly able to stay put long enough to get the proof he needed.

He was on his phone to Chantel before he was in his car.

"Get to Bloom. Make sure she's safe. Freelander was telling the truth. He didn't have anything to do with the attack on Gomez. Or The Lemonade Stand. His current coed is telling the truth, too. She only used that uniform for sex, like she said. We've got the wrong girl."

"Sam? I don't know what you're talking about. We just got word back on the knives. One tested positive for canvas residue. It had Freelander's prints all over it."

He had to think. And drive. And get the hell back to Santa Raquel. Putting his bubble out, he entered the freeway at Mach speed. Gave Chantel a staccato version of what he knew, and what he was sure of even though he had no proof. And then said, "Just get to her, Chantel. Keep her safe until I get there."

CHAPTER THIRTY-ONE

As soon as he hung up, Sam called Bloom. He got her voice mail. She never picked up when she was with clients.

He told her to call him before she left her office.

His next call was to Gomez. And then to the captain. He wanted a "be on the lookout" out for Jean Cordoba—blond or dark-haired. He wanted people sent to Bloom's office and house. He wanted a call back as soon as someone knew she was safe.

He was stepping way over his boundaries.

Captain Salyers assured him it would all be done immediately and to drive safely.

Salyers hadn't acted surprised.

Did everyone know he'd fallen for his victim?

Or was he just seeing things that weren't there?

One thing was for certain, this whole love thing wasn't something he'd choose if he had the choice.

And if he got Bloom out of this safely—when he got her out of it safely—he was going to have a talk with her.

He understood that she needed to be alone. To

heal. He got the irony in the fact that when his ex-wife had loved him desperately and needed him to love her in return, his driving need had been his job. And now here he was, needing Bloom to love him, and her driving need was to be on her own. Doing her job.

Still, he was going to be honest with her. Because the last man she'd slept with had done nothing but lie to her. Hide from her. Betray her. She deserved to know she was loved.

And then maybe he'd think about moving. He'd never lived anywhere but Santa Raquel. Maybe he should head down the coast a bit. See what kind of crimes they had to solve down there.

He wasn't even halfway to his exit when his phone rang.

Chantel. Not Bloom.

"Sam? She's not home."

"She's at the office. She never answers when she's with a client."

"We tried there, too. We've also been calling her. She's not picking up."

He started to panic. Something he hadn't done on the job since his father was killed. "She's shopping," he blurted out. "You know where she goes, you've been with her. Go there."

"I've already got someone headed that way," Chantel told him. And the tone in her voice finally registered with him.

She knew more.

And it wasn't good.

"What's going on?"

"We've got Jean Cordoba, Sam."

So why did she sound like she had something bad to tell him?

Unless…

No, she'd said she was sending someone to the store where Bloom shopped.

That meant they didn't know for sure…

"She's out of her head, Sam. On something. She just keeps saying that she had to do it. For Ken. So he'd love her again. Said she wasn't worried about the bimbo. That was just a fling. Her real problem was Bloom. Freelander just couldn't stop talking about Bloom. About making her pay. Jean figured if she did it for him he'd love her again."

"Where'd you find her?"

"A couple of blocks from Bloom's. There was blood on her hands."

"And Bloom's place?"

"The painting over the fireplace was slashed. There was some blood on the mantle."

Everything inside of him went blank.

"Bloom's car was in the garage, Sam. We have no idea what Jean was driving or how she got to Santa Raquel. She was walking when we found her. It looks like she might have done something with Bloom, Sam. But we can't get her to tell us where she is."

His whole life sat in that moment. In the balance. Without Bloom it meant nothing.

"Go home, Sam."

Hearing Salyers's words as he left the interrogation room, Sam had to clamp down on his jaw to keep from letting his captain know, in very clear terms, what he could do with that command.

"I mean it." Salyers, who knew him well, followed him down the hall to the break room where he was going to get a cup of coffee for himself and a glass of ice water to dump over Jean Cordoba's head.

He didn't care what she had in her system. She was not passing out until he found out where Bloom was.

Salyers stood over him as he poured stale coffee into a foam cup. Chantel, with a cup of her own, watched from the table. "You are not going back in there right now."

After more than six hours of interrogating the girl, Sam still had no idea where Bloom was.

He knew that Jean had talked some of her brother's guys into helping her get Gomez out of the way. And that she'd been planning to use the gun they'd also given her to scare Bloom that night she'd come out of her office. She hadn't been going to hurt her. She'd just hoped that by scaring her, like Kenneth had been saying he wanted to do, she'd get the professor's attention again. If he could see what a great partner she'd be, seeing to his needs, he'd marry her. He was out of prison. Divorced. She just had to remind him how good she was for him.

The news had come in disjointed spurts. But it had all been there.

She'd been responsible for the guard down at The Lemonade Stand, too. But Freelander had ordered the hit on Lila's car, separate and apart from Jean. The guys had told her about it and Jean had just gone along as insurance that the job got done right. To show him what a good team they made.

The young men who'd helped her had thought they'd be earning points with her brother. Instead, they'd ended up hurt worse than either guard had been. Juan hadn't been pleased that they'd acted without his say-so.

Freelander hadn't been angry with Jean, though. He'd had sex with her to show his gratitude. She'd worn the uniform she'd ordered to surprise him— the same one she'd worn on the jobs. She'd thought she'd won him back. But then he was gone again.

He'd been the one to slash the paintings. That had happened just as she'd said.

After Sam came looking for her, she'd told her brother about being in love with Freelander. He'd been really pissed, but he'd told her he'd take care of her. He'd told her what to say—and what not to say—when she'd talked to Sam the first time.

But he didn't understand how much she loved Kenneth. Or believe how much Kenneth loved her. But she knew. He'd used his one phone call from jail to call her...

It all rattled around in Sam's brain. All of it. He was missing something. Hadn't gotten far enough in someone's brain.

"I have to get back in there," he said. And ran into Salyers. The man had stepped right in front of him.

"Captain..." He sidestepped, trying to get past him. So did Salyers, his arms crossed.

"He's right, Sam. You need to go home. At least take a shower. Change your clothes. I'll keep at her. We'll find Bloom." Chantel's voice reached him. It didn't change his mind.

"And the blood? While I'm driving home and taking a shower, Bloom Freelander could be bleeding to death."

"Maybe Jean's telling the truth. Maybe all that blood really did come from that cut on her hand. Maybe it really was from the knife she'd had in her hand when she'd slipped climbing up on the mantle..."

Blood samples had been sent to the lab for testing. It could be twenty-four hours or more before they'd hear back.

He looked at her. "Do you believe that?"

She looked down at her coffee.

"And you?" he asked Salyers. "Do you?"

"What I believe is that you aren't effective here right now. If you want to find Dr. Freelander, you need to go home and shower and let someone else have a chance with Jean Cordoba."

He'd never been spoken to in such a tone.

"Just grab a shower, Sam," Chantel said. "Come right back. I'll call you if she gives us any clue…"

ONE THING GOT through to Sam. He was ineffective. He'd managed to get a hell of a lot out of the girl. She'd turned on her lover. On her brother. He had enough testimony to prove that Freelander had purchased illegal drugs with the intent to harm. That he'd sold them. And that he'd continued to write illegal scripts because when he'd been released from prison and had tried to wipe the East Side gang out of his life—even going so far as to end his relationship with Cordoba's sister—he'd found that the gang owned him.

He had everything but Bloom.

Yeah, he was ineffective. How had he managed to turn the girl on everyone she loved, and still not get her to give him the only thing he wanted at the moment—Bloom?

The woman he loved.

He drove home with his bubble going, wiping tears from his eyes as he pulled through his gate. He had to find her.

Life was nothing without Bloom in it. Even from afar.

He'd settle for from afar.

He just had to find her.

Lucy must have sensed that all was not well. She didn't jump up on him exuberantly the minute he opened the door, though she'd been alone for more than twelve hours.

There were no messes on the floor, either.

"Good girl," he told her, letting her out and then heading straight back to the shower. By the time he was done, she'd be done, and he'd be out of there.

He'd stripped his tie off in the car. Threw his coat and shirt at the bedroom wall as hard as he could, stepping out of his shoes as he did so.

"Sam?"

He froze. Salyers and Chantel were right. He was losing it. He'd just heard...

"Sam? What's going on?"

Afraid of seeing an empty space, Sam spun around.

Bloom stood there, in bare feet, and with tousled hair, but otherwise looking as though she'd come from work.

But her car was at home.

"Are you okay?" He stared. And then moved closer, studying every inch of her. Without touching.

He saw no blood. Not on her skin. Or her clothes.

"I'm fine," she said. And then gave a nervous chuckle. "Other than the fact that I think I'm losing my mind. Half the time that is. The other half I think I'm finally seeing clearly…"

He didn't get anything she'd just said.

"Sam? Are you angry with me for being here? I took a chance…"

She turned. "Maybe I should go."

"No!" He lunged and grabbed her arm.

When he noticed her looking at his grip on her, he loosened it but didn't let go.

"How long have you been here?"

"I have no idea what time it is," she said, glancing around. "I fell asleep in your bed. Well, the bed that was yours when I was here…"

She glanced behind her toward the spare room.

He stared at her, trying to make sense out of a nonsensical situation.

"I only had a couple of appointments this morning and came here straight from work. I…I've been doing a lot of thinking, Sam, and when I was in my office, counseling others…I knew what I had to do. We teach what we most need to learn, did you know that?"

He shook his head. Held her arm. And continued to watch her.

"I knew if I didn't come straight here I'd talk myself out of it. I find that I'm a little too good at the cerebral thing and that I need to get better at being willing to take on the pain so that I can feel the joy."

He caught the cerebral part of it. Wished she'd hurry up and get on past it.

"I still had your gate remote and the house key," she said. "I haven't seen you since I picked up my stuff earlier in the week and…"

She'd made that sound like an accusation. Like he was supposed to be in touch with her. Had she been waiting for him to ask for his key back?

"You came to return my key?"

"No. I came to talk to you."

Oh. "You could have called."

"I know. And I thought about it, of course, because I think about everything, but I needed to talk to you without you having a chance to try to figure me out or think about what I might say and what you might say and…"

"You didn't want to be manipulated."

"Maybe. I don't know. I just wanted to…surprise you."

"To see if I was happy to see you." Understanding was like a warm river cradling a freezing man.

"Yes."

She had no idea how happy he was to see her.

"Your car is in your garage."

"My battery was dead this morning. I didn't have time to wait for a new one to be delivered so I called a cab. And then had one drop me here. Outside the gate, of course. I didn't open the gate until he was gone."

She'd been in a cab. One she'd called. And then in his house.

"So what did you come to tell me?"

"Are you okay?" she asked again. "You look awful."

Her honesty beguiled him. Or maybe just the fact that she was alive did that.

"I've been working on a tough case..."

"All day?"

His throat clogged, preventing speech, so he nodded.

"I figured it was something like that, which was why, when I started to get tired of waiting, I took a nap. I knew I might not have the guts to try this a second time."

"Try what?"

"To tell you that I love you." The words came in such a rush they made him dizzy. "Now, don't get all uptight or anything." She held up a hand, still spewing words almost faster than her mouth could pronounce them. "I'm not putting anything on you or expecting anything. I'm not going back on our agreement. I just had to tell you. As part of my therapy. I'm accepting the pain so I can…"

She paused. Tears filled her eyes, and Sam thought he might die from the sight.

"I just… I've been… Madge…and then Lucy and…you…"

She was making less sense than Jean had all day. Only this time, it made perfect sense.

He didn't say anything. There was no way to make her past easier. No way to help the little girl she'd been. But he could help her now.

He took her in his arms, still surprised when she fell willingly against him. She was crying so hard her entire body shook—his Bloom, who was always so calm and controlled. He made it to the side of the bed with her. Lay down with her. Cradled her against his chest for as long as it took.

And when the sobs calmed, and the tears dried, he spoke.

"I love you, too, Bloom. I was going to tell you, just as soon as…"

Lucy barked. He sprang up.

"What?" She looked alarmed.

"I left Lucy outside." He quickly remedied that and met Bloom in the hallway. Lucy wasn't all of it. "And I forgot all about work," he said. "Chantel, the captain, everyone, they're interrogating Jean Cordoba."

He had to call them. Immediately. He couldn't

find his cell. Remembered throwing his jacket against the wall.

"Jean Cordoba?" Bloom was over by the wall, getting his phone out of his jacket pocket and handing it to him.

She waited while he made his call. And then stood there interrogating him until she knew everything that had happened.

At that point, when he was thinking he should grab a shower and they probably ought to think about something to eat, she grabbed him by the belt buckle and pulled him toward her, walking backward to the bed.

"You're in love with me." The smile on her face wasn't arrogant. It was just...calmly knowing.

"Yes."

"You forgot all about the job the second you saw me here tonight."

He'd just said so.

"And I love you, too."

They were at the edge of the bed.

"I still want to hear more about that," he told her, his throat dry. She loved him. He hadn't counted on that part.

"Oh, you will," she told him. "I have a feeling I'm going to be spending the rest of my life analyzing the whole love thing."

Sounded like a worthy lifetime goal to him.

"But first, we have some business to take care of." She pulled him down to the bed.

She wanted to have sex?

He did, too, of course, but after the day he'd had, he...

"I need you to let me out of that agreement we made, Sam." She teared up again, but kept going. "I need you to know that I need you. I want you. And I have a feeling I'm going to become very interdependent with you."

With one finger, he wiped her tears. "My sweet, smart, beautiful Bloom," he said, feeling reborn as he opened himself to her. "I love you. I need you. And I'm going to spend the rest of my life protecting that heart of yours. You have my word on it. My life is all about you, Bloom."

"And mine is about you, Sam."

"Forever."

"Forever."

He leaned forward to kiss her, a kiss completely filled with love, and felt a paw on his thigh just before a big wet nose touched his chin. And Bloom's.

Lucy.

Obviously, she approved.

* * * * *

LARGER-PRINT BOOKS!
GET 2 FREE LARGER-PRINT NOVELS PLUS
2 FREE GIFTS!

◇ HARLEQUIN®

Romance

From the Heart, For the Heart

YES! Please send me 2 FREE LARGER-PRINT Harlequin® Romance novels and my 2 FREE gifts (gifts are worth about $10). After receiving them, if I don't wish to receive any more books, I can return the shipping statement marked "cancel." If I don't cancel, I will receive 4 brand-new novels every month and be billed just $5.09 per book in the U.S. or $5.49 per book in Canada. That's a savings of at least 15% off the cover price! It's quite a bargain! Shipping and handling is just 50¢ per book in the U.S. and 75¢ per book in Canada.* I understand that accepting the 2 free books and gifts places me under no obligation to buy anything. I can always return a shipment and cancel at any time. Even if I never buy another book, the two free books and gifts are mine to keep forever.

119/319 HDN GHWC

Name _____ (PLEASE PRINT) _____

Address _____ Apt. # _____

City _____ State/Prov. _____ Zip/Postal Code _____

Signature (if under 18, a parent or guardian must sign)

Mail to the **Reader Service:**
IN U.S.A.: P.O. Box 1867, Buffalo, NY 14240-1867
IN CANADA: P.O. Box 609, Fort Erie, Ontario L2A 5X3
Want to try two free books from another line?
Call 1-800-873-8635 or visit www.ReaderService.com.

* Terms and prices subject to change without notice. Prices do not include applicable taxes. Sales tax applicable in N.Y. Canadian residents will be charged applicable taxes. Offer not valid in Quebec. This offer is limited to one order per household. Not valid for current subscribers to Harlequin Romance Larger-Print books. All orders subject to credit approval. Credit or debit balances in a customer's account(s) may be offset by any other outstanding balance owed by or to the customer. Please allow 4 to 6 weeks for delivery. Offer available while quantities last.

Your Privacy—The Reader Service is committed to protecting your privacy. Our Privacy Policy is available online at www.ReaderService.com or upon request from the Reader Service.

We make a portion of our mailing list available to reputable third parties that offer products we believe may interest you. If you prefer that we not exchange your name with third parties, or if you wish to clarify or modify your communication preferences, please visit us at www.ReaderService.com/consumerschoice or write to us at Reader Service Preference Service, P.O. Box 9062, Buffalo, NY 14240-9062. Include your complete name and address.

HRLP15

LARGER-PRINT BOOKS!

REQUEST YOUR FREE BOOKS!
2 FREE WHOLESOME ROMANCE NOVELS
IN LARGER PRINT
PLUS 2
FREE
MYSTERY GIFTS

✱✱✱✱✱✱✱✱✱✱✱✱✱✱✱✱✱✱✱✱✱✱✱

HEARTWARMING™

✱✱✱✱✱✱✱✱✱✱✱✱✱✱✱✱✱✱✱✱✱✱✱

Wholesome, tender romances

YES! Please send me 2 FREE Harlequin® Heartwarming Larger-Print novels and my 2 FREE mystery gifts (gifts worth about $10). After receiving them, if I don't wish to receive any more books, I can return the shipping statement marked "cancel." If I don't cancel, I will receive 4 brand-new larger-print novels every month and be billed just $5.24 per book in the U.S. or $5.99 per book in Canada. That's a savings of at least 19% off the cover price. It's quite a bargain! Shipping and handling is just 50¢ per book in the U.S. and 75¢ per book in Canada.* I understand that accepting the 2 free books and gifts places me under no obligation to buy anything. I can always return a shipment and cancel at any time. Even if I never buy another book, the two free books and gifts are mine to keep forever.

161/361 IDN GHX2

Name	(PLEASE PRINT)	
Address		Apt. #
City	State/Prov.	Zip/Postal Code

Signature (if under 18, a parent or guardian must sign)

Mail to the **Reader Service:**
IN U.S.A.: P.O. Box 1867, Buffalo, NY 14240-1867
IN CANADA: P.O. Box 609, Fort Erie, Ontario L2A 5X3

* Terms and prices subject to change without notice. Prices do not include applicable taxes. Sales tax applicable in N.Y. Canadian residents will be charged applicable taxes. Offer not valid in Quebec. This offer is limited to one order per household. Not valid for current subscribers to Harlequin Heartwarming larger-print books. All orders subject to credit approval. Credit or debit balances in a customer's account(s) may be offset by any other outstanding balance owed by or to the customer. Please allow 4 to 6 weeks for delivery. Offer available while quantities last.

Your Privacy—The Reader Service is committed to protecting your privacy. Our Privacy Policy is available online at www.ReaderService.com or upon request from the Reader Service.

We make a portion of our mailing list available to reputable third parties that offer products we believe may interest you. If you prefer that we not exchange your name with third parties, or if you wish to clarify or modify your communication preferences, please visit us at www.ReaderService.com/consumerchoice or write to us at Reader Service Preference Service, P.O. Box 9062, Buffalo, NY 14240-9062. Include your complete name and address.

LARGER-PRINT BOOKS!
GET 2 FREE LARGER-PRINT NOVELS PLUS
2 FREE GIFTS!

Ⓗ HARLEQUIN®

INTRIGUE
BREATHTAKING ROMANTIC SUSPENSE

YES! Please send me 2 FREE LARGER-PRINT Harlequin® Intrigue novels and my 2 FREE gifts (gifts are worth about $10). After receiving them, if I don't wish to receive any more books, I can return the shipping statement marked "cancel." If I don't cancel, I will receive 6 brand-new novels every month and be billed just $5.49 per book in the U.S. or $6.24 per book in Canada. That's a saving of at least 11% off the cover price! It's quite a bargain! Shipping and handling is just 50¢ per book in the U.S. and 75¢ per book in Canada.* I understand that accepting the 2 free books and gifts places me under no obligation to buy anything. I can always return a shipment and cancel at any time. Even if I never buy another book, the two free books and gifts are mine to keep forever.

199/399 HDN GHWN

Name _____ (PLEASE PRINT) _____

Address _____ Apt. # _____

City _____ State/Prov. _____ Zip/Postal Code _____

Signature (if under 18, a parent or guardian must sign)

Mail to the **Reader Service:**
IN U.S.A.: P.O. Box 1867, Buffalo, NY 14240-1867
IN CANADA: P.O. Box 609, Fort Erie, Ontario L2A 5X3

Are you a subscriber to Harlequin® Intrigue books
and want to receive the larger-print edition?
Call 1-800-873-8635 today or visit www.ReaderService.com.

* Terms and prices subject to change without notice. Prices do not include applicable taxes. Sales tax applicable in N.Y. Canadian residents will be charged applicable taxes. Offer not valid in Quebec. This offer is limited to one order per household. Not valid for current subscribers to Harlequin Intrigue Larger-Print books. All orders subject to credit approval. Credit or debit balances in a customer's account(s) may be offset by any other outstanding balance owed by or to the customer. Please allow 4 to 6 weeks for delivery. Offer available while quantities last.

Your Privacy—The Reader Service is committed to protecting your privacy. Our Privacy Policy is available online at www.ReaderService.com or upon request from the Reader Service.

We make a portion of our mailing list available to reputable third parties that offer products we believe may interest you. If you prefer that we not exchange your name with third parties, or if you wish to clarify or modify your communication preferences, please visit us at www.ReaderService.com/consumerchoice or write to us at Reader Service Preference Service, P.O. Box 9062, Buffalo, NY 14240-9062. Include your complete name and address.

HILP15